BRUNO VINCENT was a bookseller and book editor before he was an author. He has co-written several bestselling humour titles for grown-ups, and *Grisly Tales from Tumblewater* is his first book for children. His favourite horror stories are *The Signalman*, *At the Mountains of Madness* and *The Sandman: A Game of You*. Bruno grew up in the countryside and now lives in a rainy city, where he hugs the shadows.

*Also by Bruno Vincent*

School for Villains

BRUNO VINCENT

Illustrated by Jo Coates

MACMILLAN CHILDREN'S BOOKS

First published 2010 by Macmillan Children's Books

This edition published 2012 by Macmillan Children's Books
a division of Macmillan Publishers Limited
20 New Wharf Road, London N1 9RR
Basingstoke and Oxford
Associated companies throughout the world
www.panmacmillan.com

ISBN 978-0-330-47951-6



3 5 7 9 8 6 4 2

A CIP catalogue record for this book is available from the British Library.

Typeset by Ellipsis Books Limited
Printed and bound by CPI Group (UK) Ltd, Croydon CR0 4YY

*For Mum and Dad*

# THE ORPHAN

The crossroads, with its ceaseless traffic, was where Tumblewater began. Crowds of people and horses and carriages poured themselves towards one another at a reckless rate, and rushed into the middle. Sometimes they would clog up in a jam, dozens of carriages knocking against each other like logs in a river, and men would lean from carriage windows and bellow at their drivers, who in turn would shout at their horses, or each other. The rest of the time everyone plunged forward in a headlong dash and, mixed up in a great heaving mass, somehow found their way through to the other side, and continued on their journey.

On the side of the street boys swarmed, men and women walked, signs swung and singing (of a very unmelodic sort) drifted out from tavern doors. Blind beggars cried out for money and counted coins with their thumbs ungratefully, street sellers hollered their sales pitches, there was the creak and trot of wheels and feet and the jingle of every kind of conversation.

A baker carried an enormous unbaked pie on a plate on his head towards a house where a lady would pretend she had made it herself. A butcher passed, pushing a pig ahead of him and saying patiently, 'Come on, Clarence. Come on, lad,' and as he went by the fat glint of a blade showed from his back pocket.

And lastly there was the rain. Right now it drifted as softly as snow. Later on it would be hammering hard, and after that drizzling gently, but it would always come. The road was mud and the roofs were damp and mossy and the sewers ran full almost to the brim, and the gutters wept and drains chuckled all day and night. As they always had, and always would.

Much of this was visible to (although not all of it was noticed by) the man who had just stepped down from the coach, which presently clattered away. He was clean and well dressed, and he looked sprightly and energetic, all of which marked him out from the crowd, who were as a rule shabby and grey in appearance, and watchful and suspicious in attitude. His name was Finbarr Vane, and it was his first time in the city for more than twenty years, since he was a boy.

He took a few steps along the street in either direction, enjoying the spectacle and the excitement of being in the crowd, then stopped and looked at his pocket watch. He was early to meet a friend, and thought he might take a look at this part of the city while he was here. As he tried to decide which way to go, he saw a young boy standing quite alone on the corner. The traffic passed a few feet in front of him, pedestrians passed a few feet behind, and no one seemed to take the slightest notice of him.

The boy looked lost and forlorn. He was quite short and skinny, and more than a little pale. He stared into the distance in an absent sort of way, his shoulders slightly hunched.

The man watched carefully for a few seconds, until he was quite sure that the boy was alone. Then, becoming worried, he came forward, leaned down to him and said: 'Excuse me, little chap. Are you lost?'

The boy turned and the man was quite startled by the intensity of the grey eyes that looked up at him. They were clear and piercing, and although the boy had no expression at all, the man found them terribly sad. 'Is your mother nearby?' Finbarr asked, concerned.

The boy shook his head so slowly that it made the man ask, 'You have no mother?'

The boy shook his head again.

'Your father then. Might he be near?' Once again in the same slow way, no.

The man gasped, and crouched down. 'My dear boy,' he said. 'An orphan! I'm so sorry for you. Now, my name's Finbarr, and I shall take you home. You do know the way?'

The boy nodded more confidently. 'Good,' said Finbarr. 'Lead on and I'll make sure you get there all right.'

Directing him away from the crossroads, the boy pointed down a busy side street and, when they reached the end, led them down a narrow lane. The buildings were tall down here, and had once been warehouses or factories, but some of their insides had burned down or collapsed from old age, because looking in through the windows Finbarr could see sky where the roof should be.

The poor boy, he thought to himself. If he lives here, the family must be penniless. I expect he's a drain on his aunt and uncle, or on his grandparents.

'You're quite sure this is the street you live on?' he asked. The boy nodded eagerly, and led him towards the end of the lane, where a square doorway loomed like an open mouth.

Finbarr hesitated just slightly as he stepped inside, and found the boy's hand in his. Although there was no lamp, some light filtered down from above, and he could see all of the doors were shut. None of them had a number, or a name plate, and they didn't exactly look like they led to apartments, but the orphan led him on until they reached the stairs and so they went up together.

At the landing there was an open door ahead of them and Finbarr asked, 'Is that it?' but the orphan shook his head and walked on. Finbarr looked in through the doorway as he passed, and saw the shape of a man stretched out on the floor in the shadows. Frowning, he moved on and followed the orphan up a second staircase. The boy pointed at a door halfway along the wall.

'Here?' Finbarr asked. The boy nodded. Finbarr thought he seemed happier, and pleased to be home at last (although the truth was the boy's expression had not changed one bit).

Finbarr knocked on the door. It gave a curiously hollow sound. He knocked harder, and called out, 'Hello!' No response. Perhaps they thought he was the police or the bailiff, here to evict them.

'I've brought the little lad back for you!' he called

through the door. 'The one who doesn't speak!'

He locked eyes with the boy and again felt the impact of those colourless little buttons, which seemed to penetrate so sharply – he was still not sure why. The boy made a pushing motion.

'Ah,' said Finbarr. Perhaps there was a deaf grand-parent inside or an invalid unable to rise and answer the door. Or perhaps it was just very stiff? He stood back and bumped the door quite hard with his shoulder. He bounced clean off it – it seemed as hard as stone, and left a sharp pain in his shoulder. He looked back at the boy whose eyes seemed to say, 'That's it – just a bit harder!'

Suddenly feeling a bit ridiculous to be standing in a strange corridor like this, he stood further back and launched himself at the door with more strength than was needed.

It gave way with a dry snapping sound and light flooded all around.

Finbarr Vane had a moment to realize that he had jumped clean out into mid-air, and the ground was far below and rushing up to meet him at a terrific speed. He let out a cry of fright that lasted less than a second.

The orphan stood in the doorway, looking down, as Finbarr crashed into the rubble below and his cries gave way to silence. The watery eyes did not change, and whether they showed shock, or terror, or sadness, or no understanding of what had happened, neither you nor I could have said.

After a while, the boy turned and walked carefully down the stairs, out on to the lane and back to the busy street. There he vanished among the shouting, running, rattling madness of the crowd. Until he emerged again, moving slowly and cautiously, to take his place again on the corner of the street.

Minutes and hours passed. If you came across him now, you wouldn't know he'd been there for so long, because, apart from the slight hunch in his shoulders, he didn't slouch with tiredness, and his eyes didn't frown or develop bags from fatigue or distress. He simply stayed there, staring slightly upward, with an expression so blank passers-by thought, 'My, that boy is deeply contented' (if they themselves were deeply contented) or, 'Gosh, he seems very unhappy' (if they were very unhappy) or – in one case – 'My God, he's got bad toothache' (from a man on the way to the dentist).

A woman with neatly tied-back hair, wearing a cheap but clean blue dress, hardly noticed him as she passed, but stopped when she had gone on a few yards, and something made her turn back.

She knelt to look in the orphan's quiet eyes and said, 'You seem lost,' in a voice gentle but cheerful, as though they were old friends.

He nodded.

'Do you know where home is?' she asked. He nodded again and glanced over his shoulder in the direction he'd taken Mr Vane. Then he pointed the other way, over the crossroads and down the hill, towards the river.

The lady was called Miss Fort and she was a governess to three small children in a house a few miles north of Tumblewater. She led the orphan away through the confusing jumble of streets towards the dock, and perhaps the ghost of a smile tilted the orphan's lips for these few minutes as they held each other's hands, or perhaps it did not, but at last they turned along a wooden jetty by the water's edge.

They walked beneath the blackened masts of twenty or more river boats that leaned over them. All sorts of slippery characters wearing very thick clothes and oil-smeared faces stared out from the decks of their boats where they were eating meals out of tin pots, or dividing up their pay, or playing games of cards on the tops of boxes. They turned to look at the orphan and Miss Fort as they passed, showing faces as crinkled as rotting wood, but they had no curiosity in a woman and a little boy, and turned back to their pursuits.

'What *fun*,' said Miss Fort encouragingly as they walked over the planks, 'to live on a boat.'

The light was dingy in this little boatyard overhung by warehouses and cranes, and beyond the last lantern hanging on the jetty Miss Fort struggled to see for a second. Then she was shocked as she caught sight of the shoddy, forgotten boat that the boy was leading her towards. It was small, its mast was peeling and had no sail, and there was nothing on the deck – not one discarded match – to suggest that anyone ever lived or came here. It looked quite desolate as it rocked gently in the gloom.

But he kept leading her forward, past that boat, until she saw there was *another* beyond it, right at the end of the pier, even smaller and less welcoming than the first. It bobbed low in the water as though unsure whether to sink or float, and its bare deck showed only the snapped remains of a mast and a hatch standing open. From it came little gulping noises of water swilling around inside. In the failing light she saw the boy's hollow grey eyes staring fixedly at the boat. He pointed at it.

How *horrifying*, she thought. No wonder he drifts away to stand at the crossroads. She decided to give him a few pennies before she said goodbye.

'Come on, then,' she said with a cheerfulness she didn't feel, and leaning out, pulled the boat towards her until it was close enough for her to get on board. She stepped on and called out, 'Hello?' quite loudly. No noise or light came from the hull of the boat, and she looked back at the boy who pointed again at the open hatch. She put her feet on to the ladder awkwardly and began to climb downward, looking a little more doubtful with each step.

Suddenly there was a deep splintering noise, and the ladder shook. She gasped as first it juddered then collapsed altogether, and she fell down into the dark. The boat rocked from side to side, shaking the lid of the hatch so that it shut with a heavy thump.

She screamed and screamed again, but the sound was completely muffled by the tar-lined lid. And in falling down she had broken a hole in the rotten keel of the boat so that the water suddenly rose around her in the darkness, and with her legs trapped in the hole beneath her, it was quickly above her head. As it filled with water the boat began to lean backwards and slide quietly beneath the surface.

The boy watched without moving. Within a few seconds the tiny boat was half sunk and a couple of minutes later it was gone entirely. The boy's eyes rested on a smooth circle in the water surrounded by gentle ripples. After watching for a while he walked slowly back along the jetty and disappeared into the streets.

It was as the little boy was nearly at the top of the hill again that he crossed a frail wooden bridge over a deep canal. The planks rattled pleasantly under his feet, so he jumped up and down on them for a bit, as if enjoying himself, and dropped a few stones into the water.

On the other side of the bridge, he stopped in front of a sign against the wall. It read:

DANGER
WEAK BRIDGE
CARRIAGES – DO NOT CROSS

His little grey eyes travelled over the words, but he showed no sign of understanding them. His gaze fell instead on the string holding the sign in place, tied in a pretty bow. He went over and pulled at it until it unravelled smoothly, and walked away up the street, making a cat's cradle with it in his hands. He didn't notice as the sign toppled over the railing it had been tied to, vanishing from sight.

When he had gone about a quarter of a mile further on, there was a great rattling, shouting, jingling sort of noise, and looking up from his game the boy saw a coach approaching. It was filled with loud, merry-making travellers, several of whom were leaning out of the windows holding bottles, one of them doing this while also being fast asleep.

'Look!' shouted a female voice. The orphan glanced up and found that everyone inside the carriage (most of whom up until that point had been singing a very loud and very rude song) was staring down at him. The voice was that of a flushed, well-built lady who seemed in very high spirits, and who now looked down lovingly at the young lad.

'*Dear* little boy!' she cried. 'Have you lost your daddy and mummy?'

A short conversation followed which involved the orphan saying nothing at all (only nodding and shaking his head) and the travellers saying a great deal, often all at once. Having won the deep and heartfelt sympathy of everyone aboard, the boy was told that he was going to be escorted home, and that they refused to hear otherwise (which of course they wouldn't, as the boy never said anything). The decision was announced by the woman and greeted with a cheer from everyone inside, which was so loud that the sleeping man woke, banged his head on the window frame and dropped the bottle he'd been holding on to the cobbles.

'Now,' said the well-built woman, leaning clean out of the window to talk to the boy, 'you know where it is you live, don't you?'

He looked up from the broken pieces of the bottle and the red liquid which left dark stains between the cobbles, thought for a moment, and then nodded.

'Show us, then,' the woman said with her most ingratiating smile (revealing similar red stains around her teeth). The orphan pointed back down the street towards the bridge he had crossed, and began to trot away in that direction. All the inhabitants of the coach called to him to come up and ride with them, but instead he refused and trotted happily alongside, so they followed, drinking and laughing and chatting to each other.

Now, as the strange little boy and the coachload of drunkards go off down the street together, I'm going to lead you in the opposite direction, a short distance back to the corner of the crossroads. This point was just about the centre of the city, and here was where the four poorest corners of four larger districts met. All around people continued to trudge, carrying suitcases and baskets and the burden of their own stories. They made their way home, or away from it, towards the shop or the graveyard, or the school or the prison, tramping on through the rain to find out what would happen to them next.

It now began to rain a little harder, and the murmur of the crowd became drowned out by the drumming of raindrops on hats and umbrellas. And then, slowly, there began to be heard cries and screams far away in the distance, which came closer as the seconds passed, and were soon among the crowd.

'A coach has crashed!' a man shouted. 'A bridge has fallen in!' and people stopped in horror, and others paused, wondering if they'd heard him right.

'Many dead?' asked one, but the man was unable to answer, and could only say, 'Please, just come and help! Quickly!'

Some people went running with him, and many more walked behind, hoping to see something dramatic. A call went out for the fire engine to be fetched, and three policemen ran through the crowd towards the fire station. There was muttering and gossiping in the street for a few minutes, but the crush of people kept coming from four directions, the rain lashed down even harder, the voices gradually lost among other voices talking of other things. There was hardly a mention of it in the air by the time a small boy walked cautiously out to the corner of the street. He stopped just outside the line of the pedestrians, but safely within the edge of the traffic, and stood there, looking out at the crowd with his vacant grey eyes, all lost and alone.

Some time later a carriage pulled up at the other side of the street outside the doors of the gigantic Black Lamb Tavern, where Finbarr Vane had stepped down. From the carriage jumped a nervous-looking lad of about sixteen, just as the rain started to become quite violent. His satchel splashed him as it was dropped from the roof, and picking it up he rubbed a spot of mud from his cheek as he looked around him.

It was me.

How I came to know the story you've just read, I'll have time to tell you later. But first I've got to explain myself, and what happened next in my own tale. So I'll tell you.

As I wiped the speck of mud from my face, I looked up into the huge and looming shadow of the Black Lamb. It was the day before my medical studies were due to begin, and I still had to retrieve a suitcase from the post office and find my lodgings before nightfall which, under the glowering thunderstorm, felt like it was already upon the city. During the last mile of my long journey, the rain that had been drizzling down for several hours had hardened into a furious shower. I called up to the driver through thundering rain: 'Is it always like this?'

'Like what?' he called back through the noise.

'Like this!' I waved my soaked arm around, but the rain came down so hard into my face that I couldn't look up at him any longer, and couldn't hear his response above the oily crack of the whip and the horses' trudging as they moved on.

I sheltered in the doorway of the tavern for a few moments with my satchel under my arm until I heard the lock being snapped shut behind me, and saw, inside, a shadowy figure retreating away from the glass. I grabbed the arm of a passer-by.

'Please,' I said, 'where is the post office?'

The man shook my arm off roughly and glared at me from beneath the brim of his hat for a second before pointing down the hill. 'Straight down, turn left, second right, first left and right again at the bottom,' he snapped. 'You'll be lucky though. They close in fifteen minutes.'

I thanked him, took a deep breath and ran out into the rain, which buffeted me like a strong wind. Because I had to keep looking up to see where I was going it was soon trickling through my hair, and over my face, and down my neck and through my clothes. Two carriages passed in quick succession, sending up splashes of muddy water. I instinctively shielded myself from the first splash, but the second I just let break over me in a wave, knowing it couldn't make my clothes any wetter. At least I had a spare suit for my first day at the medical college, pressed and (in my imagination) warm, in the suitcase that had been sent ahead the previous day.

Halfway down the third street I had been directed down, something alarming happened. The path became steeper all of a sudden, and the cobbled paving began to give way to lumpy mud. It became darker too as the houses on either side of the street crowded closer to one another, and yet somehow the rain had become even fiercer. I dived into a doorway for a moment to catch my breath and could see that the roofs above were so steep that the hundreds of gallons of rain falling on them gathered and hurtled downward in a spray of streams, hitting the cobbles so hard that they sounded like breaking glass.

In my mind I heard the man's voice again: 'Fifteen minutes.' I took a shaky breath and threw myself into the street, jogging over the stones as carefully and quickly as I could. As I reached the next turn I gasped, clutching at the side of a building, and my feet slipped from under me. This was the turning I'd been told to take, yet it was totally dark and incredibly steep. I couldn't even see the bottom. There were no cobbles for my feet to grasp, just pure running mud so that even as I looked down with horror I slid helplessly forward.

The mud ran over my shoes and under my arms, and all discomfort was overwhelmed by fear that I would smash into something and break my neck at any second. I tumbled over and over, and at last felt the ground levelling out beneath me as I slowly came to a stop. All around me were tall dark buildings, their windows boarded up, and as I dragged myself to my feet I glimpsed a single light, fifty yards away. Ignoring my disgusting appearance, I ran as fast as I could towards it (which wasn't very fast, as I was weighed down by about thirty pounds of mud).

The light came from an open door and inside was a tiny waiting room with a hatch in the centre of a shabby wall. Through this stared the face of a gloomy old man. I asked breathlessly whether this was the post office. He nodded. I almost collapsed on the counter in gratitude.

‘Please,’ I said, ‘I’ve come to collect a package. It’s for Daniel Dorey.’

The man observed me glumly for a moment before turning round to bellow my name into the back room. Over his shoulder I could make out a group of grubby little men gathered around a table, sorting methodically through torn paper and string and open boxes, surrounded by hundreds of objects, small and large.

‘Pot of jam . . .’ one man was saying in a bored voice, ‘and some pencils. Not much of a present for “dearest Lavinia” if you ask me.’

‘Listen to this!’ shouted out another, holding up a letter, ‘“My darling Bertie! How I miss your kisses!”’ All of them broke out in a nasty giggling, before one of them, opening another envelope, shouted: ‘Here’s a pound note!’

‘That’s mine! I saw it first!’ they all shouted, and at once threw themselves into a pile of hair-tugging and nose-pulling.

‘I’m sorry,’ said the old man gloomily, ‘they’re murdering each other again. Boys,’ he warned them, turning round. ‘BOYS!’ he shouted. Three of them had taken up position sitting on the fourth (who had managed to hide the pound note somewhere down his shirt), playfully punching him in the face as hard as they could. Now they stopped. ‘What?’ said the one on top.

‘Package for one Daniel Dorey.’

They stared stupidly at him.

'Package for one Daniel Dorey!' he repeated.

'You mean he's *here*?' asked the topmost little man again, as the man at the bottom began to struggle for breath.

'He's actually come to *collect* it?' asked the new owner of the pound note, who came round from being crushed to death to express his outrage. 'All the way *here*?'

'What else do you think I mean, you stupid little brutes? *Fetch* the thing!'

In one sudden movement, all four men leaped up and began searching industriously through the piles of parcels, muttering my name over and over, and scurrying up ladders to inspect higher shelves.

'When did it arrive?' one of them asked absently, lifting a parcel above his head to peer to the back of a shelf.

'It should have been today,' I said.

They froze.

'Today?' asked the old man, sounding rather awkward.

'That's right – this morning, I think.'

'Ah,' he said. 'Then you'll have to fill in this form.' He rustled some papers below the counter for a moment and then thrust a sheet at me.

'But it's just blank paper,' I said.

'Exactly. Fill it in, please, with your name, your current address and your method of payment.'

'Payment?'

'Quite so. Storage is one penny.'

'But you haven't even stored it overnight! It only arrived a few hours ago!'

'Overnight storage would have been twopence.'

I was by now so tired and cold that I simply didn't have it in me to argue, so I filled in the form, signed it and handed over a penny. He rubber-stamped and signed the form before giving it back for me to sign *again* (at which point I gave him a very tired look) and writing out an entire copy, signatures and all. Behind him all this while I could hear the strained whispers of the funny little men. One of them kept saying, 'Quickly, quickly!' At one point something was dropped and there was the sound of glass shattering, after which they went absolutely silent for a few seconds, before returning to their hushed exertions. I craned my neck to see past the gloomy old man, but no matter how hard I tried he seemed to shift his shoulders so that I could not, without ever looking up from his paperwork.

Finally, in a rather well-spoken voice, he said, 'Your receipt, and your parcel. A pleasure doing business with you, sir.'

'Thanks,' I said uncertainly as I looked at what he was handing over to me. It had been a neatly-filled

suitcase when I had sent it. Now it was a bundle of possessions roughly tied together with five different types of string that bulged dangerously in every direction. I had no idea how to carry it except to thread my hand through one of the bits of string and hope it didn't all fall apart. Not wanting them to see my disappointment, I went straight to the door without looking back, before realising that I still didn't know where my lodgings were located, except that they were nearby. I turned round to see a CLOSED sign being lowered over the counter.

'Excuse me,' I called through it. There had been the sound of people clearing up, but suddenly there was silence again. After a second a voice cautiously said, 'Yes?'

'Could you tell me where Proker Lane might be? It's where I'm staying this evening.'

Silence reigned again for a few seconds as one of the little men considered my question. 'Where it *might* be? I can't say for sure, but it *might* be at the top of the hill, just round the corner from the Black Lamb Tavern,' said the voice. Then that same low giggling broke out among the men again.

'Thanks very much,' I said quietly as I walked into the street, pulling my muddy coat as close as I could and feeling the cold once more. City folk certainly seemed very odd, I thought, as I began my walk back up the hill.

*

I won't tell you in detail about that journey – the fear and trepidation of the shadows to a boy who'd never seen the city before, the tiredness, exhaustion and the cold. But after many wrong turns, and what felt like a whole day's hard work, I reached the top, discovered the street and finally, with inexpressible relief, found a white door at the top of a set of scrubbed-clean stone steps. Behind it, I knew, were the rooms of the landlady who had been paid in advance for my first month's lodging. By reputation my guardians knew her to be decent and respectable, and not too expensive. I knocked, and a few seconds later the door opened.

The woman who answered was tall and stern in startlingly clean clothes; the insides of the house radiated a warm light and, it being dinner time, from behind her the comforting scrape of cutlery against plates was accompanied by the smell of delicious food.

She looked at me for a second, said, 'No thank you,' and slammed the door.

I knocked again, and called out, begging that she talk to me for just a moment. I peeped in through the letterbox and saw people eating in the dining room, and heard their laughter too. But for all I could tell she might be plagued with dirty young boys knocking at her door and begging for food. However unfair it was, I knew I might have turned myself away, seeing myself in this filthy condition.

I gave up, and sat on the bottom step, resting my face in my hands, ashamed. There was nothing I could do, nowhere to go, no one who knew me in the slightest. Wondering miserably what would become of me, I shook with fearful sobs and, leaning against the railing, wondered if I could get away with sleeping here on the doorstep, even for a while . . .

'You all right, lad?'

A hand gently rocked my shoulder and I woke to find myself looking at a man who had crouched down to my level. He was tall and thin, and as shabby as I was. The grime on his face made it impossible to tell his age, but there was something gentle in his eyes, and he didn't speak to me in a challenging way, but quite calmly, and before I knew what I was doing I had told him about the door being slammed in my face. He looked up at the house, snorted and said, 'No great loss to you, *that* place, full of pompous types who think they own the world. Come along with me and we'll find you more friendly lodgings in five minutes.'

'I haven't got any money,' I said. 'Or not enough to . . .' I felt dangerously close to tears again, and frustrated with myself.

'Don't worry about that for now,' he said. 'I know someone, a very kind woman called Nuala, who'll be glad to put you up for the night in a lovely place called

Turvey House, and who'll let you set about paying her back afterwards. How does that sound?'

I thought it sounded so wonderfully kind I could hardly trust myself to answer, and as he walked off I followed, dragging my ball-like sack of possessions with one hand and holding my satchel under the other arm. The rain had long since calmed to a steady drizzle, and the small favour this man was showing me made me as giddy as though I'd won a thousand pounds – or fifty pounds; either sum was unimaginably vast to me. (It still is, in fact.)

He led me down a turning, away from the more respectable streets through a web of smaller alleys that stretched away behind, hundreds of little houses and shacks and huts thrown together with no thought or design so that the road twisted in a different direction every ten yards.

'My name's Daniel,' I said. 'What's yours?'

'Shh,' he said.

'That's a funny name,' I said.

He turned and came back to me. 'Daniel, keep your voice down,' he whispered. 'There are people asleep all around us, not the sort who take kindly to being woken. And others too, who stay awake in the dark hours, with evil on their mind. My name's not important right now. But people – well, people around here tend to call me Uncle.'

'All right,' I whispered back. 'Sorry, Uncle.'

He smiled. 'Don't worry. Just follow me carefully. It gets confusing at this point.'

We set off again, and now the streets drew even closer together while the occasional lamps with their sickly orange light grew further apart. Although I hadn't thought the houses we walked past were exactly enviable, these ones were in noticeably worse condition. The smell of the place was so terrible that we peered suspiciously where we trod, and the little houses were squeezed together so tightly there was hardly room to get through.

Slipping momentarily and clutching at a barrel to steady myself, I ran to catch up and found the alleyway completely dark. I opened my mouth to call out to Uncle, but stopped myself in time and instead felt my way along a wall as fast as I could, my heart beating loudly, listening for his footsteps above the sloshing of my own feet. Hearing something, I moved faster, only for a dog to break out barking at my side. Against the silence of the night it was terrifyingly loud, and I ran as fast as I could with my parcel of possessions knocking against my back and the satchel against my side. I crashed against one wall and then another as the dog chased me up the path until its chain yanked it back with a cruel throttling noise.

Desperate to escape before someone came to investigate, I took the first turning I came to, slipping down some half-visible lanes of cramped and decrepit shacks, fearing I heard the growl of a human above the dog's painful roar behind me. I saw a low opening through a thick stone wall, so I crouched and ran through.

I came out on the other side into a quiet cobbled lane that curved gently upward. It felt out of place in this slum of muddy streets, and I stopped to look around. A lamp post opposite cast light on the houses' clean doors and windows. I breathed clean air, and felt the fine spray of the rain on my face. With dreamlike certainty I walked up the road until a large house appeared on my right. For the first time since I'd entered the district I saw a property surrounded by walls and a gate, behind them the high and beautiful stone face of a powerful and imposing building. Something about it made me stand stock still.

A light was on in an upper window and as I stood against the railings, the cold of the iron bleeding into my hands, a dark-haired woman appeared in the window. She moved so slowly that it lent her beauty a terrible sadness and, without knowing why, I was filled with dread. As she looked down from the window, a shadow appeared behind her.

My heart jumped as the shadow resolved itself into the grey personage of a bleak-faced old woman. She uttered a few words and the younger woman's gaze fell. All expression left her pale features. Then, before I knew

what was happening, the old woman reached up and pulled a black cloth over her head in a cold, clinical movement.

The beautiful young woman offered no resistance. I gripped the railings and shouted up at them as the older woman led her gently away from the window, and the light went out.

I backed away, still trying to understand what I had seen, until I found the deep stone wall again and the passage through it. Emerging back into the filthy passageways, I walked for a few minutes without thinking, letting my feet take me through the darkness, until at the end of a street I saw a lamp and spotted Uncle sitting beneath it. With a burst of energy, I was upon him in seconds, and found him looking up at me with relief. He made no remark about me getting lost, causing the dog to bark and nearly getting us both into trouble, but said he had sat himself down in this godforsaken spot to wait for me just in case I came his way again. He seemed so kind and patient that as he got up again and led me away I felt a reproachful pang of guilt for not telling him about the apparition of the girl that I'd seen. But there was something so mysterious about how awful it made me feel, that I wanted a chance to think about it first. I was harbouring another secret from him too, about my reasons for being in Tumblewater, but he would know the truth before too long.

After a few minutes, we were out of the dangerously close alleyways and back on roads paved with cobblestones, though ones that were narrow enough for a boy to spit across.

'This is the poorest part of the city, where it always rains,' explained Uncle. 'Where you always have to look out for yourself, because . . . Well, never mind. But stay close from now on, won't you, Daniel?'

I nodded and walked in silence behind him. It *always* rained here?

He knew what I was thinking. 'Yes,' he said. 'It always rains; we don't know why. Now, we're not far away from your new lodgings, but there's about enough time for a story, I reckon, if you would like to hear it?'

'Very much,' I said, glad for anything that would distract from the pain of pulling the parcel behind me over the stones.

'Good – this is one I heard just the other day,' said Uncle. 'You'll hear a lot of stories if you spend any time in Tumblewater, but I ought to mention that they're all horrible, and nasty, and scary. I don't really know why that is the case, but it is.'

'But that's the best kind of story,' I said. 'Go on!'

'Well, good, I will. I call it –'

(Now, I'm going to tell you the story myself, but not word for word how Uncle told it to me, because – well,

partly because I don't suppose you'll be any the wiser whether I do or not. But also because if I tell this tale – and any of the others that follow it, in fact – in my own voice, and take out the throwaway remarks and the bits where the teller stopped to cough, or went back and repeated the last bit until they could remember what happened next, then we'll both enjoy it a lot more, I think.)

# THE MAN WHO TAUGHT ENGLISH LITERATURE

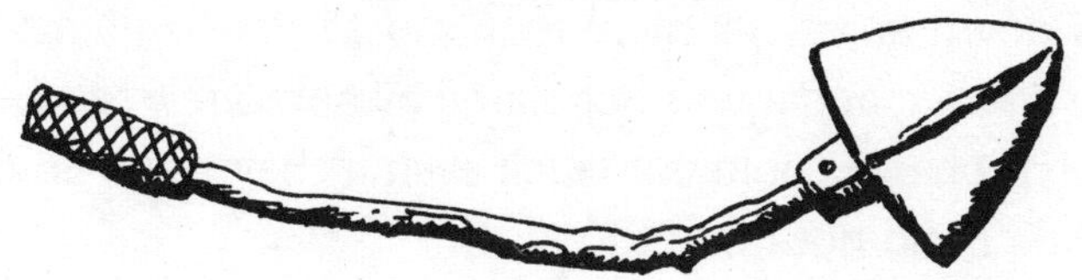

If you walked along the darkest, dingiest street you could find in Tumblewater, and struggled through its failing light, and ignored the washerwomen throwing dreadful insults as you passed, and stepped over the diseased dogs and overcame the wailing of unattended babies – if, in short, you followed the streets through to the centre of the Old District, you would find yourself at the school.

All of Tumblewater's children attended school. That is to say, when their parents threw them out of the house each day they all went to the school building to shout and scream for a few hours. It was, after all, a warm and relatively dry place, it seemed less likely to fall down at any moment than most other buildings in the district, and it was populated by only a few teachers who probably could not teach even if they tried. So the children did not mind too much.

It was called the St Windsmuth School for the Underprivileged, and to many of the pupils it must have felt very much like home. There were no books, for instance, either to read or write in. Nor did it have any pens or pencils, or chalk for the teachers to use on the blackboard. That it had desks at all seemed almost lucky.

A young boy called Henry inhabited the furthest corner of the Junior Class. Whereas most little boys place themselves at the back of the class to avoid the teacher's glare and to get up to unsuitable activities, Henry sat there because in this classroom all the naughty boys (which was everyone apart from Henry) sat at the front, so they could pelt the teacher with whatever objects they had brought from home, found on the way to school or picked up off the classroom floor. Those without physical objects to hurl instead made a very good substitute of the vilest and most horrible language they knew.

'You stupid idiot!' shouted Oliver, a portly little snot-nosed boy.

'Teach us something, you fat pig!' screamed James, a tall, spotty brat.

Henry hunched at the back of the room, hoping no one would notice that he was reading. He had a secret passion for literature, and his father went without food to provide Henry with books in the hope that his son would educate himself.

One day, after the rest of the class had run from the room at the sound of the church bell, which signalled the end of lessons, the teacher wiped the egg from his glasses and was astounded to find little Henry reading at the back of the room. Reading! And not just any book – *Dracula*, by Bram Stoker, which was then quite a new book.

'Do you like that book, Henry?' he asked.

Henry looked up, astonished. 'Has class finished?' he asked. 'I must get home!' and with that he took the book and ran out of the room.

The teacher, touched that he had at long last found a boy interested in reading books, went home in his best mood for years. When he got there, he told his wife, who had died of typhus some twenty years before, and whose skeleton he had propped in the chair in one corner, all about his discovery. She said nothing in return, because she was quite dead, but he took her silence to be one of approval and satisfaction.

You see, the unfortunate truth is that many decades of abuse by the vile offspring of the town had driven Mr Pelmettle (for that was the teacher's name) quite out of his head. So there he sat, chatting to his deceased wife, and wondering how he could best encourage his little protégé, and we cannot be too surprised that the plan he eventually struck upon was a mad one.

Therefore, after his meagre supper (which was the same as it was every day – walnut stew with peas) he set out into the rain and wind to find some way of illustrating the qualities of that excellent story – Bram Stoker's *Dracula* – so that it might stick irrevocably in the boy's mind, and encourage him on to greater things.

Being of a limited circle of acquaintance (or, as one of his repugnant pupils would have put it, a 'Billy No-Mates') and also being of an unusually morbid disposition, Mr Pelmettle made for the local graveyard. He had long ago befriended the gravedigger, Mr Grum, and now sought his advice.

'Mr Grum!' called Mr Pelmettle when he spied the man, only visible in the dark and flooded graveyard from the waist up. Grum sloshed slowly around to see who was calling him.

'I see I catch you working, Mr Grum,' started Mr Pelmettle, a little nervously. 'The flood is, er, worse than usual?'

'What do you want?' asked his friend.

'Er – ah – I wondered whether you might have any ideas as to where I might find some bats around here.'

Grum stared at him for a moment as though not sure if he had heard him right. Then he pointed with the handle of his shovel towards the bell tower.

'Up there,' he said, and turned to continue with his work.

Excited, Mr Pelmettle slipped away to fetch what he needed. A little while later he returned and then climbed to the top of the church steeple with a boathook between his teeth.

Catching the bats took a long time, because bats are wily creatures who see in the dark (also, a boathook is not the ideal instrument to kill them with), and a few times he nearly fell clean out of the church's belfry. But he kept his balance and eventually he was climbing down the steeple again, with four dead bats in his pockets.

Next he made his way to the slaughterhouse on the east side of Tumblewater, and broke in. He filled several large cider bottles with spare blood, which the slaughterhouse kept in large vats so that it could be turned into delicious black pudding for people's breakfasts. The sun was nearly up by this time, so instead of returning home he went straight to school.

Unfortunately, it had never occurred to him (or to anyone else) that he might be dangerously mad. He was, though. Utterly. I feel I should stress that once again at this point.

Just as he got to school, the church bell rang down the lane, and the boys began to tumble up the stairs and into the room, armed with their usual arsenal of rusty spikes and horrid insults. Mr Pelmettle assumed his position, cowering behind the lectern at the front, and waited for it all to end. Eventually the second bell came, the boys piled out and Mr Pelmettle poked his head round to see Henry, once more reading at the back of the room.

He stole into the staffroom, which was a forgotten little place at the back of the classroom, not much larger than a cupboard, and put on a long dark cape (which he had fashioned earlier from one of the curtains), poured blood down the front of it and over his face too, and hung the dead bats on the inside of the cloak. Then he crept back out, stood in front of Henry (who was still immersed in his book), flung the cape back and opened his mouth to let out what he imagined to be an accurate impression of Count Dracula's mad cackle. But then he saw that the book had changed. The boy was avidly reading a weathered, second-hand copy of *Frankenstein* by Mary Shelley.

'*Frankenstein*, is it?' said Mr Pelmettle, amazed. 'A fast reader!'

He hadn't stopped to think about his appearance before he spoke, and as Henry caught sight of him the shock he received lifted him bodily out of the chair and dropped him on the floor six feet away. Speechless with terror, he tore from the classroom before Mr Pelmettle could explain.

That night, Pelmettle put behind him the slight embarrassment of scaring the boy half to death, and settled more determined than ever to the task of encouraging the boy's reading habits. Finally, after much discussion with his wife, he decided that yesterday's plan to bring *Dracula* to life in front of the boy's eyes, although thwarted, was a sound one, and could be applied to this new book just as effectively. Therefore he set off for the graveyard to see if he could make his own Frankenstein's monster. Even now, it did not occur to Mr Pelmettle that he was insane, although he was. More so than ever.

When Mr Pelmettle arrived at the graveyard again, and presented Mr Grum with a rather unusual request, the gravedigger replied, 'Suit yourself. Fresh ones is in the cart,' and flicked his head towards a wooden vehicle piled up with anonymous victims of the latest plague.

'I can help myself?'

'It'll cost you,' Grum warned, sloshing back round to work on his grave.

'Anything!' called Mr Pelmettle, who went over to the cart and started selecting various body parts – hacking them off with a saw he had brought along specially. When he had what he wanted, he settled up with Mr Grum and walked to school through the driving rain.

All night Mr Pelmettle worked hard, sewing away in the staffroom, and as the sun rose, invisible behind the grey clouds and cold rain, he wiped sweat from his brow and tied the final stitches in his creation. He stood back to admire his work – and was pleased. It didn't look *quite* like Frankenstein's monster, admittedly. He had had to make do with body parts from a dark-skinned hunchback, a buxom serving wench and a young boy who'd had his neck snapped, but overall he felt that the effect was pretty good. The creature kept slumping forward, however, so Pelmettle fitted its ample bosom into an old jacket of his and hung it from a nail to keep it upright. Then he propped its lolling mouth open with a pencil to make it smile (he didn't want it to be *too* scary, after all), and stood back to gauge the effect.

'No,' he muttered to himself. 'That just looks weird.' And he took the pencil out again.

Nevertheless he was sure that Henry would be delighted, and intrigued, and spurred on to read more. When school began, he again sat out the barrage of insults and projectiles, and once the boys had gone at the end of the day, peeped round the lectern to find the room empty.

No Henry? he wondered to himself. Why, the lad has not missed a day's school in four years. I wonder what can be wrong?

Mr Pelmettle felt very disappointed not to have displayed his Frankenstein's monster after all the work he had put in and, even more than this, afraid that he might have lost the one good pupil he'd ever had.

So as he stepped out of school, rather than head towards home, he turned down the dark and narrow streets towards the boy's home. He pulled his cloak around him against the rain and stopped a few times to ask directions from boys loitering on the steps of the houses.

Eventually he stood looking up at a tall deserted building with dark windows. The number was scratched in chalk next to the doorway (from which the door had long ago been ripped) and he noticed that he had not passed a person in some minutes. In fact, there was no human voice to be heard, even distantly, and beyond the patter of rain there was only a deep and unsettling silence.

With some trepidation, Mr Pelmettle made his way in and began to climb the stairs. Not a shred of light leaked under any of the doors, and he had to fumble in the gloom for his way, until he reached the fourth floor. Then in front of him he saw an open door, and inside the flickering of a candle.

It was a one-room apartment with some bare mattresses visible in the far corner. A man sat on the room's only chair, bent over as though in pain.

Mr Pelmettle knocked lightly on the door.

'I hope I don't interrupt?' he asked. The man stared up at him.

'This is Henry Smart's house?'

Still the man gave no reaction.

'I wish to enquire whether Henry is quite well. I am his tutor, and he was not in class today.'

The man finally spoke with a great effort. 'I don't know what I've done, sir, to deserve all this. Tell me, sir, what can I have done?'

Mr Pelmettle was aghast. 'Done, sir? Why, I don't think you have done anything unless it is to rear the best-behaved and most intelligent boy in my class. Please reassure yourself – he is in no trouble.'

'He is killed, sir.'

'*Killed?* But—'

'By a carriage, sir. I don't understand. I brought him up always to be so cautious, and to cross the street with care. But they say he ran out like – like a maniac. As though fleeing from some terrible fright, although I can't imagine what. He slipped. The wheel snapped his neck in an instant.'

Mr Pelmettle leaned against the wall, unable to speak.

'But that's not all, sir. That's not all. I went to the graveyard where they had sent his body and it was gone. Graverobbers, you see, stole him before he even went into the earth. And now I can't even say goodbye to my dear boy.'

Mr Smart covered his face, too wrapped up in misery to think about Mr Pelmettle, or even to look at him.

Watching him, the thought finally occurred to Mr

Pelmettle that he might, after all, be a little mad.

'Tell me what I've done, sir. Please, tell me what I've done!' Now the man came out of his chair. He could not quite stand straight, and he held his hands forward, beseeching Mr Pelmettle to tell him what he'd done. For every step Mr Smart took towards him Mr Pelmettle took one step backwards, until, still watching the man's stricken face staring from his own doorway, he retreated from the candlelight and into the darkness.

‘hat’s *horrible*,’ I said to Uncle. He looked at me, worried. ‘I *love* it!’

‘You do?’ he asked, a little bit pleased in spite of himself.

‘It’s so *nasty*,’ I said, shivering happily. ‘It’s worse than any story I’ve ever heard.’ I trotted alongside him and begged for another.

‘Maybe some other time,’ he said. ‘But you’ll find no shortage of stories around here. And let me tell you, my boy, you’ll hear worse than that!’

I shivered again, more intensely than before. Stories worse than that? (Or better than that, if you put it another way?) I was desperate to hear them. At that moment Uncle led me round a last corner to a row of tall, tired-looking buildings. Near the end stood a very old-fashioned house – its timbers were warped and twisted with age, and the windows were crooked, like eyes crinkled by a smile. Seeing its harmless and friendly appearance, I knew at once that these were my new lodgings. At the same time, I knew with inexplicable certainty that I would be happy here.

Even though it was the middle of the night by now, chat and laughter could be heard from a few windows above me, and the sound of a guitar playing lazy ballads drifted over our heads.

‘This is a street of night owls,’ said Uncle, and there was fondness in his voice. Strangely he hung back self-

consciously as we reached the house and instead of marching up to the door, waited until a skinny, wide-eyed old man on the steps spotted us and ran inside. He returned a second later with a friendly-looking red-haired woman who greeted Uncle happily and introduced herself to me.

'My name is spelled *Nu-ala*, to rhyme with *koala*,' she said, 'but in fact it's pronounced *Nooler*, to rhyme with *jeweller*. Don't forget.'

I nodded. Over her shoulder I saw Uncle gulp and nod secretly at me. He had been pronouncing it wrong.

Uncle gave her a ten-second version of my story, and she looked at me with pity.

'Dear oh dear,' she said. 'How awful, Daniel. Come in out of the rain, lad.' She put an arm round me and kissed me roughly on the ear. As I dropped the untidy ball of possessions at my feet, I realized how tired I was and instead of responding I let out an enormous yawn.

'So you've got a spare room for the boy?' Uncle asked.

'I always do, you know that, Uncle,' she said. 'You look tired yourself. Why don't you come in, rather than traipsing all the way back across town?' He seemed embarrassed by the question and, making his excuses, started to walk away. I ran after him to say thank you.

'It's my pleasure – I couldn't have left you like that, once I'd spotted you,' he said. 'We'll meet again soon, Daniel.' He shook my hand, and I rejoined Nuala on the top step. She seemed amused, watching Uncle's thoughtful figure retreat along the street.

'He's a funny old stick,' she said. 'Did you see how he wouldn't meet my eye?'

'Yes,' I said. 'But why is that? You seem like old friends.'

'If I was given to vanity, I'd say it was because he fancies me, Daniel. But seeing as I'm not, I have to say I haven't the slightest idea. Come on, boy, let's find you a bed.'

That's almost the last thing I remember. How I hauled myself and my strange parcel of belongings upstairs, and shut the door, and got into bed, I have no idea. I only know that the most overwhelming wave of delicious tiredness pulled me deep down into the well of sleep without any further thought on my part, except a momentary vision of the huge house I had seen, and the beautiful woman. I saw the sack being pulled over her head again and again as I slipped off to sleep. It haunted me, and I knew I would have to go back to that place. She was part of my story now.

When I awoke, I had no idea where I was.

I looked up at a tiny window, covered in grime and

dust. At the end of my bed a dim shaft of light shone down from a large hole in the roof, making the specks of rain that drifted in shine like snow. Beneath it a steel basin was nearly full of rainwater, and round the rim a family of robins was perched, chatting happily to each other in confidential little peeps and chirps.

Very slowly and carefully I crawled to the end of the bed, rested my chin on my folded arms and watched them.

'Hello,' I said quietly, so as not to disturb them.

They stopped talking at once and all looked at me. I held my breath, worried that they'd fly away. Instead, after a second, the biggest one chirruped loudly in my direction, as if to say 'shut up!' and then they all looked back at each other and carried on fluttering around, and sipping at the water, and ignoring me entirely. I smiled.

There was a sharp knock at my door, and all of a sudden it swung inwards. My landlady stood there looking impatient, and holding a cup and saucer.

'Up!' she shouted. 'Your lessons start in half an hour!'

'How do you know that?' I asked, startled.

'You told me last night. Come on, it's nearly nine! Don't mind the Robinses (that's their name) – I want you out on the street in five minutes flat. There's your suit, look!' She pointed to my clothes on a hanger fixed in a crack in the wall, put the tea down on the room's only chair and slammed the door on her way out, as though to rid my brain of the vestiges of sleep.

Out on the street in five minutes flat I was, with a map she had drawn showing me the route. It was unlike any map I'd ever seen because it didn't have any words on it, but the route clearly marked with arrows and little pictures.

I carried with me my leather satchel containing the instruments I had been told to bring along to the first day of class (a scalpel, a stethoscope, a glass syringe and a bone-saw). Somehow I had survived my first day in this tumbling, rushing place with these things intact. Now my life here was about to begin.

Running most of the way, I reached the school building with a few minutes to spare. But standing in front of it I was uncertain – this wasn't like any school I had ever seen. Streams of moving people surrounded the building, carrying all manner of goods, or pushing them in barrows, and talking and arguing. I was only now starting to realize for the first time that arguing was not always bad, and that for some people it was their normal way of talking– as if for exercise, or fun. Certainly wherever you were in the streets around Tumblewater there was heated bartering and bargaining going on all about you, and everyone seemed

to go about it in such a cheerful fashion that it didn't seem harmful at all.

The front part of the school building seemed to be some sort of unusual marketplace. A different form of business was being carried out from each window. From the second floor a thickly bearded chap in a worn sailor's jacket was bellowing, 'SEA SALT FROM THE SEA-SIDE TUPPENCE A POUND, FINE AS YOU LIKE!' in a voice as though he was at the top of a ship, and had just spotted land. A woman called out to him and he threw a paper packet down right into her basket from a height of twenty feet or more. 'Mind me eggs!' she said, as she bustled past me to hand twopence to the nearest window-merchant, who handed it above him to the next man, who handed it to the next until it reached the bearded sailor who nodded his thanks and dropped it in his top pocket. From other casements women sold home-baked bread and buns and pies from a tray, and a thin spiky-looking man was droning on about something he called ''surance'.

''Surance, ladies and gentlemen!' he called plaintively. 'So's your loved ones will be looked after when you're gone. Life 'surance, death 'surance, 'surance from injury and illness. Sickness 'surance, health 'surance, goodness and badness 'surance. Let us at the Mutual Beneficial 'Surance Company 'sure YOU!' The very persuasiveness of his voice made me suddenly feel how horrible it would be to die without insurance, even though I had nothing to pay it with and no one who would benefit from it. But the face of the man was so thin and spiky, and his eyebrows arched so much like arrowheads when he was excited, that he had the look of someone who was more likely to slip a knife under your ribs than kiss you goodnight (to use a phrase I had overheard), which somewhat undermined his sales pitch.

Round the side of the building, between lots of people packing stalls away or laying things out on tables, from old shoes and bottles to fruit (both fresh and rotten-looking) to tin whistles and songsheets, I could see a door. I squeezed through the stalls to reach it, and it opened at my touch to reveal a staircase. The address I had written down said to go to the third floor, and so I made my way upward, glancing around with apprehension. The sign by the first-floor entrance offered the services of W. Hobson, Esq: Translator, Master of the Occult Sciences & Emergency Dentist, while the second-floor sign declared that I was at the door of Madame Perkinsini's Famous Ballet School. The doors on which the notices hung were so dirty and disused that they made the words on the signs seem somewhat dubious, but nevertheless I climbed onwards, refusing to be disheartened.

At the third floor I found myself in front of a door that was rotten and peeling, with no sign at all and a

pane of shattered glass at eye level. When I knocked, I got no response, and after waiting tensely for a while knocked again. I didn't know the rules – perhaps you were just supposed to march in? – so I turned the handle and opened the door.

The corridor in front of me was dim and silent, the air pungent with damp and rot. A cat walked between my legs and with its nose poked open another door further up the hall. I glanced round it, and found myself looking at a tubby man sitting at a small desk.

'Hello,' I said cautiously. 'I'm not sure I've come to the right place . . .' He said nothing, but jumped forward on his seat and burped, then covered his mouth, looking embarrassed, and hiccupped. He was about fifty years old, with a round face and round glasses, and wavy grey hair. He wore a very old suit and a very food-stained waistcoat.

Having hiccupped, he twitched and banged his knee on the underside of the desk, and then jerked backwards and knocked against what I at first thought was the wall, until I realised it was a huge stack of paper as dense as granite. Looking up I saw it rose all the way to a high ceiling – and the top was now swaying dangerously.

'Look out!' I said.

'Don't wo—' he tried to say as a lump of paper landed on his lap, making him jump. 'Don't worry,' he went on, and a second, huge mass of paper crashed into the space just beside his chair. We both waited for a second, then looked up slowly at the remaining pile. It seemed to have steadied itself for the moment.

'Hello,' I said a little more confidently. 'I'm here to see Mr Preston. To enrol in the surgery course that starts today.'

After shuffling in his chair for a few moments to get it out from under the desk, he came out to shake hands with me.

'Quite pleased, I'm sure,' he said in a surprisingly high, whistling voice. 'Mr Preston will be most pleased as well. My name is Stamps. I'm his secretary.' He smiled widely at me, tugged the edges of his waistcoat and brushed some pie crumbs off it, hoping I wouldn't notice. Then he stood, smiling and swaying from side to side, as though he was so happy to see me he could hardly contain himself.

The man seems quite mad, I thought, and this is clearly an eccentric establishment. I wondered if Mr Stamps was being employed as a favour to a relative.

'You sent your cheque ahead?' he asked as he sat back down, making a great fuss of sliding his chair back under the desk. His eyes looked up at me anxiously from above his wide smile.

'Of course,' I said earnestly. 'And I've got all the instruments I was told to bring,' I added, patting the leather satchel.

'Oh good!' he squeaked. I noticed he was beginning to sweat. 'Some students,' he said, nervously fingering a statuette of two toads swordfighting, 'some students unfortunately find the school quite hard to locate.' He shuffled some papers around. 'The advertisement was written a long time ago, and still mentions the old name for this building.'

'I was lucky – someone was able to direct me,' I said. 'Is . . . Mr Preston in?'

'Of course! I'll fetch him.' Giving me another enormous smile, he wrenched himself from under the desk and disappeared around the corner of the paper stack. 'Classes are due to start any minute, after all!'

Clutching my satchel, I looked around the room and saw what a truly amazing amount of paper had been collected there. It lay in piles and boxes and on shelves and in cabinets. Among it other effects could be seen, such as a French horn, and a teapot, and a golf club suspended halfway up the wall keeping two pillars of paper from collapsing into each other. The cat had somehow found its way to the top of one of them, where it rested its chin glumly on the edge and looked down at me.

Looking at all this I completely forgot my studies for a moment and edged to the left to peer around the huge bank of paper in front of me. I gasped.

The wall of paper, ten feet wide or more, extended

all the way to the back of the room, in one solid block. Except I now saw it wasn't *entirely* solid, because out of this, someone – I knew at once it must be Mr Stamps – had carved their own little apartment.

Paper stairs led up to a large square-shaped hole where there was an armchair and a small table holding a bottle of port and a glass. Behind it, set deep into the white paper as though it had been half dug out of the snow, was a writing desk and on top of it a bookshelf with a row of books uniformly bound in blue leather, as though he didn't think much of stories that were in any other colour.

And then above this there were steps to an upper layer, where a hammock hung from two ceiling hooks, with a chest of drawers, down which many years' worth of candles had dripped streams of wax.

I saw this great monument of madness, and felt the cold silence of the room, and the utter emptiness of all the rooms around me. With a shock I suddenly knew that there was no medical school, that there was no Mr Preston. I felt light-headed and sick as though I was looking down from a terrifying height.

I'm alone, I thought. I'm totally alone, stuck in this huge insane city!

I ran through the room and found that Mr Stamps had locked the door behind him to stop me following. I went to the window. As I stared into a writhing mass

of people, I realized the silence of these rooms had been amplified by the muffled noise of the huge marketplace outside. And down there in its centre, pushing and shoving his way through, I saw the bespectacled Mr Stamps, hurrying as fast as he could to get away.

I pulled at the door again desperately, but it was locked fast, so I ran back through the apartment, and down the stairs.

Outside I squeezed between the stalls again, and ran into the crowd. I was (and still am) a thin and wiry being, and I slipped through quickly, being jostled by people's elbows and baskets, tripping over their feet, apologizing and receiving shouts for my trouble. Overwhelmed and feeling I was going to be crushed by the crowd, I realized that I had nothing – no money, no food, no one to whom I could turn for help. I was qualified for no job. I would be thrown out of Turvey House as soon as my landlady became aware of my situation, I was sure, and on to the streets with nothing to protect me except a leather satchel of useless surgical tools.

I refused to give up so soon after coming to the city. As I got a clout to the back of the head, I started to get angry, and fought and squeezed and slid through the gaps, without apology, pushing against the crowd so determinedly that I didn't even know what direction I was going in. It was only after ten minutes of constant fighting, when a bash from a large barrel of a man elbowed the wind out of me, that my anger was exhausted.

I drifted with the crowd, and let the smells and sounds crash over me. Roasting chestnuts, fresh flowers, cheeses, coffee and ale mixed horribly with much ranker smells – dogs and rot and old clothes and the clammy smell of people's breath and flesh. But that was nothing compared to the noise of a thousand people trying to shout each other down and sell their wares all at the same time. Pleading and aggressive, musical and monotonous (and almost all of them incomprehensible), they made an all-encompassing and never-ending roar.

After a while I fell through a hole in the crowd and found myself standing in a circle that had formed round a man and a pig. Inside it was a smaller circle of excited-looking children. The man was big and muscular with long greasy hair and his face was sweaty from shouting.

'Ask Stanley!' he bellowed over our heads. His voice was deep, as though he'd stolen it from a man five times his size.

'Stanley knows the answers, see if he doesn't. Arrrsk STANLEY!' Looking around the circle, he met each and every one of us in the eye. Then, by way of introduction, he announced, 'Stanley, the sapient pig.'

He got down on his haunches and looked Stanley

level in the eye and said as he might say to a friend, 'Stanley – which hand is the coin in?' He had been fumbling his hands behind his back and offered them both to the pig, who for his part didn't seem very interested. He sat up against the wall on his large pig's backside with his trotters hanging limply in front of him. Being 'sapient' – I was pretty sure it was supposed to mean 'clever' – seemed to bore him a lot.

He was a brown-skinned pig with bloodshot eyes, which rolled slowly to and fro in silent contemplation. His tongue occasionally licked out to snap at the two flies that kept landing on his snout, and he gave the overall impression of an ancient emperor, too lazy to speak and afraid of nothing.

Dismissively he flicked a trotter at one of his owner's hands. The man turned to the crowd and showed them that it did indeed contain the coin, and that the other hand was empty. A few of us clapped half-heartedly. Then he turned and invited us to 'ask Stanley a question, ladies and gentlemen!'

A man called out, 'What's forty minus thirty-three?'

Everyone's eyes turned back to Stanley with interest. He raised a trotter and clapped it on the floor seven times. All at once everyone grew silent and fascinated.

Another man said: 'How many days are there in the

year?' Everyone laughed, and the big-voiced man said, 'Ask him anything he's able to answer, sir, and he'll do so. He can't answer you with speech. Which is quite understandable, being a pig.'

'How many years have I been married, then?' said the same man, with a smile.

The pig clapped the floor twice, and the man nodded, and laughed.

The owner asked us again: any other questions? And a man leaned forward from deeper in the crowd. There was something about his lined face, and the mean set of his mouth, and the unforgiving hardness of the eyes that unnerved me. 'Tell me this, little piggy,' he said. 'How many murderers are there in this crowd?'

Utter silence as we all looked at the speaker, who stared down at the animal, waiting for his answer. The gaze of the pig travelled down slowly from the clouds where it had been resting, and his tongue flicked, and the flies danced for a second before resting again on the brown snout. One of his trotters twitched, and then it rapped down hard on the ground, once. The whole crowd broke up into shouting as men and children alike scrambled to get away. In the midst of the chaos was the pig's owner, holding out a cap and begging for contributions, but no one paid him any attention. I tried to run too, but before I could escape I caught sight of the man who'd asked the disturbing question. He had

grabbed another man around the throat and was pinning him to the ground.

'Bradley Fuller,' he said into the other man's ear, 'I'm Inspector Rambull of the District Police and you're under arrest.'

At that, I too disappeared into the crowd, not caring who I bumped into. Horrified though I was, I felt a sick thrill at having been in the presence of a real murderer – although I knew such people existed, I had never really thought that you could meet one – and once I was safely away from the scene I drifted through the crowd again until I found myself in front of a fruitseller's stall. Realizing I had not eaten since lunchtime yesterday, the fruit in front of me suddenly appeared delicious and – feeling the few shillings in my pocket that were all I had in the world – impossibly expensive. The stallholder had no other customers for the moment and eyed me carefully.

'Help you, lad?' he asked warily.

My stomach bubbled emptily and I felt a little sick, asking, 'How much are the apples?' even though I knew I couldn't afford them.

'Three a penny,' he said, still suspicious. He watched my hands hovering near the fruit, so I stuffed them back in my pockets. Only a few minutes ago I had been about to start a prestigious education that might one day make me a gentleman – now I couldn't afford an apple and was being watched like a thief. The unfairness of it made me turn my face away angrily.

'You OK, lad?' asked the stallholder in a softer voice. 'Can't afford nothing?'

I shook my head miserably.

Before I knew what was happening, he'd clouted me on the shoulder with one of his massive hands (I reeled for a second before realizing he was being friendly) and dragged me back behind the stall. He pointed to the man with the stall next to him who was packing up his goods.

'Stick some of them spuds in a bag for him,' he said, 'and when you're done you can help me. You shift them fast enough maybe we'll spare you a bit of our lunch.'

I didn't hesitate but grabbed the sack on the ground by my feet and began helping the man (who pretended not to notice I was helping him) pile the potatoes, cauliflowers, onions and carrots into bags and stack them next to each other on his barrow – which was like the ordinary wheelbarrows I had seen back in the countryside but ten times larger, and taller than a man. The next thing I knew the man who'd made me the offer was packing up his stall as well and I was helping him. Then, with the market dying out all around us and the road opening up, we were all moving together and to my amazement the men pulled the barrows – which

looked as though they needed horses to move them – with their own arms.

We moved in a fleet of half a dozen stallholders. One of them, seeing me staring at this display of strength, laughed and said – 'Hop up!' I almost didn't believe him but was ready to accept a lift so as he paused for a minute I sat on the edge and felt the huge weight of the barrow buck and roll as he leaned forward.

One of the men had no barrow of his own – his goods were piled on his friend's cart – and he walked alongside happily, lighting his pipe and glancing at me.

'You're from out of town, right?'

I nodded.

'And you've never been here before?'

I shook my head.

'Then you won't have heard the tale of the Orphan? You being a young lad and seeming all lost reminds me of it,' he said.

I'm not *that* young, I thought, annoyed. But nevertheless I said I'd like to hear it, and as we went through the lanes out of the back of the market towards the home of the costermongers (a word I hadn't heard before, but he assured me that was the name of their job), he told me that bloodcurdling tale. And that's how I knew the story I told you at the beginning of this book.

'What do you think?' he asked as he finished it. I was chilled by the idea that I might have been so close to such a frightening little creature as the Orphan, and felt full of questions.

'But does he *know* that he's killing the people? Or is it all a terribly unlucky accident?' I asked. 'Does he realize that they die at all? Or is he some sort of ghost who will always be there, disguised as a murderous little boy? Is there any *truth* in it?'

Every question seemed to amuse the man more.

'Any truth?' he responded. 'Go back up to the crossroads and have a look for yourself.'

I felt a delicious shiver as I made a strange realization: it didn't matter if the stories were true or not – I almost didn't want to know, in case they *were* true. At that moment we were arriving at a short street of tiny, dirty cottages where there were lots of young children playing. The second they saw the men, they all ran into their houses shouting, 'They're back! They're back!'

As the men unloaded their goods, I sat on a stool near a brazier in the middle of the street where a fire burned noisily, and warmed my hands. Children came forward to throw bits of kindling over my shoulders now and then, and the men came back out carrying chairs and stools to sit around the fire. Without speaking, the children sat in the gaps between the chairs and on the laps of their parents and on the window ledges as their fathers ate their lunch and exchanged stories from their day's work (although it was only

lunchtime, I quickly realised they'd all been up since long before dawn).

The man who had brought me here sat beside me and introduced himself as Jed Field. 'Sandwiches,' he said, looking at his lunch sadly. 'That's a surprise. Eat them for me, would you?'

'Thanks, but I'm all right,' I said, but I couldn't help glancing at them hungrily.

'Really,' he said, pushing them closer. 'I hate the damn things.'

I took one gratefully.

'You want a sip of this?' he said, offering me a tin of soup. 'It's flavoured with Slumgullion.'

'What's Slumgullion?' I asked. At once all of the children (there must have been twenty or so around me) let out an uproarious cry at my stupidity, and started asking me questions like: where had I been living all this time? Hadn't I heard of the Slumgullion? Didn't I know *anything*?

'Wait, wait, wait, wait!' I shouted, laughing. 'Be fair, I've only been here for a day!'

'I was joking,' Jed explained. 'The Slumgullion is a monster, made up to frighten the kiddies.' The children heard him and all shouted in protest.

One of the other men butted in. 'It's a *real* monster that lives in the water,' he said, looking grave. 'Shaped like a man but with a lizard's skin, strong as an alligator and with teeth as long as your thumb.'

'Where does it come from?' I asked.

'Nobody knows,' he said. 'It lives in the sewers and attacks only at night, and leaves terrible bite marks on its victims. None who've seen it survive – we only know it from the wounds it leaves on its victims and people who've heard it slipping and sliding about the streets at night. And if you ask me,' he said quietly, so that everyone had to lean in and strain to hear his final words, '. . . it's a . . .' He looked pale and frightened, as though he couldn't continue, but the children urged him on. ('Don't be afraid,' one of the littler ones said.) 'Well, if you ask me,' he said, even quieter than before, so everyone had to crane their neck to hear, '. . . it's a . . . load of utter *rubbish*!'

The children broke out again in a chorus of anger and disapproval, and the costermonger smilingly ducked the scraps of bread that they threw at him.

The fire warmed everyone as the men settled into their lunch. The street was so narrow that people on either side of it could easily talk as though they were in the same room. Except, I now noticed, one girl who sat on a doorstep alone near the top of the little street. She glanced occasionally towards the rest of us, as though she hardly knew we were there, and then her attention returned to the corner, unwavering and intense.

'Why doesn't she join us?' I asked.

'That's poor Jenny,' said Jed quietly. 'She's waiting for her father to come home, and he never will. He was a simple candlestick-maker, and a good father. One day the police arrested him for stealing. He refused to admit to it, so they found him guilty anyway, and hanged him.'

'*Hanged* him,' I said to myself. 'That's awful!'

'No one has the courage to tell her, and it's been more than a year now. Seeing her there, waiting for her father's lantern to come round the corner every day, reminds us that the same fate could touch any of us at any moment, if that is the wish of Caspian Prye.'

'Caspian Prye?' I asked.

Now *everyone*, all the men and women and children, stopped talking and looked at me. 'You really don't know nothing about this place, do you?' asked Jed.

I shrugged helplessly.

'Well – Brigley tells it better than me.' The children gathered around the seat of a big, curly-haired man and urged him to tell me Caspian's story.

'But you've heard it so many times!' he protested, but that just made them ask him all the louder. 'All right, all right,' he said, picking up his plate and dabbing a potato in gravy. He popped it in his mouth, chewed, swallowed and addressed himself to me.

'Well, then. Caspian Prye is the landlord of all Tumblewater, meaning he's the owner of all our land. He owns the bricks in our walls and the mortar that holds them together and the mud you wriggle your toes into, little Lucy Pessell.'

A girl in the crowd squeaked and huddled closer to her father's legs.

'Now the one thing that Caspian Prye has in common with the Slumgullion,' he went on, 'is that no one we know of has ever clapped eyes on him. All we know of him is through his *men*.' Brigley pronounced this word with just about as much disgust as a man could heap into one syllable. 'His *men* who come and tell us the rents have gone up, and his other men who come to turn us out of our houses or –' and here he lowered his voice, with a glance towards little Jenny (we all looked at her too, still staring at the corner of the street) '– or to take us away to prison, or worse.

'Now, nasty landowners are two a penny,' he went on. 'Once upon a time, Caspian Prye was nothing more than one of those. An evil, lonely man lost among the miles of corridors in his enormous house, never happening across another human, never having to worry what people thought of him, going quite mad in his solitude. Someone with no purpose but to squeeze every penny out of us so we could hardly afford to eat, and to make sure we remained poor and miserable. If it wasn't for him, rather than sticking your toes through the holes in your shoes into the mud, Lucy, you might be wearing ballet shoes and performing at the opera house. And

you, Jane Cramb, instead of rattling a stick along the railings might have been making wonderful music on a grand piano instead.'

The girls stared at him, amazed by the idea of these transformations.

'But then one terrible day from the darkened windows of his carriage he saw a girl on the street, and decided that she would be his wife. She had dark hair and pale skin like porcelain, the composure of a duchess and a smile that would calm an angry bear. And so on and so forth . . . I ain't so good at describing girls anyway,' said Brigley, although to my mind he was doing a very good job. And all of a sudden my heart started to race, because something about his description made me think of the girl I had seen in the window.

'At the thought of having a wife, Caspian Prye saw himself changing his ways. He imagined being a good and kind landlord, presiding over a prosperous district of happy people. So he invited the girl to his house and introduced himself, and assumed that because he was very rich and she was very poor, she would fall in love with him at once. But, my little lads, that isn't the way into a girl's heart, you know,' he said.

'No one's ever tried it on *me*, I'm sure,' said his wife. He bit her hand playfully and when she cried out he kissed it better, pulled it round his neck again and went on with his story.

'But the girl was repulsed by Caspian. He didn't realize what had happened to him in all those years away from human company, never seeing a living soul, and leaving notes for his secretary each night so he didn't have to speak to anyone. And eventually, after the longest time, he lost even the idea of other humans. Which is to say, he became so strange and twisted that at last he *forgot he was a person at all*.'

There was an awful silence as we waited for Brigley to explain what this meant.

'Now you children,' he went on, after another mouthful of stew, 'you know that our bodies grow back to what they understand? So, if you cut off a finger in a threshing machine, as my poor brother Gerald did, then it grows back perfectly as it did before.' Several of the younger children nodded in acceptance of this delicious lie.

'Right,' said Brigley. 'Just like we all know that men who keep dogs come to have the same face as their pets, in time.' At this the oldest of the men was awoken by children around his chair laughing and pulling at his trousers. He snorted awake and in alarm gathered up the dog that had been snoozing at his feet, holding it close and inadvertently showing Brigley's argument to be true.

'So therefore it is said,' he went on, now almost whispering, 'that because after years of madness and

solitude Caspian Prye no longer knew he was a man, his features no longer knew how to arrange themselves, and had grown so that he did not any longer even *look like a man*. And that is the strange unhuman figure that the girl saw. She was terrified, and could not meet his eye, and had to say no to his offer of marriage. And, so the story goes, Prye locked her away in one of his many buildings, and started searching for a way to trick her into accepting him.

'There the girl remains to this very minute, somewhere in the buildings around us in Tumblewater, in a secret, cursed chamber. So whenever you walk along these streets, look upward at the windows. You might just see her looking down at you.

'That's not the end of the story,' continued Brigley, 'because from that day on Caspian Prye became like the very Devil, and took his revenge on Tumblewater. He took over the police force and turned them into the mean thugs and bullies we know. He changed the law so that almost any crime was punishable by death. Look at the dreaded Ditcher's Fields cemetery by the river, where the crowds can see a dozen so-called "criminals" hanged every week, and their bodies hastily buried with no funeral. The place is filled to overflowing with his victims.'

'Enough!' shouted the man who had told me the story of the Orphan. He had put down his lunch and was looking quite disgusted. 'Enough, enough. I have to work all day to put money in his pocket; it doesn't mean I have to hear about him as well. Someone tell a story.'

Straight away three or four of the men volunteered, each asking the crowd of children which tale they wanted to hear. I felt the warmth of the fire, and the comfort of the food in my stomach. There was nothing I wanted more than to be told a good story. Now more than ever, because as the man whose story was chosen – the sleepy old man with the dog – began to speak, I felt his words enwrap me like a cloak, and for those few minutes forgot everything that had happened to me in Tumblewater, and the horrors I had heard about Prye.

'Now this one is about a poor lost character like Daniel here, but one who is even younger than all of you kids. Do you want to hear it?'

The crowd replied emphatically that they did, at a very high volume.

So the man began the tale of . . .

# THE FOUNDLING

At the top of Tumblewater Hill there was a windmill. It was a large building, which, instead of looking rather picturesque as windmills quite often do, was in fact impressively ugly, looming against the sky and towering over all that was around it. The middle of a city is a funny place for a windmill, but it had been built a long time ago and the city had gradually grown around it. Now it looked despondent and forgotten among the newer, smarter factories, which perhaps accounted for some of its ugliness.

The rain fell down upon the enormous brick edifice of the mill, just as it did on everything else. ('Edifice, Lucy Pessell?' said the man at this point. 'Why, let's just say – the front.') On the roof it made a roaring din, which all but deafened the men who laboured around the huge and dangerous machinery.

The three clerks who worked in the little office, though, were tucked away at the back of the building, and could only hear the rain battling against the large windows that overlooked the cobbled street outside.

The oldest, roundest and kindliest of the three men was Mr Welling. He had worked in the same job for forty-two years, for which he was grateful, and he took a jovial, friendly interest in his younger colleagues – Mr Tuck, who was a thin, tense man of about forty and young Dick, a pleasant but rather simple lad, a few weeks shy of his seventeenth birthday.

Each of the clerks' desks faced the window, so that when a delivery of grain was made they could look down to the wagon and count the sacks, and make sure they were not being short-changed by the farmer. Then one of the clerks would withdraw the money from the huge safe and hand payment over to the farmer's delivery lad, who would usually be standing in the corner, dripping and cursing and wringing out his cap into the washing bowl the clerks had placed there specially, to stop their floor from getting wet.

Every day Mr Welling arrived to find the office precisely as he had left it, and precisely as he had found it every other morning since his first day at the mill as a boy of sixteen. Every evening he rose from his desk at six thirty, having remained for an extra half hour to double-check the books, and to make a couple of discreet corrections to Dick's ledger. Then he would put on his coat, look out at the rain, shiver, take a little tot of brandy from his hip flask to protect him from the cold, collect his umbrella from the stand and set out into the streets.

On this particular day, Mr Welling went through the above routine in every detail, and when he left he wove through the narrow lanes towards home feeling a little more distracted and unhappy than usual. Approaching his sixtieth birthday, he was only a few years away from taking retirement, and with each passing hour he longed for it more. After a lifetime's hard work, he pined for the modest pension he had managed to save for himself, and the chance to spend long winter days (like this one) by the fireside with a newspaper, or a good book, and maybe a little treat like some biscuits and cheese.

So much did thoughts of retirement consume him that before he knew it he was at his front door, holding the umbrella with one hand and fiddling in his pocket for the keys with the other.

As his hand scrabbled among the tobacco pouch, the matchbox, the pipe and other assorted items, his eye fell on the little torrent that whished past his door day and night, splashing over the bottom step. After a few seconds, still unable to find the keys and moving his hand to search in another pocket, he realized he had been staring at a little package that was bobbing in the stream, stopped from flowing downward by the step's edge. It was about the size of a loaf of bread and wrapped in a coarse, mud-covered cloth.

Curious, he leaned down and poked it with his finger, and then jumped backwards with fright at the sound of a baby's cry.

'Good lord!' he thought to himself. 'Someone has lost their child!' In a state of alarm he gathered up the package, found his key and bustled inside, with water dripping all down him.

Inside his kitchen, he placed the bundle down carefully on the table, removed his coat and hat as quickly as he could, and ran to the cupboard in his bedroom to fetch a blanket.

Weak and tremulous cries kept coming from the bundle as he returned with the blanket and stripped away the sopping swaddling clothes. The cries grew weaker and, fearing for the child's health, he wrapped it up carefully and then held it against his shoulder, patting it gently as he had seen women do, and speaking softly to it.

'There we go,' he said. 'All right now, everything's all right.'

Soon the baby slept soundly against his shoulder.

Well, that's all very well, he thought, but what am I to do with it? Its mother must be sick with worry. I must find her at once.

As gently as he could he laid it in an old picnic basket, which he had almost forgotten he owned, and which he first lined carefully with blankets and bedsheets. Then he made a fire and lit it, and placed the improvised cot on a kitchen chair close to it, so the baby might be warm. He also lit a candle and placed it nearby, to add to the meagre light of the fire, so that the baby might not be alarmed by darkness when it woke, although he had no idea whether children were afraid of the dark (as he had been and, secretly, still was) when they were just babies.

When he was satisfied with the arrangement, he put on his coat again and set off to find the police station.

As a law-abiding citizen who kept himself to himself, and had been lucky enough never to be the victim of a serious crime, it was only when he reached the end of his street that Mr Welling realized he had no idea where the police station was. He had to ask directions three times, feeling more guilty and suspicious-looking with each request. He found it, eventually: a small building between a tailor's shop and a derelict butcher's. A blue lamp hung above the door and there were bars over the windows, rather making it seem as though the policemen were themselves locked in or the rest of the world locked out. Mr Welling wondered briefly to himself whether a district with such a terrible reputation for crime deserved a larger police house.

He squeezed in through the tiny door, closing his umbrella and sending water cascading on to the floor, only to find it seemed even smaller inside than out. The interior was brightly lit and whitewashed so starkly that everything in the room seemed to be shining white, except for the single policeman who looked up at him with an impatient and suspicious expression.

'My friend!' said Mr Welling breathlessly. 'Something terrible has happened. I have discovered a lost baby on my doorstep. No doubt you already know of this? It must be returned to its parents as soon as possible to spare them any further worry.'

To Mr Welling's astonishment, the policeman did not move, or speak, or do anything at all. In the small space between the counter and the wall behind him, he grew a little uncomfortable.

'Didn't you hear me? I have discovered an infant. Lost and alone. He must be reunited with his parents!'

The policeman remained perfectly still, as though

he had not heard a sound, for several seconds. In disbelief, Mr Welling looked around for someone else to help him, but the room was so small there was nothing else to see. At last, the officer spoke.

'Bring him here,' he said with a cool voice. 'We know what to do.'

'What do you mean?' asked Mr Welling. 'There has been a report of a missing child, has there not?'

The policeman looked at Mr Welling in sour disbelief, and spoke confidentially. 'Listen, mister. You seem like a regular sort. I wouldn't go getting mixed up in all this – we get eight or ten of these a year, little abandoned ones whose mothers don't want 'em. Just bring it along and leave it with me. The workhouse will take care of it well enough.'

Mr Welling stood back, appalled, and bumped into the wall. 'Whose mothers don't *want* them?' he fairly shouted. The thought made his stomach turn over. 'In *this* day and age?'

The policeman sighed and looked away, running his hand through his hair, as though he was trying to explain something very simple and obvious, and it made him inexpressibly tired.

'Sir –' he said, but Mr Welling would not hear another word. He was out of the door and almost running home, all of a sudden worried about the candle he had left burning so close to the crib.

'Oh dear, oh dear,' he thought to himself. 'The workhouse. I have heard such terrible things about the workhouse. No, I cannot allow it. That policeman did not know my name and did not follow me home and, if they do find me somehow, I shall fight them for it!'

His mind was quite made up. In his quiet and lonely little world he had forgotten years ago that life could be so cruel, and that the people supposed to protect us – be they mothers or the police – could be so indifferent. He would bring up the baby himself, and nothing could change his mind.

With this new responsibility, and the thoughts of what changes this would bring to his life, Mr Welling could not sleep a wink. Which is just as well, because the baby boy woke up crying at roughly one-hourly intervals throughout the night.

By dawn, when the child woke for the seventh time, Mr Welling realized that it must be hungry, and that he had no idea how to feed it. He rooted around in the rackety kitchen drawers for a long while before he came up with a system that he was rather pleased with. He found an old copper funnel which he scrubbed until it shone, and into this he forced a clean cloth, which he pressed down with a pencil until a tip of it stuck out of its end. Then he poured small amounts of warmed milk down the funnel so that the baby could suck at the protruding tip, just as it would if it was being fed by its mother.

Arriving at work, though, he found things more difficult than he had hoped. The baby cried periodically throughout the day, and each time he had to stop his work and calm it or feed it milk, while ignoring the incredulous looks of the younger clerks. He allowed them to think what they liked, and hoped they assumed he was looking after a niece or a nephew they had never heard of.

Late in the afternoon, during which he had found it almost impossible to concentrate on work and had got quite behind with his accounts, he took his customary brief walk on to the floor of the mill to see how the men were getting on. They were always pleased to see him, and always happy to get away for a moment from their grinding hard work. Today some of them were converting a stack of huge timbers into a giant new vat for the flour. As two of the workmen came over for a chat, Mr Welling placed the basket down on a shelf by his side and felt it whizz out of his hand. With a high-pitched scream he realized that what he'd taken for a shelf was in fact a moving belt that drew wood towards a giant saw, the kind which could cut through planks as thick as railway sleepers. The man who operated the machine was at Mr Welling's elbow, and had not noticed anything was wrong so with three giant bounds Mr Welling plunged forward in a desperate leap, his hand plucking the basket from the belt just as the whirring blades nibbled at its side.

He held it tightly, taking deep breaths, as the workmen gathered round him and stared down at the screaming child.

*

The following evening Mr Welling carried the basket with him to the market. He moved between the covered stalls with care, picking out the few fruits and meats he could afford each week, and checking the prices between different stalls so he could save himself a few pennies, as he always did.

Walking home, he was pleased with his haul. He had six apples, four pears, three lamb chops, a lemon, a pound of potatoes, half a pound of carrots and – his treat – a few ounces of raspberries. He felt so hungry he couldn't recall the last time he had looked forward to dinner so much.

And then –

'My God!' he said, and set off running back towards the market. Where was the baby? He asked at every stall. Fat, indifferent women stared back at him as though he was stupid. So he asked again, all the louder. Other stallholders, grimy men with beards and cheap clay pipes, ignored his questions and instead offered him plums or gooseberries 'at the best price on the market'. Still Mr Welling asked louder, grabbing other shoppers by their elbows, asking everyone who went by, until finally a little grey-haired lady pointed across the way. He saw it, his old picnic basket with its beloved cargo, hanging over the edge of a travelling butcher's stall he had briefly stopped at earlier, unnoticed by the arrogant owner as he showed off to the crowd.

'Now I ain't offerin' you four sausages for sixpence,

ladies and gentlemen,' the man was shouting, 'I ain't even offerin' you *six* sausages for sixpence . . .'

The same second that he saw it he watched, open-mouthed, as the basket tilted forward and teetered on the edge for a second so that Mr Welling caught sight of the carefully wrapped bundle inside. He cried out to try and catch the butcher's attention and dashed forward as he saw the basket fall. A heavy cart drawn by four horses was passing close in front of the butcher's stall. With all his breath he shouted, 'HALT THERE, HALT!' and threw himself bodily beneath the horses. In the terror and excitement of seeing the basket fall and the wheels slipping in the mud, and the frightened neighing of the horses, and the thundering of their hoofs all around him, he lost consciousness.

When he came round, a couple of friendly stallholders were wiping the worst of the mud from Mr Welling's suit and trying to help him to his feet. A few less friendly people, including the angry owner of the cart, stood around talking loudly about his lunatic actions.

'What's a madman like you doing free on the streets?' shouted the nearest. 'Get on out of here, mate – before you get yourself hurt.'

'And not by a cart,' said another.

But once he knew where he was he had other worries. 'My child!' he said, and darted back beneath the cart to see if the baby was anywhere to be seen.

First he saw the basket on its side in the mud, empty. Then he saw the child, which had come to rest within a few inches of a muddy wooden wheel. He looked down and felt a happiness that was piercingly sad, or a sadness that was piercingly happy, as he saw the baby's mouth wide open and trembling. He realized that the sound he could hear was not the ringing in his ears from knocking his head but the high-pitched wail of the poor little creature.

He picked up the bundle and hugged it to his shoulder right there, with his head pressed against the underneath of the carriage. 'Dearest child,' he said, 'I'm so sorry. I'll look after you better from now on.'

And so he clambered from beneath the dripping side of the cart in front of the onlooking strangers, who stared at him until they saw the baby clasped to his shoulder. Then they started to mumble to each other and wander away into the rain. He recovered his dropped shopping and umbrella, and walked home fully laden and happy.

It was when he reached the front door, though, that Mr Welling met his next difficulty.

He had five wet bags of shopping in one arm, with which he was also holding the umbrella. And in the other he had the baby. How he was to open the door, he had no idea. So, with the shopping bags fit to fall apart, he lowered the child gently to the top step, so that he could search his pockets for the keys. Once he found the keyring, he held it by the thickest key and let the others fall away, and then unlocked the door.

As he pushed it open, he looked down, and for the third time in two days his heart stopped – he saw his umbrella knock against the baby so that the little parcel slid smoothly from the top step and into the wide rushing stream of rainwater that perpetually gurgled in the gutter below, the very one he had plucked it from in the first place. It bobbed lightly for a second as though deciding where to go, and then dived in a sudden gulp down the wide-mouthed drain.

Mr Welling remained stooped, his mouth open once again in horror, staring at the letter-box-shaped hole down which his single reason for living had just disappeared, as swiftly and silently as a leaf.

This time he did not panic. He placed his bags and umbrella inside the door and went out, shutting it behind him. Then he ran up the street to the nearest manhole, and banged on the door of the man who lived opposite, who was the local gravedigger, and a friend of his.

'What is it?' the man said, opening his door suspiciously, a candle beneath his big, drooping nose.

'Mr Grum, quickly!' Mr Welling shouted. 'You must help me open the manhole at once! A disaster! A baby has fallen down!'

'A live one?'

'A what?' asked Welling. 'Yes, of course, a live one!'

Mr Grum hurried back into his house, his nightcap bobbing behind his head, and a spade was produced. He followed Mr Welling into the street and they both set about loosening the lid as quickly as they could. Finally, Mr Welling heard a growl in the metal below his feet and leaned back on the spade with all his strength to flip the iron lid over. It had seemed so flimsy when he had walked over it a hundred – no, a thousand, ten thousand – times, yet now he saw a whole dark world that had been hidden beneath him, its mouth open at his feet.

'Go, quickly,' said Mr Grum. 'I'll be here.'

In an instant Mr Welling was climbing down towards the foetid running waters that fairly screeched with smell. He held the gravedigger's candle above his head, for when he reached it the water came up to his chest. By its light he could see forward through the curtains of rain dripping from the grates above, and his other hand was cupped above the flame to prevent it from going out.

After wading for about a hundred yards, he reached what he thought was roughly the spot beneath the drain where the baby had vanished. He was wet through, to the last hair on his head, and just about as cold as a man could be. Here the tunnel emptied into a larger chamber, with drain holes sending water cascading down from all corners of the ceiling, and six or seven other tunnels shooting off in all different directions, some of them swilling thick water into the room, some of them sending it pouring away into the dark. Mr Welling felt perfectly lost and hopeless for a moment. The baby had been swallowed up and he was sure he would perish down here from cold and fright and confusion.

Then, through the constant dripping, he thought he saw a snatch of white cloth. He fixed his glasses closer against his eyes and looked again. There was something lodged on a shelf on the other side that was a similar size and colour to the baby – and the whining noise he could just hear over the crashing of water was one he knew well.

He found a gap in the wall, where some bricks had fallen away, in which to place his candle. Then he set out, swimming breaststroke across the chamber, the only way to swim that he could remember from his one trip to the seaside fifty years before. In a few minutes, blinking the water from his eyes, he had the baby in his arm. He set out to return, which, swimming one-armed, took a lot longer, because he kept finding himself going round in circles.

Finally, by the light of the flame, he reached the other side of the chamber. With lots of coughing and choking, he tried to push the baby safely on to the ledge and keep his head above water at the same time. Spitting out water as he drew himself up, he collected the nearly burnt-down candle, and began to struggle back through the dark dripping tunnel towards the open manhole, until he found himself staring up at the face of Mr Grum in a tiny circle far above.

When he had climbed up the ladder and wrapped himself in the blanket his friend had brought along, carefully cradling the baby all the while, he thanked

Grum dearly and retreated back to his house. Here, he got the fire going and warmed some milk on it, fighting to keep his eyes open all the while. Then he fed the milk to the baby, and put it down in the cot, keeping watch until the little thing closed its eyes. Finally he got into his own bed and, after replaying the day's harrowing scenes in his head a dozen times, he fell asleep.

That Friday afternoon, an exhausted Mr Welling sat at his desk, facing the onslaught of rain against the window. He had never really noticed the sound of the rain before. Or, if he had, it had never really got on his nerves.

Now it was another story. Feeding the baby warm milk every few hours (including in the office, where he had to put up with the disdainful looks of Dick and Mr Tuck) had deprived him of any real rest whatsoever. Now, the ceaseless clattering of drops against the pane sounded to him like rats nibbling against the glass for hour after hour.

Half past six finally arrived, though, and he was glad to be taking the baby home. He was so tired he barely knew who he was, but at the same time he was happier than he had ever been in his life. His accounts were in turmoil, his files were scattered over the desk, and rather than accepting his well-meaning advice his colleagues now sniffed with an air of suspicion whenever he ventured to make a suggestion. But none of it mattered. He had another human life in his care, a reason for being, something to give meaning to his years of retirement.

This single happy thought ran through his head during his journey home, and again as he opened his front door, balancing the baby's basket on one hip, his brief-case dangling by its handle from his little finger. He shuffled inside, set the sleeping baby down on the kitchen table, and beside it placed the small packet of flour that he was given each week for free by the mill's owners. With it he always made his one loaf of bread, which he would eke out for seven days of frugal lunches and suppers.

As he opened and closed the various kitchen cupboards, another wave of tiredness overcame him and he stopped for a moment, putting his hands over his eyes. A feeling of sympathy and understanding for every young mother in the land filled him. How could they manage it? What would it be like if he had *two* of these little things to look after? Dizzy with exhaustion, he mixed and kneaded the dough, holding the baby in one arm, knocking things over with the other and generally getting himself into a bother.

When the loaf was ready to bake, he put the baby down, threw the bread into the oven, lit the fire and settled in the armchair for a few moments' peace.

He awoke suddenly an hour later, in a panic.

The bread would be spoilt, and he would have to waste money buying more! He launched out of his chair and rushed to the kitchen. He took the stick he used to lift open the oven door when it was hot, unlatched it and was about to pull it open when a thought came upon him. He lowered the stick and stared at the oven door for a second, perfectly silent.

The little apartment filled with a silence louder than the roar of water in the cavernous sewer. Mr Welling had not yet known an hour when the baby had not made a noise. He stood slowly and walked back to the drawing room. The fire had died down in the grate and the basket sat on its stool, glowing in the soft orange light.

Very slowly, Mr Welling advanced until he could see into the basket, and all of its contents.

He saw old blankets, folded to make a mattress. And old bedsheets, arranged to make warm and comfortable bedding. And a humble, battered tin, filled to the brim with rising dough.

I saw from the looks of the children that they were just as appalled as I was by the story's horrible ending (although I suspect it took them a few seconds to grasp its full meaning). There was a sneaky satisfaction to be seen on their faces too, as though (again, just like me) they enjoyed it because it was so awful.

'Can I ask you something?' I said quietly to Jed. 'Does *everyone* in Tumblewater have a story to tell?'

'Everyone knows a few that they've heard,' he nodded. 'Look at this.' He held out his hand for two seconds and it became instantly spattered with rain. 'How much time do you think we spend indoors? And how many toys do you think I can afford after paying rent on my house and rent on my barrow and buying my fruit? You need to have some way of keeping the children entertained,' he said. 'Telling a good story keeps them quiet – and what's more, it's free. You can see why we've become good at it.'

'I suppose so, but why are the stories always so ghastly?'

He laughed at me. 'Put it this way – how does it make you feel when you hear about something really *terrible* happening to someone?'

'It makes me sorry for them, of course,' I said.

'And afterwards?'

'Well . . .' I thought about it. 'Well, it makes me feel lucky not to *be* them, I suppose.'

'*Exactly*,' he said. 'You've got it. Life isn't exactly a bed of roses around here. So hearing a good, grisly story – especially one set in Tumblewater – makes you appreciate what you've got.'

I remembered how much I'd wanted the story to start so I could forget my own predicament for a moment. Jed was right. But now that I thought about my problems again I realized I had to go. I thanked Jed wholeheartedly for taking me in at the moment when I most needed it, and feeding me, and treating me like a human being. I promised I would be back.

As I walked back towards my lodgings, I couldn't stop thinking about the stories I'd heard and Jed's insistence of how many more there were. I had always loved stories, listening to them, telling them and reading them whenever I had the opportunity. Grown-ups told me that no use could ever come of it, so I had given up dreams of writing tales of my own, and settled on surgery as my future career. Now, as I trudged back to my lodgings with nothing in front of me but the most dismal prospects, I couldn't help but be excited by these grisly tales, and the idea that there were many others to discover in Tumblewater, possibly more than I could imagine. Was there something about living here that

made people more imaginative, more gory, more grotesque?

One of my faults was (and still is) that once I'm interested in something I can't leave it alone. As I mused, I wondered whether the Slumgullion (from listening to the children it seemed to have lots of names – the Creature, the Beast, the Slurgoggen) could be true, and most of all realized I wanted to know more about this man Caspian Prye as well as the girl I had seen in the window, especially if there was a chance they might be connected. I was surrounded by stories on all sides, and although I was penniless it made me more determined to stay here, find some way to survive, and find out what would happen next. And then I told myself to stop being so blooming overdramatic, and to concentrate on remembering Jed's directions and finding my way home.

When I arrived, a short man was leaning against the railings outside Turvey House, his back bent uncomfortably. He looked pained, as though he had tied himself in knots working out the odds and angles to this or that and had got his body twisted up in his calculations. When he saw me, he unwound to his full height, which was still quite short, and approached cautiously.

'You are Mr . . . ?' he said uncertainly.

There was something in his expression that was pleading but shrewd as well, and I didn't answer. His eyes were a very pale green and disconcertingly beautiful, but otherwise he was dirty, and there was something slick about him, as though he was a creature that lived in the water, but was walking on dry land. I waited for him to speak.

'You are,' he tried again, 'a young gentleman who has some . . . medical instruments?'

'Yes,' I said, startled. 'How did you know that?' He squirmed and smiled shyly. Three of his teeth were missing.

'A friend told me, sir, and I heard you might sell them, that's all.' Then, as though he was sickened by his own ingratiating smile, he became all of sudden impatient, looking over my shoulder and jumbling out the rest of his words. 'You *would* consider selling them, I think? Then follow me – I know someone who will buy them.' And he began walking away at quite a speed. I ran to catch up.

'Yes!' I said. 'I do need to sell them, as it happens.' I was mystified that such a small piece of news could travel so far and fast.

After we had walked for a few minutes he led me down a cold, quiet street of closed shops.

'Who is it you're taking me to?' I asked.

He turned and gave me a compassionate smile, and the twisted hunch of his back made him seem humble once again. 'You'll get a good price, lad, don't worry.

We'll get you some money.'

He had led me down a narrow alleyway to a tiny enclosed space behind four buildings, with dirty forgotten windows looking down at us from each side and small backyards filled with rubbish, piled up over our heads.

Switching his attention to a locked door, which was reinforced by a heavy iron grille, the green-eyed man took a strange instrument out of his pocket. It looked like a long and twisted metal finger with a sharp end and he wedged it between the door and the frame with a great squeaking, wrenching noise. He worked it down into the lock, which after several heavy twists snapped open. As he did this, his look became intensely fierce, and I realized again how quiet and dark it was around here, and how the windows looked so empty you couldn't believe anyone had looked out of them for years and years.

The door swung open and the man gave his awkward, pleading smile again. 'I always have to do that,' he said. 'I really must get this door fixed; it *is* a pain.'

'What's your name?' I asked suspiciously.

All the cunning and craft disappeared from his eyes at once, and he let go of the door. He bowed his head. 'I do beg your pardon,' he said, most politely. 'Pisk. Mr E. H. Pisk. Your humble servant, sir. Now let me show you in, and see about these items you want to sell.'

I was shocked by my own rudeness. What had got into me? Here was a man who had sought me out to perform what might be a life-saving favour, and I seemed to be accusing him of something!

Inside the dim and dusty shop, Mr Pisk lit a lamp, and blew the dust off the till drawer where the pennies were kept. We were surrounded from floor to ceiling by a multitude of strange or unusual objects. Swords and helmets, a stuffed pelican (the beauty of the creature marred somewhat by the pipe someone had glued in its mouth) and two judges' wigs on a crystal ball were the first things I saw. It was a pawnbroker's shop, meaning whatever money I got for my instruments I could buy them back, if my fortunes changed. I felt even guiltier for having doubted Mr Pisk – this was better than I had hoped.

As he searched through some drawers beneath the counter, my eye was drawn to a big, ungainly shape that hung in the middle of the wall above me. In the gloom I could just make out that it was a very large and ugly cuckoo clock. The second hand was elaborately carved and above its ticking I saw that the door where a cuckoo would usually appear was much larger than normal. On a scroll above the wooden gates was carved 'THE ANIMOUL'.

For some reason (it being a couple of minutes to the striking of the hour) I wanted almost desperately for

'the Animoul' not to appear, and to get out of the shop as soon as possible. 'It's a shame the owner's not in,' Pisk was saying, 'but he lets me transact business in his place. I'm a close friend of his. Now, let's have a look at your things.'

Only recently lit, the lamp was still just glimmering weakly, so it was in the semi-dark that I put my satchel on the counter in front of him and carefully removed my instruments. He handled each one roughly before putting it to one side.

'One scalpel, one stethoscope. A glass syringe and a bone-saw,' he said, writing them down.

'Now, these items are quite commonplace,' he said, returning to his former impatient manner. 'You'd be lucky to get more than a shilling for each, from anyone.' And he backed up his words with a very hard and knowing look, as though ready for my arguing back.

I felt my heart rising up my throat in desperation. 'I beg to differ, Mr Pisk,' I said as calmly as I could. 'I believe they cost two whole pounds, together, when new. Which they still are – they've not been used.'

'I know,' said Pisk, 'but the very fact of you owning them makes them second-hand and almost worthless. Why would a reputable surgeon buy a bone-saw second-hand, when it might have any number of diseases hidden between its teeth?' and he gently rubbed the tip of his finger against the new blade to illustrate his point.

I couldn't think of anything to say, and felt confused and angry with myself at not being able to think straight. 'What can you give me, then?'

He shrugged again. 'Maybe I can stretch to two shillings a piece. So that's eight in total.' He grabbed the lantern and took it towards the back of the shop, where we had come in. 'Wait here,' he said. 'I'll have to pop round the corner to fetch the money, as I don't have a key to the safe. I'll just be a second.'

He yanked the door open and slammed it shut behind him before I could say anything, and I was alone with the ticking of the foreign clock. My heart, which had been racing anyway, now began to pound even faster. There was something wrong about this. Panic began to itch inside me, and I crept towards the door he had closed. Heavily built to protect against burglars, with the massive iron grille on the other side, I could hardly imagine that it would move for anyone, let alone me, as I twisted the handle. It didn't turn. How had Pisk made it open? My panic worsened as I started to feel trapped.

Then I heard a voice on the street outside. 'Thief!' it cried. I wondered whether someone had just escaped from one of the shops nearby, and tried to peer out but the window was made of clouded glass and only shapes were visible. 'THIEF!' came the shout again, and I recognized the voice, bewildered. A figure ran past,

hard to make out, still shouting. 'A robber in the shop! Come quick! Police!' It was Pisk.

I didn't move, still totally mystified, thinking perhaps he didn't mean me. But the walls of the shop closed in around me, and the Animoul clock sounded like it was tutting at my stupidity. Of *course* he was talking about me. But – but what had I done? As I remembered the costermongers' stories of false arrests, I realized that I had to get away fast. Then a noise stopped me. It was the gentle creaking of wooden wheels coming to a halt. I was already near the back of the shop, but I looked again at the front window.

A carriage had pulled up outside. It looked oddly out of place and it took me a second to notice in what way it was unlike any other I had seen: it was white, and so were the horses that were pulling it. A figure climbed out of it quite slowly and at leisure, ignoring Pisk's cries, which still rang loudly down the street, and walked up to the glass.

Nothing could be seen clearly through that shop window, misted as it was and thickly grimed on the outside. But the face came closer until its two pale eyes, pressed to the glass, were almost distinguishable. There was a faintly detectable strangeness about the features, as though they had been stretched or the face's whole shape had been twisted, which made me think I knew who this was. My heart stood still. The man peered in at the glass for several long seconds, trying to see me in the gloom of the shop, so I held my breath and didn't move, watching the indistinct movements of the eyes as the dark pupils flitted left and right, searching for signs of life.

Pisk's voice grew louder as he came back towards the shop. At this the man's face withdrew, he walked calmly to his carriage, and it pulled quietly away before Pisk arrived back with half a dozen shouting men, all hungry to catch a thief.

Everything was crashing in on me. I turned and stared up at the back door. Above it was a semi-circle of dirty glass. Already I could hear footsteps coming and see light flickering against the walls from lanterns being held against the front window. To my side was a ladder used to reach the higher shelves, and I pulled it away from the wall and moved it to the door. I ran up it and found my legs were still weak with nerves after seeing the strange-faced man, so I took a deep breath and forced myself to get control, then climbed until I was level with the little window. I steadied myself and kicked as hard as I could, but my foot slipped against the thick dirty glass with a squeak and I nearly lost my balance.

More lanterns were shining light into the shop now, making me visible, and one by one the men began to shout louder as they caught sight of me. Gripping harder, I swung with all my weight and stamped at the

glass. This time it shattered and fell away in chunks. I kicked out the sharp teeth left in the frame. The front door was being opened behind me and one of the voices sounded more in charge of the others, like a policeman's. I crouched on the top of the doorframe and ducked through the gap, kicking away the ladder and hearing it crash to the floor. Above me was a drainpipe, which I clung on to, and to my side the roof of an outhouse built against the back of the shop.

One thing I had always been able to do was climb, ever since I'd first learned how to walk. I could find my way up the side of a building almost as easily as I could a tree (no matter how often I was told not to). Now I didn't think twice about it, springing and grabbing and hauling myself upward between window ledges and pipes, finding cracks in the brickwork for my hands and feet, past the dead-eyed windows, until my hands were on the tiles of the roof and I could pull myself up to safety.

I was lucky: the roofs were all roughly the same height, not too steep and quite easy to run across. I was already three houses down before I looked back and saw a few people in the tiny yard behind the shop, searching for me. They thought I had vanished into the streets, and it didn't occur to them to look upward. I climbed carefully behind a chimney pot and watched them for a few seconds, until they drifted back into the shop. Then I crawled carefully to the front edge of the roof and peeped down into the street.

People were gathered around the shop entrance, but beginning to disperse now that they were denied the excitement of a capture. A policeman stood sentry at the door. It was only when I looked directly beneath me, however, that I saw Mr Pisk. He was crouched in a doorway, and as I saw him he backed away, carrying my satchel of surgical instruments close to his chest. My heart started beating wildly again, and I struggled hard to stop myself from shouting out. Without taking my eyes off him my hand found a loose tile, held it above his head and let go. Then I got up and ran as fast as I could, not even waiting to see it shatter on his head, or hear the satisfying roar of pain.

Eventually, far enough away to feel at least half safe, I climbed carefully down on to the roof of a shack that had once been a blacksmith's shop, now shut up like most of the buildings in this sad, deserted part of the district. No one saw me except two beggars on the other side of the street who were so fascinated by my movements that they fell asleep straight away.

As I looked down from this lower roof to work out how to get to the ground, I was grateful to see a familiar figure coming down the street. Uncle was walking with a much shorter, fatter (but equally shabby) man, and when they saw me they came forward to help me down.

Uncle introduced his friend as Mr Codger. I shook his hand and asked them both if we could walk away as quickly as possible. They didn't ask any questions, but agreed at once.

Within a minute or so we were three short streets away and winding still further on a route as complicated and unpredictable as I could make it, without slowing. As we walked, I told them of the day's adventure. They were sympathetic when it got to the part where I was swindled by Mr Stamps in his apartment made of paper, and listened with smiles on their faces when I said I'd decided I wanted to collect and record the stories of Tumblewater. But the smiles faded swiftly when I mentioned my narrow escape, and they listened in silence, looking grave and unhappy. When I had finished, they said nothing. I couldn't believe they weren't outraged.

'Isn't it awful?' I said. 'Is there no one we could report this to?'

Instead of answering, Uncle guided me with one hand into a side alley and sat me on a barrel, where a coffee seller handed us cups of hot coffee through his window. When he saw Uncle, he became deferential and took extra care over our drinks and refused to take any money. He nodded to Uncle instead and said:

'You looked after my cousin, sir, when the police came for him. You remember Saul Matthews? My wife and I are indebted to you – three cups of coffee doesn't cover it,' and he disappeared back behind his hatch. Uncle smiled awkwardly at being the centre of attention, and Mr Codger changed the topic of conversation.

'Now,' he said quietly, sipping his drink. 'In answer to you: no, there's no one to tell. You're wanted by the police now, don't you see? The law reports to Prye.'

A nasty chill wriggled up my spine. 'How could he have known I was there, though?'

'Daniel, it's sad to say but Prye has made people all around so hungry and miserable that some are forced to act as his spies just to get enough food to live. His "men" are not just men, but women and children too, and they are everywhere, just trying to survive. Hardly a fly buzzes in Tumblewater that he doesn't know about. That's why we have to be extra-cautious in everything we say, and when we have the chance to help each other out we must – like poor Saul Matthews, who was as innocent of his charge as any of us.'

'Us?' I thought. Had Uncle been accused of something too?

Codger took up the refrain. 'The only thing you can do is keep out of trouble and hope he forgets about you. Daniel, you must try to understand who you're dealing with. Caspian Prye is not a normal man. But if you catch his attention, even though he has no reason to single you out that we know . . .' Uncle paused, giving me a

chance to contradict him. I felt again the shameful pang of holding my secret back from him – yet it was my business and mine alone, and my proud heart wouldn't let me share it with anyone (not even you, just yet, but I will come to it, I promise). I avoided his eye.

'Then,' he went on, 'you have to become invisible and wait for his attention to wander away. Which it will, and soon – Prye's anger is provoked by someone new every day or so. Every few hours, it sometimes seems.'

Raindrops plopped on the surface of the coffee as I stared into it.

'Now listen,' said Codger, trying to be more positive. 'Let's presume that this blows over if we keep you out of trouble for a few days. What you need, then, is to get a job as soon as possible and earn yourself a living.'

I agreed.

'There's a little publisher on the south-west corner of Tumblewater, where you'll be in much less danger of being recognized. The owner's a strange old gent, but he's our friend, and we can only ask. If he doesn't have any work for you, he might have some good advice. And he's sure to buy us a good lunch, whatever.'

'That's true,' said Uncle, who seemed quite inspired by the idea. 'He'll surely do that.'

'But it's four o'clock in the afternoon,' I said.

'That never stopped a publisher having lunch that I

heard of. Strange folk, they are. Always penniless, but they never miss a chance for some good food.'

I thanked them both again, and said truthfully that I couldn't imagine where I would be without them, even though I'd done nothing to earn their kindness. They bowed modestly.

'Don't mention it,' said Uncle. 'And don't try to imagine where you'd be without us; it's not a happy thought. Now let's go. We'll take a back route and keep to ourselves. And as we'll be walking right across Tumblewater and young Daniel says he loves them so much, why not tell a story, Mr Codger?'

The other man ruminated for a while, making a few grumbling noises as though he was searching around in the attic of his brain for something suitable, and finally said yes, he thought he knew a story about the right length for our journey.

'It doesn't have much of a happy ending, mind,' he said. 'Nonetheless—'

'But none of them do,' I muttered. 'That's why I like them!'

'But, nonetheless, here's the story of . . .'

THE BOY
WHO PICKED
HIS NOSE

Once upon a time there was a boy called Philip, who was a very well-behaved little boy of about nine or so years old. His mother was very proud of him in every respect, except one. Once in a while she would see him with his finger up his nose, and this displeased her – that was a habit for dirty little boys, and her son was not one of those.

'If you start doing filthy things with your fingers, you never know where it might lead,' she said when she caught him at it for the hundredth time.

'But it itches!' he protested.

'Even so,' she said. 'Use the hanky I gave you for your birthday.'

They were walking through the market as they had this conversation, and Philip (because he was, in all respects but one, a good little boy) was helping his mother carry the bags of shopping. The market was very busy that day – the busiest, in fact, that Philip had ever seen it. People had flocked in from nearby towns because an exotic band of traders was passing through, offering foreign herbs and spices and beautifully decorated clothes that were not normally available to local people.

Philip struggled to keep up with his mother as he was jostled by the crowd. His eyes were drawn to the stalls and he was delighted by the objects on sale, and startled by the strange faces of the people selling them. But his nose did itch abominably. Unable to get his handkerchief from his pocket, he kept trying to rub his shoulder or his elbow against his nose to scratch it. But he couldn't reach it with either and, at his third attempt, one of the bags under his arm spilt oranges all around him. Desperately he reached down to grab them up and one of the other bags fell as well, pouring tomatoes in a little pile.

He looked up and found his mother had vanished ahead of him into the crowd. Hurrying to scoop all he could back into a bag, he was banged into by people's knees and feet.

'Get out of the way!' shouted one woman, who had nearly toppled over him.

'Mother!' he called, feeling himself beginning to cry. He did not like calling out for help because he wanted to be big and strong. He had been the man of the family since the day his father, a fisherman, had lost a battle with a swordfish at sea, and he wanted to help protect his mother. Nevertheless, as he saw tomatoes being squished to pulp beneath the trampling boots all around, more and more tears squeezed out of his eyes and, pulling all of the remaining bags close to his chest, he wriggled between the legs around him and hid in the space between two stalls.

He did not know how long he sat there crying, waiting for his mother to find him. He pulled out the white cotton handkerchief to wipe away his tears and to blow his nose, but when she still did not appear, the tears kept coming and the itching in his nose grew worse. Looking furtively around, and seeing no one in the bustling crowd paying him the slightest attention, Philip slowly raised his little finger and put it into his left nostril.

Ah! The itching stopped. He felt tingling joy as he rubbed and twisted his finger around for longer than he had ever got away with doing before, pushing it all the way in. For a moment he even forgot his sadness that he had lost his mother, and he didn't worry about anything in the world except scratching away that itch.

When he had been going at it for some minutes without any sign of his mother (and without the pleasure of itching getting any less at all), a shadow fell across Philip's lap. He looked up and saw a huge round-headed man with great curly thickets of dark brown hair and a leathery face of dark brown skin. Philip gasped deeply and – click! – felt his finger pop in even further, and become stuck.

'Hellooo,' said the man in a deep voice. 'Why, you seem like an unhappy little chap.'

Quite sure that his finger was stuck, Philip tried to look as natural and relaxed as a little boy could in his position. 'I've lost by bubby. I bead … by buther,' he said, trying to sound as grown up as possible.

'I'm sorry to hear that,' said the man. 'Let me help you find her.' And with that Philip stood, but with one hand stuck to his face found he was unable to manage all the bags of groceries. 'I'll look after those,' said the man kindly, and taking them up in one hand he scrunched them rather roughly into a ball and placed it in one of the huge pockets of his dark brown coat. Philip felt that his mother might be unhappy at the fruit and vegetables getting damaged like this, but was sure that the joy of seeing him again would make it all right. The man shook the juices of the squashed fruits from one hand and with the other gently guided Philip between the stalls and down the street. Philip walked along happily.

'By dabe's Philip. What's yours?'

'Oh . . .' The man's face clouded over and he went silent for a few seconds. 'Mr Leg,' he said finally.

'Bleased to beet you, Bister Leg,' squeaked Philip, who was, after all, a very well-behaved boy.

'And I am pleased to meet you,' replied Mr Leg in a dark brown voice.

Mr Leg guided Philip left and right through small turnings in the streets so confidently that Philip thought he must know exactly where his mother was. Perhaps he was even a friend of the family whom Philip had failed to recognize, and knew a spot where his mother would be sure to go when she found she had been separated from her little boy.

As they took yet another turn, Philip noticed that the rush and noise of the market had died away behind them and that there were scarcely any people on the street at all. It must be a short cut, he decided, remembering from previous visits to town that the short cuts his mother took him through were invariably along dark, narrow streets like this one.

'Nearly there,' growled Mr Leg, his voice darker and browner than ever, his hand pushing Philip along the street not quite so gently as before.

Philip wanted to ask where they were going, but with the ache in his arm from holding his hand up to his nose all the time, and Mr Leg pushing him along at quite a speed, he could not get the words out. As they turned round a corner, he noticed with alarm that this new street, even darker and narrower than ever, ended in a brick wall.

'Here we are,' said Mr Leg, and stopped abruptly. Philip looked up at a shopfront so grubby with soot and grime that he couldn't see through the windows, let alone read the name on the blackened sign that hung above him.

His arm ached from holding his finger up, and his legs ached from rushing down cobbled streets, and he seemed further away from his mother than he had been before. He suddenly felt very lost, and less grown-up than ever. Tears started to well in his eyes again and he was just fishing his hanky from his pocket when the gargantuan hand on his back thrust him forward through the doorway.

The door closed behind them with a little ring. Philip's sobs stopped in his throat as he looked around. He was in what looked like the cleanest, brightest butcher's shop in the country. The white walls and the white tiled floor shone so brightly he almost had to cover his eyes. Behind a counter of clear glass glistened an astonishing array of juicy cuts of meat. Some sat in pale slices on enormous platters, some bulged in giant chunks from bowls dripping with red juice. His eyes running over this selection of meats, which was far richer than anything he had ever seen before, Philip noticed that none of them was labelled. How then might a customer know which creature he was eating? He followed Mr Leg's gaze and found himself looking at a very clean, bald little man whose head only just came over the counter. He looked like a cheerful sort of person and Philip instantly felt relieved. He *had* been led to a friendly place, after all.

'Good day!' piped the bald man in a high voice. 'What do we have here?'

'This little chap's lost his mother,' grumbled Mr Leg, looking down at his feet. 'I believe you can look after him while I go to find her?'

'Of course!' chirruped the man, coming round the end of the counter and bending to greet Philip. 'Let me introduce myself,' he said, extending a very clean, white hand. 'My name's Mr Pot.'

'Bleased to beet you, Bister Pot,' said Philip, shaking the hand. He was shocked by how cold the hand was, and how his own hand stayed cold even after he returned it to his pocket. But the man's smile was warm, and he regretted that he was meeting such a friendly person in such embarrassing circumstances.

'Wonderful!' cried Mr Pot, who then stood and said

to Mr Leg, 'How much do I owe you?'

'Settle up next time,' muttered Mr Leg. His voice was so dark it sounded like the branches of a great tree creaking in a night-time breeze, and one could barely make out the words. With a tinkling slam of the door, Mr Leg was gone.

'Well now,' piped Mr Pot, taking Philip's hand and leading him behind the counter. 'Let's have a look at you. Step up here,' he said, ushering Philip on to some scales, and then watching as the needle spun round to tell his weight. 'Wooooh!' he said. 'We *have* been eating well!'

'Hab we?' asked Philip.

'We hab,' said Mr Pot, holding his nose. 'Now,' he said, bending down to look Philip in the eye. His eyes had a bright friendliness, but he was quite serious as he asked, 'Have you been doing something that you shouldn't?'

Philip looked at the floor. 'I but by figger up by doze,' he said quietly.

'That's not a very nice thing to do!' said Mr Pot, standing up straight again, the smile back on his face. 'That's what naughty boys do. And you don't strike me as one of those. *Are* you a naughty boy?'

'Doh,' said Philip honestly. 'I dote dink so.'

'That's good to hear,' said Mr Pot. 'But you have done something bad, and something I'll bet your mother's told you not to do. And bad things have to be punished, do they not?'

'I . . . suppose so,' Philip admitted.

'Well, they do. And, if you have your punishment now, then there's no need for your mother to know anything about it when she gets here. So, do you want to know the way we punish them around here? We make them climb a ladder. Can you do that?'

'Ob course!' protested Philip, who was both insulted to be asked and relieved that the punishment was so easy. Mr Pot, still smiling, nodded over Philip's head and, turning round, Philip saw a narrow wooden ladder that he hadn't noticed before.

Eagerly he climbed up, careful because he only had one free hand with which to grip the rungs (the other was really aching now). He reached the top and leaned against the spotless white tiles on the wall. Up here near the ceiling he was near the bodies of the animals that hung down, and which he refused to look at, in case he got scared. Turning round on the ladder's platform, he looked down at Mr Pot, who was holding the ladder firm and smiling up encouragingly.

'I'b at the top!' he called.

'Good boy!' said Mr Pot, sounding impressed. 'Now, can you see the hook in front of you?'

Philip brought his eyes rather dizzily all the way up to a large silver hook next to his head. It had lots of scratches on it, as though it had been used to carry heavy things for years and years and years.

'Yes?' he said doubtfully.

'Put your arm over it.'

Philip grew uncertain, and wondered for a second whether that was really a good idea. It sounded like the sort of dangerous thing that adults were always telling you *not* to do – but Mr Pot had been so friendly, and Philip was so desperate to complete his punishment, that he ignored his doubts. Reaching out with his free arm left him balancing only on his feet. His knees quivered weakly.

'Not *that* arm,' called Mr Pot playfully. 'The other one!'

Still holding on to the ladder, Philip angled his elbow over the edge of the hook.

'Is it on?' piped Mr Pot.

'Yes,' called Philip.

'Good,' said Mr Pot, and drew the ladder away.

A sharp pain shot along Philip's arm as it took all his weight, along to the tip of his little finger, still stuck in his nose. His feet dangled and kicked, but couldn't make contact with anything.

Below him Mr Pot began to whistle, opening and shutting drawers, weighing things in his scales and sharpening his knives with a scratchy metallic sound that Philip could feel in his teeth.

'Bister Pot?' called Philip. 'Bister Pot! Bister Pot! I'b stuck!'

Philip thought he heard the voice below him say, 'So you are,' under its breath. He wriggled his body on the hook, and the pain along his arm and hand was horrible enough to make him nearly faint. He would never ever pick his nose again – he knew that for sure. Perhaps if he wriggled enough his finger would slip out and he would fall with a painful bump and have a bruise to teach him his lesson. As he tried again to squirm free, he knocked against the other hanging bodies, and, despairing, felt his finger stuck as sure as ever.

Beneath him he heard the gentle ring of the doorbell and turned his head to see if it was Mr Leg come to rescue him, or even his mother. But no. It was a very short fat man with a huge moustache. He was licking his lips, and looking at the meats on display.

'Good day, Mr Pot,' said the man.

'Good day to you,' said Mr Pot. 'Are you after anything in particular?'

'I *think* so,' said the man, 'but I can't be sure. What in particular might you have?'

'Well, if you want something special, I have . . .' said Mr Pot, and waved an arm up towards the ceiling. The moustachioed man's gaze rose.

'Yes, of course! An admirable suggestion,' he said, nodding vigorously.

Philip wriggled and twisted and turned, but the pain only got worse, and the movement made him swing around on his hook until he could see that the other hanging bodies were not pigs or sheep, but little boys like him. Each had his arm over a hook, and a finger stuck up his nose, or in his ear. Philip's head felt dizzy and light as the hook spun him round so he could see the shop again.

He could not scream or shout or get any words out of his mouth at all. His body went limp as he felt himself begin to faint. The last things he saw were the bright, eager faces of the two men looking up at him, and in Mr Pot's hand an extraordinarily long stick with a carving knife tied to its end.

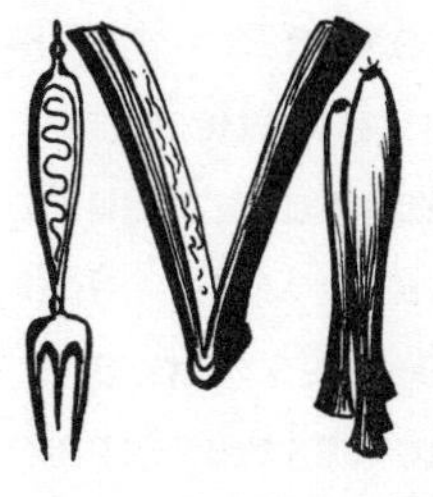

r Codger seemed such a kind, mild sort of person that the shock of the awful ending, delivered in his quiet voice, made me shiver so violently that my teeth knocked together. But however chilling he might be, he had perfect timing: the end of the story came just as we rounded the corner and saw the publisher's office ahead of us.

It wasn't quite what I would have expected of a publisher's building, just a dirty shopfront on the corner of a street, made up of little square windows much spattered with mud from the horses' hoofs, and little visible inside except a wall of clutter crammed against the glass. The sign read JASPERS & PERIWETHER.

Codger went in first, then Uncle, both taking off their hats, and I heard a voice cry happily, 'Ahh!' at seeing them. I followed as meekly as I could. Inside, the room was almost overflowing with damp. Drops fell from the ceiling into a series of buckets and pans and flowerpots, which were scattered on every shelf and part of the floor. The walls might have been white once upon a time, but the damp had crept downward and upward and across from each side, staining them with clouds of murky brown. Aside from mould and water, there were books in piles everywhere, supporting desks, keeping doors open and holding up candles. In one corner some books had been arranged into a long, perfectly flat shelf, upon which further books had then been piled. On top of this was a funny sort of octagonal lamp, which made something stir in my memory, although I could not quite think what.

In the middle of all this mess was a large desk and at it sat a wiry, alert-looking old man. He was very small and his face was deeply lined. His wispy white hair, apparently the only thing in the place unaffected by damp, stuck outwards from his head in every direction, as though he'd arrived here a moment ago after an extremely energetic horse ride. Seeing me, he cried, 'Ahh!' again, and his sharp features shone with a charming happiness.

'I don't know you, sir,' he said, coming round to shake my hand enthusiastically as the door banged behind me. 'But I should like to. My name is Jaspers. Horatio Jaspers.'

I shook his hand. 'Glad to meet you,' I said. He immediately forgot about me as he shook hands with the other two.

'Good to see you good to see you good to see you!' he shouted, returning to his desk. 'What we need is a cup of tea. CRAVE-ERRS!' He bellowed the last word up at the ceiling and ushered us into some chairs in front of his desk. In response to his call, a short man wearing thick spectacles and a rather nervous look appeared in the doorway.

'Cravus, there you are. Four glasses of tea!' For a second Cravus seemed unsure what Mr Jaspers meant, so the old man shouted, 'AT ONCE! Be gone!' and flapped his hand until Cravus went away.

At first sight the most remarkable thing about Horatio Jaspers was the fact that he seemed to be working hard on a densely written manuscript even though he was surrounded by the most excessive noise and commotion: the cascading of water into buckets and pots all around, the rattle of wooden wheels and clopping of hoofs outside and the metal creaking of large machinery from the next room, which I assumed was the printing press.

Opposite Jaspers's desk I now saw a tower of rotting paper quite the opposite from the exact, well-ordered one I had seen in Mr Stamps's apartment earlier in the day. That had looked like a brick wall; this was more like a crashing wave, with billows of sodden pages curling over each other, piled haphazardly up above the shelves and cupboards and over the door, looking like it was about to pour down and engulf the office below. Underneath it, an alert-looking blond boy not much older than me was talking to a sad-looking red-haired fellow.

'Have you considered putting in a collapsing windmill?' the blond boy was saying.

'That would hardly make sense,' said the other man.

'You should,' said the boy conclusively. 'Collapsing windmills are all the rage in publishing these days. You can't fail with one. And does the heroine have an evil sister?' he continued, with a pretence of idle curiosity.

'No,' said the ginger man, more despondent than ever. 'I don't think that a book of recipes—'

'Put one in,' said the boy, leaning over the desk. 'No book is published these days without the heroine having an evil sister. They sell like hot cakes, evil sisters do. I'm only thinking of your sales.' The red-haired man looked as though he might be about to cry, and made some feeble protestations, but without paying him the slightest attention the boy opened a big ledger and turned to other business.

'Now, with regard to money,' he said briskly. 'You understand we can't afford to pay you a bean . . .'

As I watched this conversation progress, it occurred to me that I should show interest in Jaspers's work so I said, 'It must be so interesting working on books all the time, Mr Jaspers.'

In the middle of lowering himself into his chair, he stopped still, and I saw Mr Codger and Uncle fidget nervously. I wondered what I had done wrong as I saw a severe expression settle on Mr Jaspers's face, and harsh lines twist into a look of disdain.

'Interesting?' he asked. '*Interesting?* What did that ever earn a man in wages? Don't think this is some

beautiful *storybook*, my lad. It's a book about the history of socks and it's TOSH!' With a louder shout than before he grabbed the manuscript and flung it angrily into the pile above the door so that it rested on the curling lip of the great wave of paper. Beneath, the red-haired author jumped and looked round nervously.

The blond boy said to him, 'Please, Mr O'Sullivan. There's much to discuss.'

'TOSH!' Jaspers yelled even louder. 'All of it. I tell *you*, my lad, I've got three tons of paper in the warehouse upstairs and forty gallons of ink in the basement *down*-stairs, and nothing to use it for. If you can find something worth printing, you're a better man than me. And now, gentlemen, I think it's time for a late lunch.' He looked at his pocket watch, which was tied to his buttonhole with a short length of cheap string. 'Or an early supper. Either way, let us repair round the corner.'

So repair round the corner we did, trying to duck out of the rain under the umbrella that Mr Jaspers swayed above his head, to a quiet, dark little restaurant where we settled at a corner table. He immediately ordered a number of dishes, none of which I'd ever heard of. Both Mr Codger and Uncle grew a little more hollow-eyed and hungry-looking at the name of each dish, which made me think we were in for quite a feast, and I realized I was extremely hungry too. The second the waiter disappeared Mr

Jaspers collapsed into a gloomy mood again.

'Words!' he said. 'Words, words, I need words. Thousands of them. *Millions* of the damned things! Where will I find them around here, where not a soul can read or write except me, Cravus, and the weird blond boy I hired one day by accident after a particularly good lunch? What a time to be a publisher,' he sighed.

'How d'you make money, then?' said Codger, piping up most unexpectedly. 'If folks around here don't read or write?'

'Good lord,' muttered Jaspers easily, 'I don't try to sell books *to* these people; I'm not an idiot. The books I publish (when I can find them, and I'm not being bothered by idiotic authors writing about the history of bathplugs) are for people outside Tumblewater, and are about the people *inside* Tumblewater, you see? So long as I can find someone to write them, they sell like hot cakes.'

I nodded in agreement, remembering what Jed Field had told me about the grisliness of the stories people told in Tumblewater, how they helped the people feel happy with their lot. I was about to mention this when Codger spoke first.

'Well, now, Mr Jaspers,' he said, picking his words carefully as though to make up for his previous rather blunt remark. 'That's exactly what we have come here to discuss with you. You see, well, I mean . . .'

Uncle broke in. 'Mr Jaspers,' he said, 'I think we've found your answer.'

'I should like to hear it,' the publisher said. 'Although if it's your life story I can tell you in advance I'm not interested. The last thing people want is another depressing book. They want *excitement* and *heroics* and BLOODY MURDER!' His voice rose to a shout, causing a terrified silence in the little restaurant. 'Sorry about that,' he said to the other diners, looking round. 'I do get carried away. You were uttering . . .'

'Mr Jaspers, may I introduce Daniel Dorey?'

'We've met,' said Jaspers without looking at me. 'I don't need another copyist, thank you. Cravus serves me well enough.'

'Mr Jaspers,' pursued Uncle, 'you don't understand this, perhaps, but among the streetfolk here in Tumblewater there's quite a culture of telling stories.'

'Horrible ones?'

'Very horrible,' agreed Uncle.

'With dastardly doings and bloodcurdling conclusions?' asked Jaspers, reluctantly interested.

'I've never known dastardlier doings (if that is a word),' said Uncle. 'And as for endings . . . Well – Daniel, tell him yourself.'

I had been rehearsing this moment in my mind, and forgetting my hunger for a moment (although it didn't help that the food arrived while I was talking) I told him the story of 'The Boy Who Picked His Nose', which had pretty much the most bloodcurdling conclusion I could think of, and followed it up with the tale of 'The Foundling', which came a close second in that regard. Those tales together should have put him off his food if anything could, but throughout he kept chewing and frowning as more dishes were delivered.

Mr Codger looked on all the while, nodding encouragement, and after I finished he kicked me beneath the table and said under his breath, 'You done that better than I could have, lad. Well done.'

I blushed, and watched Mr Jaspers for a reaction. Everything depended on him. Minutes passed as Jaspers ate, and finally he looked up from his food.

'You like the leeks?' he asked me with a sharp eye.

All my life I had totally and utterly hated leeks. Until he said the word, I had no idea that that was what I was eating, only that it was delicious. He saw my uncertainty.

'Me neither,' he said. 'But they do them in this delicious sauce . . .' He scooped a spoonful of leeks in the delicious sauce and stared deeply at it for a moment, before swallowing it down and closing his eyes, so as not to distract from the deliciousness of the flavour. Opening them again, he fixed me with the same sharp look.

'You're enjoying the lamb chops?'

This second question put me at just as much of a disadvantage, because at that exact moment one of those very lamb chops was in the process of choking me to death. Nevertheless the importance of an answer was sufficient to make me regain control of my throat by the sheer force of will, and to discreetly cough the offending bone into a napkin. I nodded enthusiastically, with water running from my eyes. Jaspers nodded back, and applied himself again to his food, seemingly satisfied.

Unable to contain himself any longer, Codger asked, 'Well – did you like Daniel's stories, Horatio?'

But the publisher was chewing thoughtfully on a hunk of bread he had dipped in sausage gravy, and not paying us the slightest attention. He closed his eyes and said, '*Delicious.*'

The three of us held our breath as he swirled the last bit of bread around the plate and put it in his mouth. After a few more seconds of chewing, he said, '*Exquisite.*' And then he was suddenly businesslike again. 'You have more of these tales, you say?' he asked sharply.

'Lots,' I lied. 'And I mean to discover many, many more. I've only been here a day, Mr Jaspers,' I said, 'but I don't think there's a limit to the number of grisly tales that one person could find in Tumblewater.'

Still he stared at me as blankly as though I was speaking another language, or as though he had just woken up from a daydream. I went on:

'I'll wager you this: if in two days' time I haven't got enough tales to fill a book, then I'll shine your boots and polish your glasses for your trouble, and never darken your doorstep again.'

Still the three of us waited. Mr Jaspers finished his glass of wine, let out a deep, satisfied sigh and said in a loud voice as though he was addressing a public meeting, 'The funny thing is, I myself know a similar type of story. It's supposed to have happened to the friend of a friend of mine, right here in Tumblewater. Would you like to hear it?' He didn't wait to hear our answer, but cleared his throat to start talking.

I couldn't wait any longer. 'I'm sorry, sir,' I said, with as much respect as I could, 'but you will hire me to write these tales? You are interested?'

'Oh, shut up, boy, for a moment, while I try to remember the story. Yes, that's it, I've got it. Now, if I had to give this story a name, I suppose I would call it the tale of . . .

# THE TONGUE

It was under strict and repeated instructions that the colonel directed the deliverymen through to the glass conservatory at the back of the house, as though they were a company of soldiers being drilled.

'Careful . . . *Careful!* . . . Man on the right, keep a straight back! . . . God help me, I'm not having this doorway repainted because of you!'

The deliverymen probably would have been more surly and indignant had they not been completely startled by the colonel's strictness. They might even have been tempted to break one of the valuable-looking vases 'accidentally' to teach him a lesson. As it was, Colonel Truff was far too experienced at commanding men to let them get away with anything. Before they knew where they were, the enormous crate – far larger and heavier than the grandest piano – was set down in the conservatory, they had each received a single shilling tip and the door had been firmly closed behind them.

'You are dismissed, Mrs N,' said the colonel to his little mute housekeeper, who had stopped her sweeping to watch, with no idea what was going on. At his words she looked at him with alarm, so he added, 'For the afternoon, I mean. Have a few hours off.' She nodded, relieved, and shuffled off to the basement.

The moment he was alone, Colonel Truff went into the conservatory and locked the doors behind him. Then he set about the enormous box with a hammer, carefully prising away the planks one by one until he could lift off the lid and allow the sides to fall flat. What he saw made him sigh proudly. The roar and smoke of battle could not compare to this; the majestic sight of a towering Arctic iceberg faded in comparison; forty years of travel and adventure, of terror and wonder, were as nothing. For, as a man who always kept his word, now in his first year of retirement he had honoured a promise he had made to himself when he had been a ten-year-old boy.

There, on a bed of soiled hay, surrounded by a thick foliage of tropical plants and flowers with which he had filled the conservatory in preparation for this moment, stood his very own hippopotamus.

The creature nodded tiredly as it became accustomed to the light and the colonel rushed forward to pet it, running his hands lovingly over its brow, feeding it bunches of spinach leaves and water lilies.

'There, there,' he said. 'Daddy will look after you. You must be so tired and hungry after the long journey. We shall feed you and let you rest and you'll be fit as a fiddle in no time.'

Mrs N, meanwhile, was such a forgetful and anxious creature that the second she got downstairs it slipped her mind that she'd been given the afternoon off. So she picked up her mop and bucket and trudged back up to give the drawing-room floor a going over, also forgetting that she'd already done so twice that day. In the middle of mopping she turned round to see Colonel Truff next door in the conservatory, hugging a hippopotamus. The sight made her jump backwards so violently that the mop flew up and got stuck in the chandelier, and she fell down in a faint.

All of a sudden, perhaps because in old age men are said to become children again, and perhaps because he had lived a long life without ever having a wife or children, Colonel Truff found himself overcome with a protective love for his hippo.

He did not change in any other way. He was still gruff and stern with tradesmen, innkeepers and the like, to his friends he seemed as stiff and emotionless as he had ever been, and he continued to regard little Mrs N with complete bafflement (as she had always regarded him). But every time he unlocked the conservatory door he became loving and paternal, so much so that even he would not have recognized himself a short while before.

Over the coming weeks he threw himself into action, buying up all the supplies he could find of spinach leaves and water lilies, and other foods he had read that the hippo would like. Boxes of nettles and truffles and mushrooms and celery arrived. He made chicken soup and pineapple juice and liquorice water and poured them into the trough for the hippo to drink from.

Truff noted that Mrs N made no comment about the creature, so he assumed she was happy for it to be there. (Of course, she made no comment about anything else either, so perhaps he was fooling himself.) At one point, he had seen her standing in front of the conservatory door with the broom in her hands, staring at the filth spread out over the floor as though a whole new world of work had opened up. But he had relieved her by giving an order that the conservatory was the one area that was not to be cleaned under any circumstances.

He was delighted that the hippo seemed quite comfortable bathing in the mud pit that he had dug into the floor, or lazing against the bank of overturned *chaises longues*, or munching on the leaves of the palm and bracken which overhung from the shelves of potted plants.

The colonel now relaxed into exactly the sort of retirement he had looked forward to. He rose early, ate kedgeree for breakfast, read the newspaper, wrote a few letters, walked briskly through the rain for an hour or so, lunched at his club, returned, bathed, snoozed or read books for the afternoon, and then spent the remaining time before supper with Albert. This was the name he had given the hippopotamus. It struck him as a fine, upstanding name, ideal for an affectionate pet, and it just so happened that it was his name as well.

'How are you, Albert?' he would call from the conservatory door. Hearing no response, he would tiptoe up and pat it on the head, then check its appearance.

'You're looking a little bloodshot in the eyes,' he would say. 'I'd better get you more greens.' Or: 'Getting flabby. Better cut down on the pork chops!'

Overall, Albert was the best of pets. He did not

complain or make a mess (outside his dedicated space). Nor did he make much noise apart from the occasional violent burp. He was not only docile and affectionate but so exotic and extraordinary that the colonel did not feel he had a pet so much as a unique project. Each day he would talk to Albert for a while, play him choice pieces of music on the piano or read him interesting newspaper stories. Then he would empty out any droppings and leave, giving him a kiss on the forehead first.

This happy state of affairs went on for many months through Albert and Truff's first winter together, until spring set in. Then, one day, he realized that Albert had not eaten anything for a whole week. Indeed, as he stepped back he became convinced that the wonderfully fat animal was definitely thinner. This was not an eventuality that the colonel had ever imagined. Normally very healthy creatures, hippopotamuses rarely become ill, and often lived to the age of forty or forty-five. He knew this. Now he realized something terrible. In his cherished ambition to own a hippo he had selfishly put Albert at risk. What was he to do?

That night he tried to persuade himself not to worry, and that many diseases cured themselves over time. Everything would be all right, he thought.

But another week passed, and it became worse. Albert still hadn't eaten a thing, and his shoulderblades now stood out clearly where there should have been healthy pads of fat. His hippo eyes sagged and he let out long keening sounds, like those of a dog but much slower, deeper and sadder.

Truff supposed that, given the lack of appetite, there might be something wrong with Albert's mouth. Perhaps he could help – he had after all performed emergency surgery on injured soldiers in the field, and had a strong stomach for blood. So, as soon as he had decided this, he went into the conservatory and approached with caution, making sympathetic noises and stroking Albert's head, and carefully propped his mouth open with a wooden spoon.

In the dark cavern of the mouth it was difficult to see anything at first. After a few moments his eyes adjusted and he could see the thick row of teeth on either side, the vault of the throat and the fat, pink flap of skin that was the tongue.

'Ahh!' he said. 'I think we have found our problem.' For there, right in the middle of the hippo's tongue, sat the largest and most repulsive boil he had ever seen. It was as big as a billiard ball, greenish-yellow and filled to bursting with a horrid pus.

'Ugh,' Truff said to himself. 'How disgusting. But we know how to deal with those!' And taking out the spoon he got up, patting Albert affectionately on the head and saying, 'Don't worry, old thing. We'll soon have you as right as rain.'

As he went out to fetch the equipment he would need to deal with this little problem, something caught his eye. He stopped in the middle of the dining room, looking up.

'MRS N!' he bellowed at the top of his voice. The poor housekeeper came bustling in a few seconds later, trembling. She looked at him imploringly.

'*What* – is – *that*?' he asked, pointing up at the chandelier. Steadying her glasses, Mrs N peered up, but her eyesight simply wasn't good enough. She shrugged.

'I believe it is a mop!'

Her eyes widened as if to say, so *there* it is!

'Fetch the stepladder and take it down at once, for God's sake!' barked the colonel. 'It makes the house look like a madman's.' And he went off to find the first-aid cabinet.

Back in the conservatory a few minutes later, Truff held a needle over a candle and peered over his spectacles as he administered it to the hippo's mouth.

Perhaps Albert felt no pain, or perhaps he was distracted by the spectacle of Mrs N atop a stepladder silently tangling with the chandelier in the next room. Certainly he was well behaved as Albert prodded the red tip of the boil with his needle.

'It's a tough little brute,' Truff muttered, holding the point of the needle over the candle again before trying afresh. The main body of the carbuncle seemed to be made of a soft, liquid jelly but at its top it had hardened into a crimson button. Heating the needle to red hot for the third time, Truff plunged down hard through the centre of the pustule.

'*There's* a good boy,' he muttered, stroking the hippo's head. 'It's for your own good.' He had expected a moan or a shriek or some kind of reaction, but none came. Still holding the needle, he peered into the animal's mouth to see if his surgery was working. And, slowly, it began to. The outer skin of the boil became a fainter yellow and seemed to pulse slightly. Then Truff noticed some little veins that ran up the side of the boil, which he hadn't seen before. As he watched, they became more pronounced, and began to throb visibly, as though the enormous pustule was a living thing. And all the while the hole made by the pin yawned wider until it quivered, and the skin fell back in folds. Yellow liquid began to pour out from it, on to the pink tissue of the hippopotamus's tongue. Shakily holding the pin in mid-air, Truff started back in horror, and pulled the wooden spoon from the creature's mouth so it could fall shut. He saw little bubbles blistering on the metal surface of the pin as the sickly yellow liquid dripped down it.

Albert's eyes stared up at him, as placid and calm as ever. It was as if he was somehow numbed to the pain. As Truff wondered at this, the first wisp of the smell from the boil's liquid reached him. He leaped backwards, his hand over his nose. Nothing in the terror and death of all the battlefields he'd seen, in all the appalling acts of barbarism he had encountered in the furthest corners of the world could compare to the horror of this smell. He felt faint as he reached the conservatory door and pushed it open. Slamming it shut behind him, he sat on the floor and leaned against it, breathing cold air in deep, welcome gulps.

This was worse than he could have imagined. Whatever could it be? He must act quickly.

Dr Christopher Gibson stepped between the many puddles of Mayhew Street in a merry mood. He was almost skipping. This was to be his third call of the morning, and so long as it furnished his usual fee of six shillings (and it surely would) he could retire for the day, have a spot of lunch and spend the afternoon over an agreeable game of draughts with his good friend Mr Milner, the well-known chef.

When he reached number 143, he turned in through the gate and rapped on Colonel Truff's door. He stood back, twirling his umbrella and humming a military march of which he was fond, wondering whether he would have partridge for lunch, or a cutlet of veal. When the door opened and he was admitted, he dropped his umbrella into the stand and said, as he always did, 'Well, now. What seems to be the problem?'

Instantly he knew that this was not one of his ordinary calls. Colonel Truff, who he had known as a schoolboy fifty years before, and had heard of as a famous military hero and a great example to all young soldiers, stood before him pale and panicked and almost unable to speak.

'My dear friend,' said the doctor. 'Whatever is the matter?'

'Come with me,' said Truff, ushering him through the house. 'I have something awful to confess.' He showed the doctor into the drawing room, which looked out into the conservatory.

'What is it?' demanded the doctor. 'Out with it. It can't be that bad if you are walking and talking!'

'There.' Truff pointed. 'I smuggled this creature into the country against the law. It was my fondest dream to own such an animal, and to care for it. It was foolish of me – so very foolish! – and now I'm paying the price.'

The doctor began to make astonished noises, but the colonel went on, determined to get his story out. 'Something has gone wrong. Whether it is a condition that has lain dormant in the animal since it was removed from its native land, or some horrible reaction to our environment, I don't know.'

'Good *lord*!' whispered Gibson, standing close to the glass. Albert's condition had deteriorated gravely, even in the last few hours. He seemed thinner, and somehow almost pale through his thick grey hide. Resting on his knees, he hadn't the strength to lift his chin higher than a few inches off the floor, and his eyes, now quite red and watery, stared upward. Worst of all, a greenish-yellow foam dripped from his mouth, spattering on to the floor in globules as thick as cake mixture.

'But, my friend,' whispered Gibson, 'you need the advice of a veterinary surgeon, not a doctor like me.'

'I know!' cried Truff in great distress. 'But I'm afraid they'll take him away, and then the newspapers will find out! I can never let that happen! And, dear friend, perhaps his condition has some similarity with a human ailment, which you might easily cure?'

It didn't look like anything the doctor had ever seen before, in humans or anything else. But reluctantly he gave in to the colonel's begging that he might be spared the public embarrassment of being exposed, and he agreed to have a quick look at the hippopotamus. Colonel Truff thanked him with all his heart, explained the history of Albert's symptoms, and gave him a handkerchief to hold over his mouth while he went near the beast.

Doctor Gibson had now completely forgotten his lunch, his game of draughts and his friend Mr Milner. He stepped forward with great trepidation, carefully keeping the hanky over his mouth and nose, and heard the conservatory door click shut behind him and the key turn in the lock. Even through the handkerchief the smell nearly made him sick, and each detail he saw mystified and disgusted him further. The animal seemed to be sweating, or at least water was running down its skin in streams. Its legs trembled and a soft keening sound, which he realized was the wheezing of huge weakened lungs, came from its nostrils. When Doctor Gibson touched the vivid yellow froth that bubbled from its mouth, he pulled his hand back, stared at it in amazement and began to scream uncontrollably.

Here we had better leave the doctor to the privacy of his unpleasant fate. Colonel Truff watched for as long as he could, ignoring the doctor's pleas – to be let out, at first, and then, a few minutes later, to be put out of his misery by any means. Then he went and sat in another room, and a calm change of emotion came over him as he realized what trouble he had got himself into with his ridiculous scheme. Of course it was a shame to lose Albert, and he would miss Dr Gibson's company at the billiards table, but he could not allow any of this to get out. He had some difficult decisions to make. Eventually there was silence from the next room, and Truff returned to the conservatory door to take in the haunting sight. The disease continued to advance more and more quickly and fed on the doctor with terrifying speed. After his death it took less than an hour to consume him. By then Albert was dead too, and had crumpled to half his original size.

Mrs N came back from her daily visit to the market a little after two o'clock and found the colonel in an armchair in front of the conservatory doors, drinking a large whisky to steady his nerves.

'Mrs N,' he said solemnly. 'I'm afraid we have rather a mess to clean up.'

They unlocked the back doors of the conservatory from the outside and left them open overnight to allow the fumes to dissipate in the rainy air.

Then Mrs N led Truff to an old shed he had never noticed at the back of the garden and, once inside, pointed out several shovels and two empty barrels.

'An admirable suggestion,' said Truff.

Mrs N shrugged modestly.

The following morning, after breakfast and an extra cup of tea to fortify themselves, Colonel Truff and the loyal Mrs N set about clearing things up as best they could.

They put on masks that she had prepared before bed the previous evening, which fitted over their mouths and noses and protected them from the ungodly smell with lavender and rosemary.

Even so, the scene which awaited them was decidedly unpleasant. They would struggle to put it from their minds for a long time to come. By now, both Albert and the doctor had been devoured so completely that all that remained besides a thick greyish-green sludge, which reached up to the ankles, was the occasional bone, lump of flesh or tuft of hair.

At first Mrs N held the barrel at an angle and Truff scooped the sludge in. Then when it got quite full, they stood it up and used buckets. Each of them wore thick old leather boots left over from the colonel's foreign military campaigns, which they could feel getting warm and soft as the diseased liquid ate away at them while the day wore on.

When they had filled one barrel, they started on the second. This was at about lunchtime, but neither of them could bear the idea of eating. They scooped and splattered the lumpy mixture in until Mrs N's face was bright red, and the colonel's back creaked like an old staircase. Had she been in the habit of saying anything at all, Mrs N might have remarked that she would give up her Sunday treat of a bowl of custard from now on. If his back had not ached quite so much, the colonel might have mentioned that he would think twice before ordering a Béarnaise sauce with his steaks in future. Instead, they both toiled on in silence.

At last, the floor was almost clear, except for some smudges and smears around the edges that could be cleaned up with a mop later. They had two barrels filled nearly to the brim, and Mrs N held them still while the colonel hammered the lids in place.

It took an hour's running up and down the high street before Truff found a wagon for hire. He brought it back to the house and with help from the wagon's owner loaded the barrels on to the back in a few minutes.

In spite of his strict instructions, Mrs N insisted on getting up on to the cart with him. Unable to find any way of making her stay at home, he held the umbrella over both their heads as they set off through the wet streets, pulling it down to hide their faces as the wagon splashed muddy water over people they knew. The sun was still up at late afternoon, but the overcast Tumblewater sky looked like night and the gas lamps cast their strange lime-coloured glow through the rain as the wagon rolled along.

Soon they were on the main thoroughfare, jostling for position among the grocers' carts and four-horse coaches. Swinging left and right to overtake slow coaches and dodge the odd pedestrian, both the colonel and Mrs N cast worried looks back at the barrels as they rolled heavily across the boards and smashed against each other with a sound like thunder. Yet not a drop of the poisonous liquid leaked, and eventually they passed through the borders of the city and the two of them began to relax a little.

It was a little under an hour into their journey when the waggoner pointed upward and, lowering his umbrella, Truff found himself looking with astonishment into a brilliant blue sky.

It was wonderful, as the journey went on, what the breeze of a crisp autumn day did for the nerves. They waved happily at the unattended cows in the fields, breathed the sweet rich air of the countryside, and even began to find the cart's violent jerking on the uneven roads quite soothing.

'This is the place you want,' muttered the waggoner, once they had travelled a good few miles into the countryside. Turning off the main road, he drove them down a thin track with tall hedges on either side, which led for a mile or so up to a pretty little wood on top of a hill.

Mrs N looked at Truff questioningly, so he asked the waggoner, 'You are sure this place is never visited by anyone? That it is quite deserted?'

'These hundred years or more,' the man replied without looking round. 'My family's from nearby and the belief is that this place is cursed or haunted or something. Don't you worry,' he said as the wagon reached the top of the hill and the beginning of the wood. 'They stay away in droves.'

There was no visible path through the trees, but the horses somehow squeezed between them with a rush and rustle of leaves on every side, as though they were passing through a storm. Truff and Mrs N huddled close together, looking up through the branches where they could see slivers of an early moon, and dreading the tree trunks which flew either side of them smashing into the wagon and splitting open one of the barrels. And yet, within a few minutes, they were coming out on the other side and down a scratchy field of yellowing grass. Everything on this side of the hill seemed to be poorer, malnourished, starved by the sun. Strangely, even the air seemed emptier and it was only after a minute or so that Truff noticed they couldn't see or hear any wild animals at all. Not even a single bird darted across the sky.

But the waggoner did not slow as they rode down over the bumpy surface. He kept right on with their frightening descent towards the bottom of the empty valley, where some trees straggled together in a bunch. Except, Truff saw, it was not just trees. As they came closer, a substantial dwelling became visible, almost hidden between the branches.

The waggoner pulled up short with a sudden jolt. The whole cart lurched with the weight of the barrels rumbling forward and slamming against the back of their seats. Mrs N was almost propelled into a patch of mud below them, but Truff caught the back of the bonnet tied round her neck and she jerked back with much coughing and spluttering.

'You asked for the most godforsaken spot in the land,' mumbled the waggoner. 'This is it.' And he refused to move further, sitting grimly and clutching his reins as the other two got down and rolled the barrels off the wagon.

It was not only the most secluded spot Truff had ever seen, it was also, he thought, one of the strangest and most uncanny. As he looked closer, the entire overgrown copse revealed itself as a network of buildings that must once have been a farm. There was something about the silence and the way the evening light shone on the trees and the deserted buildings that made it feel primordial, as though it had stood in this place since time began. Some of the buildings leant towards each other as though frozen in a secret conversation, the windows and doorways like empty eyes and mouths.

The farmhouse, which he had seen first, was overhung by a lopsided greying willow like a shaggy haircut, and poison ivy spread over every visible inch of wall like a network of bulging veins. Briars and weeds sprouted at its every corner; wild flowers nestled in its broken windows, growing in curls around the spikes of broken glass. And all around in the thick, twisting undergrowth the relics of ancient farm tools stuck out, covered with nests and webs and weeds.

Shivering, Truff pushed back brambles and waded through bracken to a small clearing between the derelict buildings. He pulled the hammer from his belt and said, 'This is the place.' Mrs N, pale and tired from their recent exertions, was standing a few yards outside the thicket peering in. When she saw him waving, she nodded briefly and began to roll the first barrel towards him.

When it was safely through, he held the head of the barrel facing the centre of the clearing, and brought the hammer down hard on the lid. He kept his face turned away to avoid being splattered with the diseased liquid, so he had to blindly hit the barrel six or seven times before he heard the splintering crack he was waiting for. Immediately the hole began to gurgle softly and a pool formed around the barrel. Truff retreated quickly.

The second barrel was easier. The lid split in half first time and its contents, now rotted to a thick dark gravy, flowed out over the clearing in a smooth wave.

Leaves and twigs crackled as the mixture covered them, and wisps of a strange pale gas hung above the sludge. Having watched for a second, Truff and Mrs N battled back through the branches and ran to the cart in fright, the colonel calling to their driver to leave at once. Within seconds they were off at a gallop. Although he said nothing, the waggoner made his feelings about the place known with his whip to the horses' behinds, and they moved almost as fast up the barren hill as they had down it.

As the lightened wagon rose up the hill towards the little wood, Colonel Truff placed an affectionate arm round Mrs N's shoulders.

'We make quite a team, you and I!' he said. She slapped his hand away.

'You misunderstand my meaning,' he protested, rather stiffly. But she pretended not to hear, and stared off in the opposite direction, her nose in the air.

Ignoring her, Truff turned and looked back with considerable relief as he felt the strange place retreat behind him. It was awful to think of poor Doctor Gibson and dear Albert's remains being dumped in such an anonymous pit. But then a stronger feeling surged in his stomach. This horror, this terrifying disease which he had feared would devour him and his life, was gone. No one would ever know. He was safe, his reputation was intact and cool blue night was falling over this forgotten place.

By tomorrow his appetite might have returned and he could consider lunch at his club, and start to forget about where his reckless and foolhardy hobby had taken him. A sharp breath of frosty air tasted sweet, and Mrs N instinctively gripped his arm as the wagon dived into what looked like an impenetrable bush at the hill's top. The figures of Truff and Mrs N ducked, there was a tremendous thrashing of leaves like the applause of a huge crowd and they were gone.

Peace descended at the bottom of the hill around the

derelict farm. Every plant grew a fraction of an inch, or inclined towards the last glimmers of the sun, which nestled against the shoulder of the hill. Shadow stole across the valley, until it was evening in the copse of twisted trees.

As the shadow rose over the roof of the farmhouse, a sound came from within it. It was a kind of grinding, like a heavy chair being scraped back across a stone floor. A few wild animals darted out of the door. A figure appeared, leaning against the doorframe.

He had a mud-brown complexion, a great bulbous nose and eyes which darted left and right like little creatures that had grown in his skull. He was dressed in clothes so spattered and sprayed with stains that they did not look like clothes at all, but layers of dried earth. He coughed again, a sound like the cracking of a rotted tree trunk before it falls, as he saw the messy spillage that had appeared in the clearing outside his house. He looked at it for a few moments, and noticed the chunks of flesh and bone bobbing at its top. Without moving he let out an animal cry.

Sounds came from behind one of the uncollapsed sheds. Answering his call, some sickly misshapen creatures lurched forth. They had once been hogs, but were pale and bloated as though fed by some atrocious and unnatural diet. They sniffed over the grey liquid, licked at it and then began to gulp it down.

From another outhouse, some diseased fowl, which might generations ago have been turkeys, began to emerge hesitantly, squabbling amongst themselves and pecking at the edge of the pool. Other creatures, too, crept out of the shadows: black sheep, blind and milky-eyed; furless hares lapping with nervous licks; even a lumbering bull, which came in from its resting place behind the house and the draping branches of the willow. This last animal drank up the strange-smelling food with its head tilted on to one side by a balloon-sized growth in its neck.

The farmer sat on a tree stump and watched his creatures feed. He sucked air through a pipe which had no tobacco, and chewed hard on the stem with his remaining teeth.

His mouth moved with his thoughts until eventually words began to come from it. 'Ready for market,' he said, and let out a laugh like the bark of a dog. 'Aye, ready for market, you are. Tomorrow morning we'll leave early, and you'll fetch a pretty price. Folks always wants good meat.' The black shapes of bats were beginning to gather on the branches above him now, their wings twitching. 'And you're good enough to eat, you are,' he said.

'Now,' said Mr Jaspers, looking immensely pleased with himself, 'won't you agree that's a rather good one?'

I agreed without hesitation. In fact, it was so weird and odd and twisted, I thought it might be my favourite so far.

'That's exactly the sort of story I love,' I said. 'It's even crazier than the others!'

'So – you'd like to publish these as a book?' His manner had changed from that of an irritated bank manager to an indulgent father.

'Yes,' I said, although I hadn't thought about it until that second. 'Although there'll be enough stories to fill much more than just one book.'

'We'd have to see if the first was profitable, of course,' he remarked.

'Of course!' I agreed. 'So you think you might be interested in hiring me?'

'Well, I'll have to speak to our sales people,' he said complacently. 'But then,' he added, 'I don't really have any, unless you count the simpleton Cravus and the blond boy whose name I can never remember. You've met Cravus, and I daresay he likes you, so I suppose we can discuss terms. If this is to be an ongoing series, perhaps you'd better have a desk in the office too. Sir,' he reached over a hand to me, 'you tell a good tale. You are employed.'

I shook it warmly. 'Thank you!' I said. 'I'm honoured! Thank you!' The three of us who had been waiting for Jaspers's decision relaxed, and I felt a swell of gratitude to them all. It was a miracle to have found some work so quickly, when a few hours earlier everything had seemed so impossible.

Uncle chose this moment of good humour to speak up.

'There is the small matter that young Daniel is a . . . well, a fugitive from the law.'

Mr Jaspers composed himself, looked blandly first at me and then at Uncle and waited for an explanation.

'He is wanted for a burglary he didn't commit,' said Uncle. 'I know that might dampen your spirits somewhat . . .'

Mr Jaspers laughed loudly. 'Good *lord*, no! It's *tremendous* publicity! Other publishers would kill for an author who's on the run,' and he chuckled again, looking at me admiringly. I felt a rather complicated emotion for a second – proud of myself, but also as though I was being sized up like a prize pig. Then Mr Jaspers regained a serious expression and leaned in towards me. 'For God's sake, don't get *caught*,' he said. He thought for a second and added, 'At least not before you've written it all down. Gentlemen!' he raised his wine glass to Codger and Uncle. 'This has been a very

satisfactory late lunch. Or early supper. I shall be most pleased to pick up the bill to commemorate this meeting!'

'That's good,' said Codger, 'cos we ain't got a penny.'

'Well, that's what I mean, I suppose,' said Jaspers. 'Although it's always nice to see you both, of course. Mr Dorey, you must be vigilant from now on to remain out of the public gaze. We will find a disguise for you. Perhaps you should – er . . .' He faltered and looked at the other two men. 'Does he know about the . . . ?' he asked uncertainly.

'Do I know about the what?'

Codger shook his head. 'We ain't told him yet.'

'We'll do it later,' said Uncle.

'What the hell are you talking about?' I asked, getting annoyed.

'You're better off if you don't know for now,' said Uncle. 'What you've got to concentrate on is avoiding the law and getting home before dark. Don't take this lightly, Daniel,' and he put his hand on mine and gripped it. 'Every copper's going to be out tonight looking for a lad about your age. And if they catch you, or any poor boy who looks like you, it isn't prison you'll be for.'

'Ditchers Fields,' said Codger quietly.

'*How exciting*,' breathed Mr Jaspers.

'But I haven't *done* anything!' I said, though I didn't

sound convincing to my own ears. No matter how strange and sinister it was that Prye knew about me from his spies almost before I had arrived, I was starting to suspect that he *did* have a reason for hunting me – could he know about the very secret I had been keeping from Uncle and the others?

I shuddered as I thought back to what I had heard among the costermongers. That Caspian Prye had been away from other people for so long that he had forgotten what they were like, that his face had grown into something unrecognizable. That he was *no longer human.*

With this in mind I stepped back on to the street, turning up the collar of my cloak so that it covered the bottom half of my face. I thanked the men for everything, and decided to return to Turvey House to write up as many of the stories as I could before sleep – I was determined to do a good job so Mr Jaspers wouldn't regret his decision. The three of them kept trying to say they would accompany me, but I knew they would just slow me down. I wanted to run through the back alleys. I wouldn't be spotted, and I could be home in five minutes, putting pen to paper.

As I started to trot along quite speedily, I suddenly remembered what the lamp in Jaspers's office had reminded me of. How it had come to be there I had no idea, but it was a candlestick-maker's lamp, exactly like the one that little Jenny spent her life watching out for

at the corner of the costermongers' street. I began to wonder if there was some way I could help her.

While this went through my mind, I had been darting instinctively down the darkest and most deserted alleys that I saw, avoiding any sign of habitation. But now I found the close streets eerily silent. I had slipped into an area of deserted factories, their tall rusting shapes closing out the light, all of them empty since long ago. In between them a network of slender canals ran crossways through parts of Tumblewater, constructed decades ago to bring materials into the factories and take away finished goods on narrowboats, before this area had become obsolete and forgotten. As I ran along, I heard a noise in the echoing silence – it sounded like someone running in wet, bare feet. It came from nearby, but I couldn't see anything moving in the shadow. I slowed down, persuading myself it was an echo of my own footsteps, but instead it got faster. It didn't sound like someone running away from something. It was a stealthy tread, like a creature stealing up on its prey.

I looked over my shoulder, my fear growing because the noise rebounded through the broken windows and off the high walls on every side so I couldn't tell whether it was in front of me or behind. I ran across one of the small iron bridges over a little canal to slip between two buildings and shouted in fear as a figure dashed across the entrance at the other end. As it disappeared there was a big splash and I ran forward. When I got to where it had been, there was no one there and I was alone in the silence again, except for the rippling of the water below. What light had filtered down from the sky above reflected in tiny fragments on the disturbed water, but everything else was in darkness. I thought I could hear the swish of something large swimming away, but I didn't stay for long enough to be sure. In a minute I was sprinting back towards the more populated areas – worth the risk now – and trying not to think of the Slumgullion.

'You're too old to believe in monsters,' I muttered to myself.

When I found myself near the main road again, I ducked into a side street and became a small shadow in the dusky alleyways that were at least lined with people's houses, trying to keep myself invisible, keeping a compass of my direction in my head.

I was only two or three streets from my own bed when I heard another strange sound. Still distant, it sounded like a flock of birds taking off, flapping leathery wings. I stopped in a doorway to listen – it grew louder. Tentatively I stepped into the street and looked in the direction of the sound. It grew louder again, and three or four boys about my age came running round the corner towards me. Then behind them appeared

twenty or thirty more, sprinting. As they passed me, I saw fear in their eyes.

'Run!' one of them shouted. An unknown fear gripped me, and my legs wouldn't move. The group of boys was perhaps fifty strong, all pounding past me. The last one shouted desperately, 'Run! Are you stupid? *Run!*'

Three horses suddenly sprang round the corner, ridden by three policemen, dark silhouettes with tall helmets and truncheons swinging wildly. They shouted at their horses and raced towards me. All the boys had gone, slipping round the corner and vanishing into a dozen different passageways. I sprinted across the street after them, squirmed under a low doorway as the first horse came level with me and ran into the darkness, bashing hard into a door where the lane turned. I spun in the mud, and heard the squeak of a door. In front of me like an apparition a tall, beautiful woman was leaning down and offering her hand. The room behind her was yellow with a fast-burning fire, and in a second I was inside the room, leaning back on the closed door, panting, the icy fear in my veins already starting to be soothed by deep breaths and safety.

'Thank you,' I said, gasping. 'Thank you, thank you.' I tried hard to control my breathing so I could listen for hoofs outside.

'Don't worry, they aren't near,' the woman said. My

head rested back against the door and I kept breathing deeply in great quenching gulps. She had sat down facing away from me towards the fire, and was sewing a shirt.

I looked around, still getting my breath back. Much of the room was invisible because blankets and fabrics had been draped from the ceiling like sheets left to dry. I looked at the woman again. Her hair looked darker now against the flickering light, and somehow she didn't seem as tall as when I'd come in.

I sat in the chair beside her and a second later felt a blanket being draped round my shoulders. I watched the flames as my breathing returned to normal and after a minute asked, 'Who are you? Why did you help me?'

'You've seen me before,' she said gently. 'Many times, although you didn't know it.'

I wanted to ask what she meant, but she got up and walked quietly out of the room. Alone in the warmth and quiet I began to feel drowsy, but I resisted my tiredness. This wasn't the time to fall asleep.

She came back in stirring something in a wooden cup and handed it to me. It smelt curious and unlike anything I had drunk before, but good, and as I sipped it I started to feel more like myself.

'You look very snug there,' she said, taking up the shirt again. 'You'll feel better in no time.'

I nodded and took another sip, staring into the flames.

'Tell you what I'll do while you're drinking that,' she said. 'I'll tell you a story.'

I nodded again, more eagerly.

'What sort of a story would you like?'

I shrugged. 'One about magic,' I said quietly, to see her response.

'Hm,' she said thoughtfully. 'All right, then. A magical one it is.'

And as I sat there, the fire warming me from without and the drink from within, she began in her beguiling voice the tale of . . .

# THE GIRL WHO LISTENED TO A RAVEN

Penny was a friendly little girl of nine years old who lived with her mother on the top floor of a very narrow, rickety building in the poorest part of town. Her mother worked hard in a factory all day while Penny stayed at home mending clothes for their neighbours, a job which she liked, and which also brought them a few extra pennies a week.

She was a quiet and obedient child who used her spare moments to clean up around the little apartment, scrub the floors and dust the furniture. This was so that her mother might be pleased with her when she arrived home from the factory, tired and bothered, which she always did at around seven o'clock. Her mother never noticed, however, or if she did she never mentioned it, and would always send Penny to bed after a meagre supper, at seven thirty sharp.

For the past few days, after she went to bed each night, Penny had been kept awake by a curious tapping on the little window high above her bed. Last night she had gone into the kitchen to tell her mother about it, but her mother's friend Mrs Grobble was there, who always seemed to love talking about the most awful and terrifying things, and she could not get a word in edgeways.

'Hanged him at last, they have,' Mrs Grobble was saying. 'And a good thing too. Leastways we can sleep well again without the worry of him on our streets. You didn't go to the hanging?'

Penny's mother seemed about to speak, but Mrs

Grobble answered for her.

'Course you didn't, busy woman like you, at work no doubt. *Anyway*, most terrible weird thing. Just as he was hanging there and the crowd was cheering fit to burst themselves, this bird came down – crow maybe, or a rook, it was hard to see – and settled on his head for a second. It seemed to lean right in like it was going to peck out his eye, or was listening to his voice, and the crowd went dead quiet. Then it flew right up, screaming, as though it realized what it had landed on. Quite sent the chills down me, I don't mind telling you. I haven't looked at a bird the same way since, these two weeks.'

She seemed to pause, so Penny tried to speak: 'Mummy, I—'

But Mrs Grobble carried on the next second, as unstoppable as a steam train. 'And you know what they said he done to those poor women? They said as how he would use a carving knife – and then *eat their bodies* . . .' Penny found herself feeling sick and faint, and ran back to bed to hide beneath the covers.

That was yesterday. Now it was very late and she lay in bed hearing the tapping on the window once more. Mrs Grobble was in the kitchen as usual, talking nineteen (or more) to the dozen, so Penny, who was not only quiet and obedient but also helplessly curious, decided to climb up and see what the noise was. First she stepped on the bedpost, then on to the handle and the top of the wardrobe, then she climbed over an empty suitcase and a tall chest and finally pulled herself up by a thin nail sticking out of the wall, so she could see out of the window. Through its small circle of glass she saw a black bird, much larger up close than she had ever realized a black bird could be, and which she thought must be a raven. As she looked, it tapped the pane with its beak three times. Penny waved at it and smiled.

'Hello, Mr Raven!' she said.

But the bird shook its head, as though it didn't just want to be waved to. It tapped the window again, three times.

Maybe he wants to come in, Penny wondered. So she leaned up and twisted the little lock on the side of the window, making it swing outwards.

The bird put its head in so that it could see all the way round the room before turning its little black eyes to her. Then, to Penny's astonishment, in quite a courteous voice, it said: 'Do come out and join me.'

Penny gasped, her foot slipped from the nail and she fell hard on to the chest (where she banged her bottom), the suitcase (where she bruised her shoulder) and then all the way down on to her bed where she landed with an enormous crash.

'What's going on in there?' called her mother. The door burst open and Penny's mother filled the frame, Mrs Grobble's wart-covered face peering over her shoulder.

'I'm trying to have a quiet chat with my friend!' shrieked her mother. 'If you can't keep it down, you'll have to sleep in The Box like your brother, Teddy, God rest his soul.'

'God rest his poor soul,' muttered Mrs Grobble, performing the sign of the cross.

'So get to sleep and don't disturb us, brat!' With these affectionate words her mother retreated, closing the door with a slam, and leaving Penny in dark silence. There she lay for a few minutes before she heard the noise again: tap-tap-tap. Too quiet for her mother to hear. Tap-tap-tap. Too loud for her to sleep.

Tap-tap-tap.

At last, sure that her mother and the warty Mrs Grobble were talking again, she started to climb upward, careful not to make a sound.

Tap-tap-tap.

'Don't go away,' she whispered, as she clambered up. 'I'm coming!' She reached the window and there the bird still was, looking in. She twisted the lock and pushed the window open.

'You came back,' said the bird, and bowed.

'Why do you want me to come outside?' she asked.

'I have something amazing to show you,' said the bird, 'but I can't tell you what it is. You must follow me.'

In a second Penny had pulled herself up and through the windowframe. She sat on the thin ledge of the steep roof, a drizzly rain falling all around her.

'I'm so pleased you have come,' said the raven. 'I've

been trying to attract your attention for some time.'

'I thought it was a tree branch tapping against the window,' Penny explained. 'Tell me, can all birds speak?'

The raven had been walking around on the spot and staring downwards in that distracted way birds have, as though trying to remember something. Now it stopped and looked up at her.

'Good lord, no,' he said. 'I'm the only one, I think. Most other birds are really quite stupid.'

'That's a shame,' said Penny, thinking of the pigeons she would throw breadcrumbs to some Saturdays.

'If you say so,' said the raven. 'Follow me.'

The raven climbed easily up the steep slates of the roof, but Penny found it much harder. She kept slipping and nearly falling, and tried not to think about the dirt and grime she was getting on her nightdress.

'My name is Penny,' she panted, when they were a little way up. 'Do you have a name?'

'Of course,' the raven said, becoming slightly impatient. 'Keep going, we're nearly there!'

In a few minutes they reached the top of the roof, where there was a flat section on which one could walk. Penny stood holding her nightdress around her against the wind and wishing she'd put on a coat. The rain was very fine tonight, almost like a mist, and from this height you could see down into the streets on either side and all the little rooms where families were making their dinner, or preparing for bed.

'This isn't what I was going to show you,' said the raven, whose voice was so well-mannered and pleasant to listen to that Penny wished she could speak so nicely.

The raven strutted ahead to a little shack built on the top of the roof. It seemed barely wide enough for one person to stand up in, but the raven rapped his beak against the door and said, 'Open it, Penny.'

She pulled the door open.

'What's this?' she asked in wonderment.

'It's where I used to live,' said the raven. 'Back when I was – well, that's not important.'

The little shack extended quite far back and was packed with a multitude of interesting objects and curiosities. Furs of strange animals hung from the ceiling and along the shelves were boxes of odd and glittering stones. There were jars of liquids and powders too – some dark and dusty, some sparkling as though with a strange magic. Penny also noticed many funny-shaped instruments that looked like they might be used to do unusual things, like clip a kangaroo's toenails, or remove a splinter from the inside of an elephant's trunk.

'How amazing!' she said. 'What fascinating things.'

'I am flattered that you think so,' said the bird, bowing briefly. 'Careful what you do with that!' he said. She had picked up a long metal rod with a bell on the end, and little green stones inlaid around the handle.

'Why?'

'It is a special tool to attract lightning – its design is based on the sceptre with which the kings of East Persia used to be crowned. Sometimes it contains enough electricity to kill a full-grown buffalo, so be careful.'

Cautiously Penny replaced it on the dusty wooden shelf. In the distance she heard the clock on the tower of St Hildred's begin the twelve slow strokes of the midnight bell.

'Twelve o'clock!' said the raven. 'We must hurry. See that box on the shelf? Not that box, *that* one!'

'Oh yes,' said Penny, pulling a stool close to climb up to it.

'Hurry!' said the bird impatiently. 'Open it.'

Penny twisted a tiny key in the front of the box and lifted its lid.

'Does it contain a lamp?' asked the raven.

'It does. Oh, how wonderful, I've never seen such a thing!' said Penny, holding it up. It was made of a strange silvery metal that glimmered with other colours against the light of the moon – darkish brown, purplish blue and more.

The church clock kept striking on towards twelve, now on six, now seven . . .

'HURRY!' shouted the bird, sounding less and less polite, and more like someone who had grown up with Mrs Grobble. 'Open the top of the lamp. Is there a little packet inside?'

'Yes,' said Penny, flustered by the bird's urgency and not wanting to annoy it.

'Open it – quickly! Is there a grey powder?'

'Yes. And it's slightly glittery too, like it's got flakes of gold in it.'

'Throw a handful of it over me – good! Now throw the rest up in the air, over your head!'

The clock struck for the eleventh time.

'Now strike that flint!'

As the dust twinkled around her and in her eyes Penny saw a sharp stone in one corner of the box and a touchpaper against which to strike it. In the excitement of the raven's insistent voice she grabbed them, held them above her head and struck a large spark as the final bell of midnight sounded.

All at once the dust around them glowed and sparkled – the raven's black little eyes seemed to glitter against the dancing light and its beak fell open in amazement. Then the light grew as the whole room seemed to catch fire for a second and Penny found herself dazed and on the ground, and looking up at a girl in a grubby night-dress who was covered with a light dust. The girl shook off the dust with her hands and bent down to talk to Penny. As her face came close, Penny froze. She realized it was *her* face leaning in. It spoke with a raspy rattle, more mean and unpleasant than any voice she had ever heard.

'Thank you, my dear,' it squawked. 'That feels much better.'

Penny tried to get up, but became scared as all she could feel was a feathery fluttering around her head.

She tried to stand and found herself only a few inches high, tottering about on little stalks.

'You'll get used to it,' rasped the voice. 'I did, and it ain't so bad. After all –' and now Penny saw her own face come even closer, so its nose almost touched her – 'you get to eat WORMS and MAGGOTS and FLIES, and they're absolutely LOVELY.'

Penny began to flutter her wings, trying to fly. 'You'll get used to it soon enough. Now I'm going to go and cause some mischief,' said the girl, and Penny watched her own body leave the shed and climb down the roof.

In panic, she flapped her wings hard until she began to take off. She hovered in the air for a few moments, trying to get used to the sensation. Then she flew out of the shed and up into the air. She flew round and round in circles a few times to get the hang of it and then swooped down unsteadily past a number of windows until she saw her own – but there was no one in the bed. Nearing exhaustion, she kept flapping until she found the kitchen. Miraculously her mother was standing right near the window, washing dishes. Penny landed on the ledge and began tapping the window at once with her beak. Her mother looked up, saw her and frowned. Penny tapped again and called out, but in a second her mother had unlatched the window, reached out and grabbed Penny by the neck, strangling her voice.

'Good,' said her mother, bringing the bird in. 'Bird

pie for supper tomorrow. Penny! What are you doing there!'

Penny twisted her head in her mother's grasp to see the little girl, changed into a clean nightdress, standing in the doorway. She now spoke with a prim and polite little girl's voice.

'I couldn't sleep, Mother, so I thought I might help you with some chores. Can I kill that bird for you? And then pluck and skin it for the pot?'

'A good idea for once, you little wretch,' said her mother, handing over the carving knife. 'It's about time you helped out around here.'

'Of course, Mother,' said the girl, looking up innocently. 'I just want to help.'

I was still staring into the fire, slightly dazed by the thought of what had happened to poor Penny, when I realized the woman had left the room again.

A different door opened and a little old woman came in. She sat in the same chair, and picked up the same garment of clothing the younger woman had been stitching.

'It's you they're looking for, you know,' the old woman said. 'Not those other boys.'

'I didn't do what they think I did,' I said, wildly trying to work out what she knew, and how she knew it.

'Of course not,' said the woman, looking down carefully as she threaded a stitch, 'but that hardly makes a difference. You will have to be extra careful, more careful than you have been.'

I nodded, and looked up from my cup to see she was gone. The shirt lay on the chair, the needle halfway through the hole of a button.

'You want to rescue her, don't you?' a voice said. 'The girl in the window.' I jumped, and spilt some of my drink on the blanket.

'Who's that?' I said.

'I'm here, in the corner,' said the voice. I stood and walked slowly towards it. Behind a few layers of hangings there was a thicker rug. Wide and luxuriously decorated in an intricate design unlike anything I'd seen

before, beads of coloured glass and silver pieces winked from its fur. It stretched across the corner of the room. I reached out and pulled it back. Behind it was darkness.

'Don't be worried,' said the voice. 'Come in.' I inched forward and let the rug fall down behind me. I could dimly see the outline of a shape on a chair in front of me.

'Who are you?' I asked.

'You want to rescue her,' she repeated. It was a female voice, an old one. Not frail but hardened and strong. There was something distant about it too, so that even close up it sounded as though it came from the bottom of a well.

'Who are you?' I asked again.

She waited a long time to answer and because I couldn't see it I became transfixed by what her face must look like, and fearful of it. 'You could call me Gora,' she said at last.

'Gora,' I repeated, feeling the strangeness of the word in my mouth. 'How *can* I rescue her?' I asked. 'Caspian Prye owns everything and everyone; it's impossible.'

'There are ways of getting round things. I can help you.'

'Why would you want to?' I asked, my curiosity made all the sharper by the darkness, and her invisibility.

There was a creaking noise as she leaned forward,

closer to me. 'That is my business,' she said. 'You think you know what I am, don't you? Maybe you're right. See this –' and her finger touched my forehead. The room vanished, and I saw an image of myself crouching by a grave in the deserted corner of a churchyard. A bush had grown high above it, so it was nearly hidden, and shaded from the bright sunshine.

No one knew about this place but me. The scene was so vivid I couldn't breathe. A surge of strong sadness went through my body as the invisible figure removed her finger and the vision retreated. I was back in this dark enclosure.

'How do you know about that?' I whispered.

'I didn't, until I touched you. That was just to show you I can see things,' Gora said. '*Some* things,' she corrected herself. 'Where I come from, we have many words for what I am. Many of them are good words. But in this country you say only "witch". Do you see a broomstick in this room? No. That is an ignorant superstition told by stupid people. There are witches of everything, you understand. Good witches and bad witches, and some who are in between. Witches of fire and animals and words, and anything you care to mention.'

She went silent for a second, thinking. 'What *is* your connection to the girl? It intrigues me.'

'That is my business,' I said.

She laughed quietly and in the darkness I felt as though she could see me, and was sizing me up, as Jaspers had, but with an icier and more penetrating gaze. 'There is something you must get if you want to free her,' she said at last. 'This is what I have to tell you. That man, Prye, has stolen this thing, although he doesn't know how to use it. You have to take it from him, and you can't do that without help from me. So – now drink up that brew I gave you,' she said, 'and don't speak for a few seconds.'

What choice did I have but to trust her? (For a moment I wasn't sure if I'd heard her right. The brew that *she* had given me?) I closed my eyes and forced the drink down. It was lukewarm now, and the dregs tasted totally different from the first few sips – vile, an ashy mud. As I drank, Gora muttered something in a language I couldn't understand, and as she came to the end she said the same phrase three times and placed her hand on the top of my head.

'Do you fear me?' she asked quietly.

'Yes,' I said.

'Wise boy. People who betray me do not fare well. Take this creature – what do they call it – the Slurgoggen.'

'You know about the Creature? The Slumgullion? It does exist?'

She laughed delightedly, her voice transformed into

a high, clear sound like a young girl's. 'Let's say *if* he existed, this scaly creature as big as a shark, with a man's intelligence and supernatural strength – *if* he existed, he would not frighten me. Magic over muscles, you see, boy?' She tapped my wrist with her forefinger as though she had been wagging it to teach me a lesson. 'Magic over muscles.'

I felt the dregs of the mixture taking effect inside me. I felt warmer, almost as though I glowed, and experienced a strange feeling of power. I looked at my fingertips and thought they gleamed with a blue light.

'My grandmother was a witch of light and darkness,' Gora went on. Her voice had retreated back to the bottom of its well. 'My mother was a witch of memory; she could make you remember wonderful and terrible things. I am a witch of doorways. What I have given you is the gift to walk through any door. Draw your hand across the door, from one side to the other, and it will vanish for you and you alone.'

In the darkness I touched my fingers to my lips and then made fists and squeezed my fingers into my palms. They felt just the same. Could this be happening to me? 'What is it that I need to steal from Caspian?' I asked.

'A silver box. I don't know what's inside it. Prye wishes to win this girl's heart, and he knows the contents of this box are the key to it, but he doesn't understand how. He had his men steal it only a few days ago, and

there it is still, beneath the Chief of Police's pillow, where he sleeps at the Black Lamb Tavern. Go now, quickly.'

I pushed my way back through the drapes and hanging rugs and standing by the door I saw again the friendly younger woman from before, the one who had welcomed me in.

'You're Gora too, aren't you? You are *both* of the women I've seen? I mean, both of them are you?'

She smiled again, and winked. 'Go quickly. This door won't lead back to where you were before,' she said, smiling. 'The tavern is outside. The policeman is asleep now. You should have no problem. Go!'

She opened the door and pushed me out into the night, and closed it again sharply. When I turned round I was standing in the doorway of a butcher's shop that was closed for the night.

On my own now in the cold silence of the street, and holding my hands outwards almost as though I was afraid of them, I decided I had to test whether I was under the spell of a weird hallucination or whether this was true. I stepped back and touched one side of the butcher's doorway. Then I reached over and touched the other. Nothing happened. I tried again, touching one side and carefully drawing my hand, exactly as she'd said, in a straight line across to the other. I pressed the door – it was as solid as ever.

'Damn it!' I said, and impatiently slapped the door-frame. In a swooshing movement, the entire door came off its hinges and slid away in front of me. I pushed my hand hard against the other side of the frame, and the door disappeared clean into it. I stared into the open butcher's shop for a few disbelieving seconds, and then without a sound the door slid back across in front of me, and fixed itself in its frame again.

I looked over my shoulder to see if anyone was watching me, then I looked at the door again. I swiped it open, and stepped inside. I counted to five before it closed behind me. I stared around the shop in disbelief, and started to laugh. It was impossible! And why, why, hadn't I picked a pie shop? Or a sweet shop! What good was raw bacon to me now?

Staring out of the window, my eyes focused on the huge tavern on the other side of the street where I had been dropped off yesterday. I stopped smiling. This was going to be the most dangerous, stupid, frightening thing I'd ever done. If I was caught, I'd be dead. I knew that. But I had to do it, so this was no time for nerves. Instead, I concentrated fiercely on not putting a foot wrong.

The Black Lamb was a gargantuan building, brooding at the edge of the hill by the crossroads. It seemed to have many doors to different bars, saloons and taprooms. I watched for a few minutes, trying to

work out which would be the best way to get in, then dashed across the road to a smallish side door. This looked like a servants' entrance and could possibly give me access to the rooms. I swiped my hand across it – it disappeared – and blinked for a second, still amazed that it miraculously followed my command, before stepping inside.

I found myself at the bottom of a staircase, and listened for any movement or sign that someone had noticed me coming in, but heard none. On the wall beside me I could see a board with all of the bedroom numbers, next to which the staff had written the guests' names in chalk. I scanned it briefly, suddenly realizing I had no idea what room I was looking for. Then one name caught my eye. I repeated it in my head a few times, wondering why I knew it, before I realized. There it was. ROOM 3: RAMBULL – the policeman I had seen arresting a murderer in the market that morning.

I took the stairs carefully, trying to make no noise, until I was at the first-floor landing, with bedroom doors all along it. The nearest was Room 6, so I crept along the passageway with my breath caught in my throat, feeling by turns terrified and ridiculous, so nervous I nearly burst out laughing.

What happened next showed me I might as well have done, because having never stayed in an inn, and not knowing the custom of leaving your boots outside to be polished in the morning, I was more than a little surprised to find myself toppling forward and crashing to the floor. It felt like each knee and elbow (not to mention my head) smashed into it with a separate deafening blow and that I'd made just about as much noise as I could if I'd tried, so I wasn't surprised to find the door nearest me opening and a great fat man lumbering out in his long johns.

'Mind out, lad,' he said, stepping over me. I stared after him as he clumped down the corridor towards the toilet, and saw the '3' in the centre of his open door. Scrambling up, I darted inside and found only discarded clothes in a heap on the floor. I rushed to the bed and felt under the pillows, then the mattress. Nothing. There was a chest by the bed but it was locked, and I was getting frightened that Rambull would return when I swept a quick arm under the bed and my wrist made contact with a sharp edge. I pulled the object out with both hands and slid it inside my coat, not stopping to look at it. I slipped out of the bedroom as fast and silently as I could, taking refuge in another doorway with less than a second to spare before he came trudging back along the corridor. He was still more asleep than awake, and smelt heavily of beer. When he reached me, he stumbled and gripped my arm hard, as though steadying himself on a banister. His mouth ducked close to my ear, and at the same time he spoke.

'There's a storm coming,' he said in a low, dirty growl, whether to me or to himself I couldn't tell. I nodded, breathing evenly, desperately trying not to drop the box, and his arm released me. Then he was gone.

The second he closed his bedroom door, I fairly sprinted along the corridor and down the stairs, not caring how much noise I made. I swiped the door in one swift movement, feeling the sheer joy of using the spell.

The wind and rain came in through the door with a fierce noise, and I ran into them. With a childish fear I imagined someone roused by the noise running down the stairs behind me, reaching the door before it closed. When I was halfway down the street, I ducked round a corner and looked back: the little door was shut fast, so dark and tiny and far away I couldn't believe I'd been on the other side of it a few seconds before. Everything was like a dream today. I pushed the silver box deep inside my shirt, pulled my coat round it and slipped back into the street.

I hadn't walked two minutes before I saw that Rambull's words about the storm were true. The rain lashed down more violently than before. Not heavy and concentrated, but in sudden unpredictable gusts as though the wind was taking its first deep breaths before a loud roar, as though there was a great temper in the sky about to be unleashed, and it buffeted against the low roofs around me.

I went slip-sliding through arches and down alleyways with no idea where I was going, but told myself it was in the general direction of Turvey House and I would see a landmark soon. Every window was shut up against the storm as if in dread. Then a strong gust picked me up and sent me slithering forward in the mud on my knees. For the first time my surge of confidence that I would be all right faltered, my joy at getting hold of the box began to melt away. A sliver of fear crept into me again as the wind rattled doors on my left and right.

I took a couple of turnings I was unsure about and began to doubt my direction too. I was at the top of a steep cobbled path that led down to a road bright with gaslight. Something told me not to go down there. Little rivulets ran between the cobbles, shimmering with some kind of warning I couldn't understand. But I had to keep going, that was the most important thing, so I ran down and came out into the road. What I saw stopped me dead.

Ahead, half turned towards me and his whole figure frozen in fear, was a boy. He was about my age and height and similar in every respect to me. Behind him, crowded into the cobbled passage, were fifteen or twenty huge horses breathing steam. Mounted on them were fifteen or twenty policemen in uniform, their hats

dripping with water, burning torches in some of their hands. And at their lead was the man from whom I had taken the silver box, Rambull, his face lit by the torch in a hungry leer.

For a moment we all paused, and the boys and men stared at each other.

'Run!' I shouted to the boy, and when he didn't move screamed at the top of my lungs, 'Come on! *Run!*'

He stumbled towards me as the first hoofs began to clatter behind him. I grabbed his outstretched arms and pulled him with me, but already the thunder of horseshoes had drowned out the storm, and above it all rose the angry shouting of the police as they goaded their horses like madmen.

The boy slipped and we both fell – he cried out in pain and I found my face pressed against the metal of a drain cover. I pulled him as tightly as I could against me, held him down as he wriggled to get free and swept my hand from one side to the other. The horses were so close the stones shook beneath us. As a hole appeared at our heads I pushed him down first and dived in after, and the dark throat of the drain swallowed us up.

There was a second of black nothingness as we fell, the sense of feeling weirdly weightless, and then a sudden hard smack of water as we crashed into the sewer below.

I surfaced, searching desperately inside my shirt to

see if the silver box was there, and trying to breathe at the same time. Finally my hand found it, slipped all the way round to the small of my back, and I kicked hard to keep my head above water, looking for somewhere to climb out. After a few seconds I felt a ledge and pulled the boy towards it. He climbed up and pulled me after him. We leaned against the wall hearing nothing but our own panting, drops of water falling and the pounding of hoofs on the iron lid far above.

Without speaking, we both moved along the ledge as fast as we could, scared that the men above would prise open the lid and come looking for us. After a few minutes, the boy spoke.

'I'm Benjamin,' he said between breaths. 'My name is Benjamin Bright.'

'Daniel Dorey,' I said. 'Excuse me not shaking your hand, but I can't see it.' Neither of us had the wind to say anything else for a minute, until our lungs were working normally again, and the only sound around us was our own breathing. Either the horsemen had gone or we were out of earshot. I looked back along the tunnel to gauge the distance we had walked.

'That thing with your hand – how did you *do* it?' Benjamin asked.

'Quiet a minute,' I said.

'But how did you *do* it?'

'Shut up!' I whispered – my hand covered his mouth

and held it closed. My eyes had adapted to the darkness quicker than his, but now he began to see what I saw, and he became silent too.

We must have fallen a long way because the walls rose high around us, and tunnels fed in from both sides. Above us on the other side of the water was the circular mouth of one of these smaller tunnels. Inside it we could see a dark shape, totally still and silent and looking not unlike a kneeling man.

'What is it?' breathed Benjamin into my ear.

I shook my head. Carefully we started to walk away from it, nervously watching our steps on the narrow ledge. Looking back I saw the figure's head move with us, as though watching us closely. Then Benjamin pinched my side and whispered, '*Look!*'

He pointed up at another hole a little way ahead. There were two silent dark shapes in this one, huddled together and following our progress in the same way. Able to see further now, we saw more circular openings in the sewer walls regularly spaced all the way into the distance.

'What the hell . . .' I muttered.

We flinched as we heard the snap of a match being struck some way ahead and I had to grab Benjamin to stop him falling back into the water. The flare of light was intensely bright after the darkness and we shaded our eyes for a second before we could see properly.

Dozens of people looked down at us from their hiding places in the tunnels. Whole families were crouched together in the cramped space with their possessions piled up around them, looking poor and hungry and dirty. Yet they didn't have the look of fugitives, but seemed defiant – more frightening than afraid. The man who leaned outwards holding the match over the water to look at us wore a wild beard. Weapons and climbing gear hung from his belt. He regarded us for a second and then pointed across to the wall near me. Not ten feet ahead a metal ladder rose up vertically into a hole in the ceiling, probably towards another drain cover. I nodded my thanks, but in his grim seriousness he was not impressed. I got the feeling he didn't want to help us, he just wanted us to go. As I reached the ladder he took a shallow breath and blew out the match.

Benjamin and I climbed in silence until we had vanished into the ceiling and were out of earshot.

'I've heard about them,' said Benjamin below me, 'but I never believed they existed. Apparently there are hundreds of them, never leaving the sewers . . .'

I was too disturbed to answer, and concentrated on finding the next rung above me in the darkness, until my hand rapped on the metal of a lid. I took a deep, deep breath and silently said a short prayer as I drew my hand across. The metal sprang back and we saw the

street above. We climbed out, ran like rats to the nearest doorway and sat there, shivering. It was suddenly incredibly cold, and the storm had got worse while we were underground, but at least now there was not a horse or a horseman in sight.

Knowing we didn't have the strength to face the cold and the storm, I reached up and took the risk of knocking on the door we sat against. For a minute we heard nothing, and as our hopes faded we felt the bite of the cold and damp even more bitterly. But then we heard a discussion going on behind us, two people arguing about whether to open the door or not. At last it was held open a crack, and a pair of worried eyes looked outwards – then downward – and saw the two scruffy little heaps of misery on their doorstep.

All at once the door was thrown open and we were dragged inside, placed in front of a small fire and interrogated by the house's inhabitants, who were a lovely and doddery old couple. You could tell that the husband had poor vision partly because he wore half-moon spectacles, which slid continually down his nose and which he had to push back up (always sniffing as he did so), and partly because when either of us spoke he leaned in and peered closely at us, a habit which was luckily more funny than it was disconcerting.

'You are in trouble, my lads?' he asked. Benjamin and I exchanged a look, and nodded slowly. 'We need to find a man named Uncle.' At this the man's face grew grave, and where before he had seemed kindly almost to the point of silliness, a firmness of purpose now entered his voice. 'Yes, I know this Uncle,' he said. 'A very good man. He helped out a friend of mine once upon a time. Isn't that right, old girl?'

His wife looked at him with fond impatience. 'It wasn't your friend, it was your brother!'

'My WHAT?' he bellowed, squinting as though that was going to help him catch the words.

'It was your BROTHER!' she replied.

'Can't hear a word she says. Say it again?'

But she only sighed, and took up her knitting again.

'What did she say?' he asked, turning to us. I didn't want to get involved, so I smiled awkwardly, at which he seemed to remember what he had been saying. 'Of course,' he said. 'That Uncle feller. Now I think about it I'm pretty sure it wasn't my friend, but my brother he helped. Anyhow, I know someone who'll be able to lay hands on him. You boys just wait here.' He stood and pulled his coat on.

'Please don't go out there,' I said. 'I can't let you go out in the storm. There are policemen on horseback, and they . . .' I trailed off because both the man and his wife gave me a look of sweet, indulgent amusement, as if I'd said something charmingly naive.

'Don't you worry about me,' the man said, still smiling. 'We know all about the streets. We have other ways of getting around in Tumblewater.' And then, going to the low table in one corner, he pulled it back and kicked the wall hard, twice. After a few seconds there came a clicking sound like the unlocking of a latch, and a diagonal section of the wall was pulled back, revealing a dark passage beyond.

'Thank you,' said the old man to someone inside the passage, and then he was gone, and the secret door replaced, its seams fitting perfectly so that the wall became whole again, and made me doubt the evidence of my own eyes.

'He'll be back soon,' said his wife, pulling her chair a little closer. She regarded us with fond sympathy, and saw that as the fire began to warm us, our shivering became more violent (we had been past shivering when they let us in), and our faces became more pathetic and miserable as we tried to control it, both of us looking at the fire as though to suck in warmth faster by will-power alone.

'Poor boys,' she muttered. 'I've nothing to offer you, it shames me to say. Nothing but a tale, although maybe if I tell it right it will distract from the cold as well as a bowl of soup would.'

I nodded vigorously and through chattering teeth assured her it would.

'It's not quite so horrible as the other tales people like to tell around here – or at least not at the start. But it's my favourite, so I'll tell it you – unless you've heard it before? Stop me if you have. It's called . . .'

# THE MERRY BAKERS

Once upon a time, there lived two men called Fabian and Freshpenny. They were bakers, and very fine ones – so fine, in fact, that almost every customer who came into their shop remarked that it was the finest bakery they had ever encountered, and Fabian and Freshpenny without question the greatest bakers.

As well as being brilliantly talented at bakery, both men were also exceptionally jolly and happy, so that people would not only step into their shop for the delicious cakes and pastries, but also for the cheery greetings and bright smiles they would receive. The people in the town grew slightly fatter than they would otherwise have been, but they did not blame the bakers, for they made such delightful things, and were such nice men.

As well as being excellent bakers and jolly people, Fabian and Freshpenny were the best of friends. They divided the work equally between them, Fabian making the dough, Freshpenny cutting it into shapes, Fabian baking it and Freshpenny laying it out on the shelves. As they closed the shop each day after selling their last loaf of bread, Fabian would say, 'Another fine day over with, my old friend!'

And Freshpenny would reply, 'Our best day yet!'

And then, because they had been up since so very early in the morning, they would retire with their hot-water bottles to their large double bed and sit there reading until one of them dozed off. Then the other would dutifully blow out the candle and go to sleep.

*

A few years after they first set up shop together, Fabian (who was thin, and of a more nervous disposition) began to notice that their bakery was not large enough for them to make all of the breads and biscuits that people wanted to buy from them. So Freshpenny (who was altogether rounder and more jovial) rode to the next town, which was bigger than the one they lived in, and found a larger shop for them to move to. Within a few months they were open for business in their new home.

Residents in the new town took to the merry bakers just as their old customers had. Fabian and Freshpenny soon found they were taking more money each day than before, which meant that they were able to experiment with new things – bread stuffed with nuts and chocolate, or baked into extraordinary shapes such as a ship (Fabian's greatest accomplishment) or a deer (Freshpenny's crowning glory). They drove each other on to ever more impressive feats: Fabian repeated the deer-shaped bread of Freshpenny, but served it up to the mayor with a pound of venison stew concealed within its belly. Freshpenny responded by baking Fabian's fantastical bread-ship but with a whole salmon, topped with potatoes, carrots, peas and a soft cheese sauce, laid along the boat's insides. He served this to a party of visiting sailors in a local tavern to roars of approval and much drinking of ale.

Fabian saw his plump friend returning from the inn

with such a proud, happy smile that he thought to himself how pleased he was for Freshpenny, and how lucky he was to be his partner. As he watched him bounding around the shop over the following weeks, however, and welcoming customers with his rather high-pitched voice which (he started to notice) he found rather annoying, Fabian decided that he would not be outdone. Sure enough, soon afterwards he was asked to bake a wedding cake, and he threw himself into the project with all his energy, fashioning a seven-tier masterpiece that rose taller than a Christmas tree. He fixed an ingenious piece of clockwork into the topmost layer so that, as long as it was wound up in advance, little wooden figures of a bride and groom leaned in to peck one another on the lips every few seconds.

On the day it was completed, Freshpenny watched this magisterial creation being carried away down the street, and he clapped his skinny friend on the back.

'That truly is the most magnificent cake I have ever seen,' he said. He saw a beam of satisfaction on Fabian's face, and thought to himself, not for the first time, that Fabian's moustache was more than a little unhygienic, and must surely be putting customers off.

'Thank you,' said Fabian. 'I could never have done it without you.'

'But I fear if we want to make any greater creations we shall have to find another bakery even bigger than this one, with a larger oven and a pantry wide enough to feed a whole city!'

Fabian thought it was a fabulous idea. So they began to search again, and eventually they found a town a little further along the coast, with a population twice the size of their current home, in which they rented a larger property. And so, in due course, they moved and settled in, and began to sell the iced buns and fruit tarts and loaves of bread that they had always sold, and proved as popular and successful as they ever had.

Over the course of the following year, as their business thrived and their popularity grew, Freshpenny began to find that it wasn't just the sight of Fabian's moustache that got on his nerves, but also his ridiculous duck-like walk. What's more, he was convinced that the moustache smelt. He took to sniffing loudly whenever Fabian was near but instead of taking the hint, the other man decided Freshpenny could smell some food which had gone off, and got himself into a state, waddling around the place and fussing so that Freshpenny thought he would go mad.

For his part, Fabian felt he could hear nothing but Freshpenny's whining voice. Even when he got away from the shop for an hour's walk in the countryside, he could still hear it ringing around his head like a gate on squeaky hinges. Worse than this, though, was Freshpenny's habit of slamming things.

The merry baker showed his satisfaction at the end of every day by closing the shop door with a resounding slam. But that would just be the final note in an orchestral performance that lasted from the first slap of the dough on the kitchen counter, and went through a hundred and one variations after that. Throwing the oven door open with a bang, crashing it shut, thrusting the till drawer closed with the flat of his hand so that every silver coin danced a frightened jig, clumping the bread down on the shelves and clapping people's hands in double-fisted handshakes hard enough to break their fingers. By the final snap of Freshpenny's apron strings and the jangle of his keys being thrown on to their hook, Fabian was a jumpy wreck of nerves. He pined for silence, and viewed every new day with dread.

All this time they kept up the pretence of friendship to one another, even in private, and their renown for extraordinary creativity with food continued to grow. The newspapers wrote about their bakery, the word passed infectiously from mouth to mouth, and soon buying a cake at Fabian & Freshpenny's Bakery became the one thing that everybody who came to the town had to do.

A visiting party from St Petersburg arrived: Freshpenny fashioned a huge cassock sword as long as an oar and as sharp as a razor, layered with pastry, marzipan, icing and jam. A rich merchant told them he wanted a special dessert for his daughter's birthday: Fabian crafted an astonishing rainbow from seven different-coloured arches of hard-candied sugar beneath which a swan fashioned from meringue swam between sculpted hills of ice cream. It was declared the eighth wonder of the world by all who saw it, and the guests feared to eat a bite lest they ruin its exquisite beauty (all save the merchant's daughter, who was a greedy pig and tucked in at once).

But these accomplishments took their toll. The enormous effort and the awful tiredness which followed each creation meant that their considerable irritation with each other did not remain unspoken for long. As they closed the door each day on their final customer, their wide smiles would vanish and they would snarl pettily at one another.

'Sweep up, you fat sweaty pig!' Fabian would bark, duck-waddling to the back door.

'I'd rather be *well built*' – Freshpenny would shout, as this was how he preferred to describe himself – 'than a weasly little runt!' and he would slam his broom against the wall, making Fabian jump.

There was nothing to be done. The more they craved to be away from one another, the faster the orders poured in, and business improved more than ever.

One day Freshpenny 'accidentally' tripped Fabian, who fell clean into the burning oven. Afterwards Freshpenny claimed that the oven door had slammed itself shut of its own accord, locking Fabian in. It was only at the enquiry of a concerned customer that Freshpenny reluctantly opened it, to see what the noise inside was. On seeing Fabian's hands blackened with soot, and his face blackened with rage, Freshpenny let out a rather exaggerated gasp of horror, and said:

'My lord! What a horrible accident!'

A few days later, Freshpenny was getting ready for sleep when he saw that Fabian, lying reading his book on the other side of the bed, had a funny little smile on his face.

I wonder what he's up to, Freshpenny wondered as he climbed under the covers, when –WHOOMF! – he fell clean through the floor, landing in the man-sized mixing bowl in the kitchen below.

Feeling the cut on his forehead and wiping the blood from his eyes, Freshpenny looked up to see a perfectly circular hole, which had been sawed into the ceiling, the bed and the mattress above. Into this gap Fabian's face now appeared, looking maddeningly pleased with itself.

'Good heavens!' he cried. 'These rats will eat through anything. We really must invest in a rat catcher!' Then his face disappeared again, and as Freshpenny clambered out of the mixing bowl he was sure he could hear a muffled chuckling.

Things got worse as time went on. One day, watching Freshpenny say goodbye to a little boy who had popped in for an iced bun, Fabian become enraged by the man's sickly sweet and ingratiating grin. As soon as the shop emptied, he picked up a long-handled biscuit tray and, as Freshpenny turned round from slamming the door shut, still grinning, swung it with all his strength. It hit Freshpenny's wide face with an immensely satisfying smack, knocking him out cold and denting the tray with a perfect mould of his insipid grin. Fabian took it out into the back yard, propped it against a wall and flung coals at it.

When Freshpenny awoke, he went about his business without saying a word about the black eye he now had. He let Fabian worry about what his revenge would be for a full month. Then, one evening, he slipped sleeping draught into Fabian's bedtime cocoa where he slept, and sewed his mouth shut so that when he removed the stitches, Fabian would feel about the same amount of pain that Freshpenny did, listening to his insistent fussing all day. He bounded into the shop next morning more cheery than ever, and sold more loaves and flans and quiches and rolls than ever before.

While they concentrated on their vendetta, they did not notice that all around them there were preparations for a gigantic jubilee. It was to be the town's one hundredth birthday in a few weeks and a succession of floats, marching bands, circus performers and dancing troupes were being recruited from all over the land to come and take part in the celebrations.

The first they heard of it was when the town's chancellor appeared in the bakery one day. A ruddy-faced, puffed-up man with short grey hair, he stood in front of Freshpenny (whose face was almost recovered from its bruising) and Fabian (whose moustache and new goatee beard hid the marks of the stitches around his mouth), and in a rather long and embarrassing speech proclaimed the praise and gratitude of the town to the two bakers.

'We endeavour to do our best,' said Freshpenny, performing a curtsey with a flourish of his apron.

'Only too pleased to be of service,' giggled Fabian, nervously knocking over a plate of scones.

'Glad to hear it!' said the chancellor. 'For we wish to give you a very special, once-in-a-lifetime commission. If you accept, you are to create a delicious biscuit to commemorate the great day, to be paid for from the town's coffers and handed out free to every citizen, to show how proud we all are of our greatest asset: your bakery. And – why, that mould would do perfectly! *Perfectly!'* They both turned to see what he was pointing at. There, leaning against the wall, was the long-handled biscuit tray indented with the image of Freshpenny's smiling face.

Fabian protested, horrified at the idea, but the chancellor wouldn't listen. Freshpenny himself was just as frightened as Fabian at the idea of everyone in town biting into images of his own face, and tried to persuade the chancellor against it. The chancellor's good humour faltered for a moment as he listened to both men's voices at once.

'I INSIST!' he shouted, suddenly red-faced. Fabian and Freshpenny jumped back, and didn't argue any more. 'You accept the commission,' said the chancellor, 'and we hereby make full payment in advance.' And with that he dropped a heavy purse of coins on the counter with a fat chinking sound, saluted the pair and marched out, making Fabian jump again at the sound of the slammed door.

Now, I'm sure I don't need to tell you that this was quite the largest commission they (or, indeed, any bakery) had ever received up to that point. On the best of all possible days they could hope to serve around two hundred people. But here they were being asked to bake for thousands all at once. Their fame would reach far and wide, perhaps hundreds of miles beyond the town's borders. And then there was the *money* they would be paid!

'We could buy that fancy jam-making machine I hear they've perfected in Belgium!' cried Freshpenny.

'We could hire a pastry chef to do all that tedious kneading and rolling and crimping!' gasped Fabian.

'We can have a new BAKERY sign painted!'

'And our names on the window!'

'In gold leaf!'

They danced round and round in a circle, excited, until suddenly each of them remembered who he was dancing with. And then they stopped, and their faces became serious, and a little embarrassed, and each of them went off to begin planning for their biggest day ever.

First of all Fabian rode out to a nearby town where he knew he could find enough supplies. When he reached it, he hired a coach and horses, and bought tubs of both salted and unsalted butter, and sacks and sacks of both light and dark-coloured sugars, and organized for an enormous supply of eggs to be delivered to the shop on the day before the festival, so that they might be as fresh as possible. Last of all he bought a large bag of salt, because, as any good biscuitmaker will tell you, a biscuit can be as crisp and sweet as you like, but just the tiniest pinch of salt adds the final deliciousness to its flavour.

While he was doing this, Freshpenny took the toasting tray with his face on it to the blacksmith's and had fifty biscuit moulds made from it, so that his face was in the centre of a perfect circle. Then, while these were being made, he returned to the shop and cleaned and scrubbed, and polished the outsides of their machines, and oiled the insides, and rubbed down the counters, and washed the windows, and laundered the curtains, and burnished the floor until it shone better than new.

Two days remained until the big event and both men went to bed early, careful not to tire themselves. But bad dreams infested Fabian's sleep. He saw thousands of merrymakers eating biscuits with Freshpenny's face on them; he saw the biscuits finding their way to large cities, making Freshpenny famous – the most famous baker in the world – and Freshpenny becoming rich, baking for kings and queens and forgetting him, with Fabian left behind in this shop alone . . .

He sat up awake with a start, chilled to his spine by

a cold sweat. All of a sudden, and more than ever before, he detested the image of Freshpenny's fat, smiling face. He could not bear it to be the emblem of the happiest day the town had known in all its history and, with a fresh, deep hatred, decided that he could not allow it to happen.

Checking he had not awakened his friend, he put on his dressing gown and stole down to the cellar, where there was a cupboard of dangerous poisons they had used to try to rid themselves of rats. The final bottle they had bought was the largest and the darkest, with a horrible bulbous shape made from purple glass. It contained a pure black liquid and had a label reading DANGER: POISONOUS TO ALL LIVING THINGS pasted across the front. Underneath the print, the apothecary's handwriting declared, 'For God's sake, keep away from children – in fact, from everybody!'

Fabian had already decided what he would do. He placed the bottle carefully in his pocket, relocked the cupboard and walked back upstairs, smiling to himself. Back in the bedroom, he hid the bottle in his bedside cabinet as quietly as could be, and then slipped under the covers so as not to wake his partner. Freshpenny, fat-guts that he was, always tasted his biscuit dough at the last minute, to make sure it was perfect. Therefore Fabian would allow his friend the pleasure of tasting the delicious dough of the biscuit that was about to make him famous, thereby poisoning himself.

Fabian slipped off to sleep comforting himself with

pleasurable images in his mind of how Freshpenny's stupid grin would look when he found him.

The following day Fabian watched his friend become a perfect whirlwind of activity. As Freshpenny was the one who was best at biscuits, and they were working from his original recipe, Fabian took on an assisting role as Freshpenny first placed giant blocks of butter into the churn, and then poured many pounds of sugar over them.

Fabian worked the pedal frantically to keep the mixer running as Freshpenny blended together all the butter and sugar, and then the vast number of eggs, which had to be added one by one.

They had decided to leave the shop closed for the day, and once the golden mixture of sugar, butter and eggs was ready they took in turns the exhausting process of mixing in the flour. They worked and worked, sweat pouring off them, and after long hours had passed Freshpenny began to add the final flavourings – candied ginger, cinnamon, salt and chocolate shavings.

Finally it was midnight and the man-sized mixing bowl was filled with dough ready to bake. Both men staggered upstairs towards their bed, thirsty for a few hours' sleep before the mammoth job of baking three thousand biscuits.

As soon as Freshpenny's head hit the pillow, his first high-pitched, rasping snore broke out on the night air.

Exhausted as he was, Fabian pinched himself to remain awake until the snores became heavy and regular. Then he retrieved the bottle from his cabinet and stole downstairs very quietly.

He stood over the vat-like mixing bowl and uncorked the bottle. He took a sniff. Such a horrible, vicious smell rose from its neck that it made his head swim and he tottered back a few steps before he regained control of himself. Then he approached the giant bowl again and poured a few small splashes of poison on to the top of the mountain of dough.

In the darkness he looked down at it and wondered. That little amount was enough to put paid to Freshpenny and his stupid smile forever, for sure – but the topmost layer of the dough would become dry overnight. Like the good baker he was, in the morning Freshpenny would be sure to turn the pedal to mix it up a little so that the top was fresh when he tasted it, to test its proper texture. The only way to be sure was to poison the whole lot. So in the whole bottle went, gurgling and glugging until the last few drops trickled out with a little cough.

Now he had to mix it so that it was evenly spread through the whole mixture. Able to see only by the moonlight, which gave a dim blue glow through the kitchen window, he struggled hard to move the paddle round just half a dozen times, using the last of his energy, until he knew that it was so thoroughly turned over that anyone taking a taste could not fail to be poisoned.

He pulled himself to his feet with shaking hands. He was so exhausted he couldn't even feel relief that he would be free of Freshpenny in a few hours. He leaned against the rim of the bowl and gazed down at the dough, which in the moonlight looked as fresh and delicious as any either of them had ever concocted. In fact, in his confused state, he could not believe that it was poisonous, and suddenly he became anxious that something had gone wrong. Perhaps the bottle did not contain poison at all, but a hidden stash of grog which Freshpenny swigged in secret? He dipped a finger in and held it to the tip of his tongue – nothing, just the tangy flavour of cinnamon, sugar and that touch of salt. Sure now that his plan had failed, he popped a tiny lump in his mouth, chewed and swallowed, thinking that even if the bottle did contain poison it might somehow have gone off, or been rendered harmless by the ingredients. As the morsel went down his throat, dizziness rushed upon him in a cloud, and he passed clean out, hitting his head on the floor.

Fabian woke to daylight, with the refreshing feeling of a cold wet cloth across his forehead.

'Where am I? What time is it?' he asked.

'Don't move, dear Fabian!' cried Freshpenny from his bedside. 'Thank God you're all right. Dearest friend, when I saw you had gone downstairs to work afresh on our preparations, I knew that all this disagreement was silliness. We belong together, and together we will go on to greater things!'

Fabian kept trying to speak, but Freshpenny was possessed by an unstoppable stream of thought.

'I've been thinking,' he said enthusiastically. 'We should move on. Find a bigger shop in a bigger town – a city even! Oh my friend, it all went so perfectly today – so perfectly and without a hitch!' And with that Freshpenny hugged his friend tightly, only letting go when he heard a whimper of pain. 'You are all right?' he asked.

'What do you mean?' asked Fabian, aghast. 'Surely it's morning! The day has not passed?' He began to struggle out of bed.

'Don't you worry about that,' said Freshpenny, placing a hand on Fabian's forehead, and pushing it back to the pillow. 'The main thing is that you feel well again.'

'But what time is it? You have really fed all those people by yourself?' Fabian cried, and he leaped out of bed with the strength that comes from fear, and raced down to the kitchen in his nightshirt.

'It was tiring, I admit,' said Freshpenny from behind him on the stairs.

Perhaps I'm going mad, thought Fabian. I can't tell whether it's dawn or dusk – that fat idiot might just be playing a trick on me.

He took an umbrella to use as a walking stick, and hobbled to the front of the shop, his head beating with a horrible pain.

'Did you taste the dough to make sure it was ready

for baking?' Something seemed wrong to him about the silence. He turned round, and saw Freshpenny smiling at him with a funny, knowing look that made him feel dreadful, as though he was going to be sick.

'Well,' he asked. '*Did* you taste it?'

'There was no time,' his partner replied, still smiling. 'When I saw I had to do it all myself, I clean forgot.

'But . . .' Fabian turned back to the door. Where was the noise? The celebration? His head throbbing worse than ever, he pulled the door open and looked into the street.

'I'll ride out in the morning to the city, and find a shop for us,' said Freshpenny from behind him. Speechless, Fabian stepped out to look down to the town square. Not one single cobble could be seen. In every direction there was a new multicoloured coating of cloth and leather and skin, which belonged to what looked at first glance like a sea of peacefully sleeping people.

He flinched as his partner's hand clapped him on the shoulder.

'Rest tonight, dear friend,' said Freshpenny. 'Tomorrow it begins for us again!'

hen she had finished the story, the old woman looked down at the pair of us by the fire and beamed, proud of herself for remembering it correctly. She also saw that while listening to it the two of us had thawed a great deal, and she looked extra pleased, as if the story had magical powers of healing. Glancing up I was surprised to see Uncle and her husband leaning against the wall and listening too. They must have stolen back in as the story reached its climax.

Uncle now stepped forward and thanked her for looking after us. '. . . But I can't let them stay under your roof for another minute. If the police found them here, you'd be in the worst sort of trouble.'

All the pleasure and warmth seemed to drain from the old woman's face as she nodded in reluctant agreement. The husband was more business-like, and showed us straight to the hole in the wall, which was still ajar. Uncle gestured for us to follow, but Benjamin was shaking his head.

'No,' he said, 'I won't go. I've got to get back to my parents – they'll think that I'm dead!' Everyone in the room saw the madness of this except for him. As he saw us all regarding him with the same reproachful look he got more stubborn, and began to retreat to the front door.

'Benjamin, please!' I said.

'Benjamin,' said Uncle warningly, 'if you go out there, there's a good chance you *will* be dead. The police are out in force on the streets tonight, hunting a boy who looks like you. You've seen them yourself! Although you don't know me, you must trust me, if you can. I know where we can go to wait until the storm passes.'

'Please,' I begged him. But something stopped him from listening. Perhaps the firelight caught Uncle's face at a sinister angle, and the strange secret tunnel in the wall was disturbing. Maybe the magical power I'd displayed (and hadn't explained) scared him, and the terrible sequence of events we had witnessed built up in his mind so he couldn't bear the thought of anything except getting home. He retreated further and further until he was at the door, then he unbolted it and dashed out. Uncle jumped forward to catch him, but it was too late. Wind and rain whipped in through the open door and he had already vanished. Wearily Uncle locked it again.

'Stupid boy,' said the old man sadly.

'Come on,' said Uncle to me, and turned to the old couple. 'Time for us to leave you in peace and safety.'

The old man rejected my thanks for taking us in. He said he hoped that anyone in his position would have done the same, and that I would certainly show the same kindness if ever I had the opportunity. I agreed without hesitation.

In a moment Uncle and I were in the secret tunnel. We had shut the panel behind us and could hear the table being squeaked back into position. Uncle struck a match and lit a candle from his pocket, leading me forward. I was silent, trying to make out what was around us, and feeling the strange but enjoyable weirdness of walking behind a wall, like a ghost.

'What is this place?' I asked.

'You don't need to know just now, Daniel. I suppose it's a kind of emergency system that some people in Tumblewater use to get around. People who aren't allowed to show their faces in the street.'

This must be what he had half-mentioned earlier with Codger and Mr Jaspers.

I didn't want to push him if he didn't want to tell me more, so I told him of my adventures with Gora the witch, my theft of the box and my narrow escape with Benjamin. When I had finished, he said, 'My God, Daniel. I wonder how many lives you have left – you did well to rescue that boy; that was a good thing to do.' There was something strained in his voice, as though he wanted to say more, but I didn't know how to make him. He stepped carefully over several puddles in the narrow passageway, going slowly, before speaking.

'I didn't know you had seen that girl in the window,' he said. 'But I know the legend well. If Prye somehow knows you saw her then everything makes more sense.

No wonder he's chasing you! And now the policeman's seen your face, and knows you stole the box. So there's no doubt it's you they're after.'

We both fell silent. There was something neither of us was saying: Prye had tried to have me arrested under the ticking of the Animoul's clock – when I was sure he'd come to stare at me with his own eyes – *before* the business of the silver box. Before I'd told anyone I'd seen the girl. Both of us knew I was holding something back, but now I felt Uncle trusted me to explain to him when the time was right.

He broke the silence. 'You've reminded me there's someone I know who told me a tale about the witch. It's the sort of tale you have to be sitting down for, though. Remind me to tell it to you later, if I forget.'

I said I'd love to hear it. 'What about those people in the sewer, though?' I asked. 'Do you know about them?'

He stopped as we reached a corner, and held the candle out in one direction then the other, trying to remember the way. Then, as though he finally heard my question, he turned round and held the candle between us.

'Yes,' he said, 'I know those people. Many of them I helped to escape down there. This passageway we're in now, and the tunnels those poor people live in, are part of the same network. We call it the Underground,

and I truly hope you never have to live there – it's the place of the forgotten people, the dispossessed, people who are officially dead. Now, Daniel,' his voice became softer and in the flicker of light his look intensified, 'I can't tell you more than that – and this is when you have to be brave. All of Prye's resources are being used to catch you now, even though we don't know why. We will do everything we can to keep you hidden. But if you are caught, they will make you speak. This is why I can tell you no more for the moment.'

I followed him in silence after that, my feelings swirling between paralysing fear and swaggering pride.

Prye is after *me*! I am important enough to have made him angry! And he hasn't caught me yet! I would think to myself, before my mind's eye tried to conjure up the terrifying instruments with which they would 'make me talk'.

Coming to the end of the passage, we had to climb down through a hole in the floor into a tunnel that had been dug out of the earth, and which dripped constantly from the ceiling, making the candle go out time and again so we had to pause while Uncle relighted it. At the other side (Uncle explained we were passing beneath a busy street) we came up into a cellar and through a hole in the opposite wall, into another deserted house where we went up one staircase and then rapidly down another. I was more thrilled and scared by this secret, deserted route at every turn, and told Uncle so.

'Oh, it's not deserted by any means. That's just the storm – everyone has found somewhere to hide. Tumblewater always floods during a storm, and underground, you can imagine, that's very dangerous indeed. We will have to use these passages again later, and you'll see then. They're not deserted at all. Now,' he said, coming up to a door set in the clay-earth wall and knocking on it with a coded pattern of long and short raps, 'if I give you a dozen tries, you'll never guess where we are.'

The door was opened by a scared, wide-eyed man who I'd seen before, but couldn't remember where. He left us and disappeared for a moment and I recollected who he was just as the door was filled by my landlady, Nuala, who held an oil lamp over her head, stared at us and tutted severely.

'Look at the pair of you,' she sighed.

This time Uncle let me go first, and hung back, shy of conversation with her, but muttering into my ear: 'Running Turvey House is only half of what Nuala does – it is her Overground occupation. To us in the Underground she is seamstress, dressmaker and all-round wizard with clothes and disguises.'

Nuala had been walking ahead of us through the corridors of a basement much larger than anyone would have suspected from looking at Turvey House from the

outside. She opened a door and showed us into a large underground dressing chamber, which was lined on every side by racks and boxes of clothes and costumes of every colour and description.

'I see much has changed since I packed young Daniel off to school this morning,' she said to Uncle, as though he had got me into trouble, but I jumped in and explained everything. Afterwards, her look was much more serious, and she regarded my tall protector with real pride.

'So we are to disguise the lad, is that it?' she asked. Uncle nodded, and Nuala addressed herself to me. 'You've come to the right place. We'll soon have you so that you wouldn't be known by the man whose nose you cut off.'

'*What?*' I asked.

'Just a phrase,' she said, already flicking through clothes and pulling out things for me to try on.

'The police are searching for a boy with blond hair,' said Uncle. 'So we have to make him look as much the opposite of that as we can.'

'Let's do the hair first, then,' said Nuala. 'My, it's fair!'

'Well, thanks,' I said.

'Hmm, maybe it's just cleaner than any I've seen for a long while,' she mused, peering at it and ruffling it with her hand as though something of value might drop out. 'Well, let's start with this, then.' She started to massage a thick oily liquid into my hair. 'This should make you dark-haired for six months or more,' she said, 'but I'll give you a little tub of it so you can put some on when you need to. Your hair was wild and curly before, so that makes a big difference.'

Her little warren of clothes was a marvel. In what I first thought was just a dingy basement packed with rags, I saw there was a brilliant system in place which contained (ready to be pulled off the shelf in a moment) every type of garment, of every quality, salvaged from bins and dustcarts and tips, now washed, mended and waiting for the right owner. I began to realize that Nuala deliberately dressed herself simply, to leave the best clothes for others, and had a passion for getting every aspect of a look just right.

In the corner of her shop there was a workroom with a system of pots on shelves and boxes hammered into the wall, holding ribbons and threads and needles and buttons and fabric. This was all kept in perfect order by her assistant, a red-haired girl called Josephine, who (bearing in mind I was just a muck-covered boy) proved very shy on my several attempts to say hello, each time burying herself deeper in the stitching of a lady's jacket collar.

'That makes him look fat,' said Nuala, standing back, as I tried on my sixteenth jacket.

'For God's sake, woman, *make* him look fat!' said Uncle. 'We want him to look not like himself. Tie a dozen pillows round his waist, by all means!'

'Don't be sharp with me,' said Nuala, putting pins between her lips as she made adjustments to the jacket. She stood back again. 'No,' she said. 'Definitely not. You don't understand, do you, Uncle? I can make him look like an earl, a washerwoman or an escaped madman if you like, but I *won't* make him look unstylish. Now, Josephine,' she said, gesturing the girl over. I had to stand as another jacket was pulled on over my arms. I tried to smile my thanks over my shoulder at Josephine, but she was already back at her desk, needle in hand.

For the first time that I'd tried anything on, Nuala failed to dismiss it at once and it was left to Uncle to speak first.

'*Yes!*' he said.

Nuala narrowed her eyes and looked at me with her head on one side, unsure. 'Daniel,' she said, 'pull that collar up.' I did so.

She smiled.

Uncle beamed. 'It's *perfect*,' he said.

I looked down at what I was wearing and saw an ordinary black overcoat and beneath it a threadbare black jacket and black trousers.

'I look like an undertaker!' I complained.

'Not a bit of it,' said Nuala. 'Undertakers are well

dressed. In that, you look like someone who's been a teacher at a poor school for ten years, and unmarried. With the collar pulled up your own mother wouldn't recognize you.'

'She wouldn't anyway,' I said. 'She's dead.'

'*Exactly*,' said Uncle. 'We have our disguise!'

I was getting very tired, and my chosen clothes – none of which fitted, and all of which were quite uncomfortable – were finally agreed upon. At last, as Uncle and Nuala settled down for a chat about mutual friends and Josephine served them both with tea, I slipped away and found a box of off-cuts and discarded rags where they couldn't see me, crawled into it and dozed. But Uncle wouldn't let me rest for long. In what felt like less than a minute, he was barking at me to get up and come with him.

'Remember what I told you!' he said, annoyed. 'Nuala's at risk every minute you're here. Come on.'

'You mean I can't go upstairs to my own bed?' I asked, outraged. I had only snoozed so as not to interrupt them, and to get Uncle to talk to Nuala a bit more. The idea that I couldn't sleep here seemed ridiculous.

'Of *course* you can't,' said Uncle. 'This is the first place the police will look – they could call at any moment. Remember that Mr Pisk knew you were staying here, before he led you to the pawnbroker? That means Prye does as well. Don't underestimate him.'

'All right,' I said, feeling as though I was being lec-

tured quite often today. 'There's no need to be so serious just to impress your *girlfriend*.'

He looked chronically embarrassed for a second and clipped me round the head harder than he needed to (at which I shouted 'GET OFF!'), but Nuala wasn't paying any attention to us.

As I reached the door, I looked back at the little underground dressing room, sorry to leave this cosy, friendly place. Nuala pulled the door open, and I gave her a kiss goodbye on the cheek.

'Your turn,' I said to Uncle, and he kicked me in the ankle.

'For God's sake,' Nuala sighed. 'Now listen, young man, don't go getting yourself caught by police or in any other sort of mischief, because now I've disguised you it'll only be your fault if you do. And, Daniel – I want to see you back here soon so you can tell me a story of your own.'

I promised, and we said goodbye. Then Uncle and I were back on the 'road' (a narrow corridor), squeezing past groups of people coming the other way, going down a staircase and along an incredibly cold passage, which went through the back of a sequence of deserted houses.

'Uncle,' I asked eventually, 'how did you end up involved in the Underground, as you call it? What was your crime?'

Uncle smiled in the way that adults smile when they are far from happy. 'It doesn't matter,' he said. 'I was a very young man, younger than you. I still am a young man, although I have to make myself look older with this beard and these clothes, for my own safety.'

When we reached the end of the third house, we came to a sturdy wooden door and Uncle rapped on it with his funny sequence of knocks again. It opened after a short pause, and a golden light poured out, accompanied by a cloud of smoke on which seemed to drift the smell of pastries and the sound of laughter. It was some sort of secret inn, and a sense of unexpected contentment warmed my heart more than I had thought anything could. We were welcomed in, given drinks and sat down before I knew what was happening. I didn't speak, but looked around me in a happy daze.

Uncle handed me a pastry from a plate that was being offered around, and said: 'Welcome to the Crackey Inn, Daniel.'

He was greeted by almost everyone who passed our table, stopping to thank him for something, or ask his advice, or pass on gossip about a mutual acquaintance. After this had happened half a dozen times he suddenly jumped up and called out to a man who hadn't seen him.

'Daniel,' Uncle said, excited, 'I had hoped to intro-

duce you to this man at some point – how lucky to stumble across you, Harry!'

'Don't talk too loudly about luck around here – it'll make you unpopular,' said the man into his pint pot as he sipped from it. He shook my hand.

'Harry has an incredible story to tell,' said Uncle. 'The one I was going to tell you myself later on, but now you can hear it from the horse's mouth.' Harry clearly wondered why he should be telling his story to a slip of a lad like me, but Uncle whispered something in his ear and he decided I was to be trusted. He took a deep breath. Telling the story obviously troubled him.

'I'm a carpenter,' he said. 'One day a few months back I had to visit a house to fix a table. It belonged to this little old lady who showed me up to the landing where the table was, and left me there. Now this place was piled up with junk and rubbish so I thought, all right, I'll do it quick as I can, and be out of this weird place.

'I hammered in some supporting planks underneath and put in a couple of extra legs that would hold it up for a while . . .'

I started to grow a bit awkward, wondering whether Uncle had stopped this man to give us a lesson in carpentry. But then he said something that made me listen.

'I knocked on the nearest door to tell her the job was

done. No reply. Pushed it open, and . . .' He trailed off, shaking his head. Uncle and I exchanged glances. 'The walls were fifty foot high.'

'What sort of room was it?' I asked.

'A ballroom, like you'd find in a palace. You could have ridden a coach-and-four from one end to the other and given all of the horses good exercise. Huge pictures hung on the wall showing floods, tempests, the beginning of the world. The ceiling was painted with clouds and angels, like you could see up to heaven, and it was so far up it might as well have been.'

Harry's voice stopped and he looked at us, afraid that we wouldn't take him seriously.

'I think I've been to the house you're talking about,' I reassured him.

'I didn't know what was going on. I thought I was going bonkers,' he said. 'So I went down the stairs careful as you like and saw that the old woman was talking to this guy wearing a hood. You couldn't see anything of him but his nose which had a birthmark on it like a splodge of ink. She was paying him and he was fishing little paper parcels out of a sack around his shoulder. She was sniffing each one closely before putting it in her pocket. I got the feeling I was seeing something I shouldn't and went back up the stairs.

'Well, what was I supposed to do next? There was two more doors at the end of the landing, next to the

table. Right and left. I knocked on the left one and opened it.' He paused for a second, and took a deep breath. 'There was uneven floorboards and a stove in the corner giving off strange smells. Skinned furs – wolf furs, I think they were wolf furs – hung from the ceiling. I was in a small hut, and I went to the door at the back of the room.

'Beyond that door, as far as you could see, was a field of tall wheat, stretching on for what seemed like forever. A great wind hurried through it constantly, combing it, like waves through the sea. And in the middle of the field you could hear two children chasing each other, a boy and a girl, hidden by the grass.

'Beautiful and strange as a dream it was, but I went back into the little wooden cottage. There was magic going on here, and suddenly I feared the door wouldn't let me back where I had come. I've never had such a turn, I'm telling you. Getting all worked up, I stole a big knife from a block of wood beneath the wolf furs, and went up to the door with the life half frightened out of me. But the door led back to the corridor again, thank God, and I went down the stairs in a flash. No sign of the two oldies – now there was a younger woman waiting, kind of blonde and good looking, with coins in her hand to pay me.

'I should have got away all right, but she saw in my eyes I was scared, and she knew that I must have seen something I shouldn't. She started to get angry and shouted at me in a language I didn't know. I just wanted to get my arse out of there – 'scuse my language, young man, but you see the occasion calls for it – so I showed her the dagger.

'The second she saw it, she went deathly pale,' he said, 'and stood back, letting me escape.' He patted his pocket, and then brought the dagger out to show us.

It looked medieval or even earlier – savage, even. It was just a jagged spike of iron sticking out of a rough wooden handle. As I took it from him, I felt how incredibly light it was, and saw it was rusty and blunt as well. I couldn't believe Gora had been scared of such a thing.

Harry sighed and relaxed now his tale was told. 'Afterwards I sought out others who had come across her, in all her disguises, listening to every story I could about her, and I made myself an expert on that witch. I don't care if people think I'm a loony. But I know more about her than anyone alive. Like about her and the Creature – the Slurgoggen, the Slumgullion.'

'The Slumgullion!' I said. 'She mentioned it to me! She said how unafraid of it she is.'

'Really?' Harry asked. 'Interesting she says that. Why doesn't she leave her house, seeing as she can disguise herself, if she's not afraid? Why tell someone who knows nothing about it – why say to you, Daniel, that she's

not afraid? I wonder if that's really the truth.'

Uncle was fascinated. 'Go on, Harry,' he said. 'Why?'

Harry leaned in and spoke quietly to us. 'She *made* him,' he said. 'Centuries ago he was a man. Her lover. And he broke her heart. So she turned him into the ugliest creature she could imagine so he could never be loved again. After swimming in the deep for hundreds of years, and waiting for death to release him, he came to realize he was cursed with eternal life as well. So he swam back to land, and detected her scent in the water here. Now he waits in the river for his chance to see her again, and break the spell.'

Uncle shifted uncomfortably in his seat and again murmured something in Harry's ear.

'Of course, I'm getting distracted,' he said. 'Now, I get the feeling your interest is something to do with the girl she captured away from Prye?'

'The girl I saw!' I said. '*Gora's* got the girl?'

Uncle nodded. 'She is Prye's prime obsession. He wants her. And if you know something about her whereabouts, he wants you too. You know something, don't you, Daniel?'

I nodded and said quietly, 'I think I know who she is. But I can't be sure – I need to check something first.' The men looked amazed for a second, and then Uncle reassured me.

'I won't pry – sorry, Daniel, excuse the pun – it's

your business. You tell me in your own time. Let's hear the rest of what Harry has to say.'

'It was Gora who trapped the girl in the first place,' Harry went on. 'But she couldn't make the girl fall in love with Prye – that's the one thing her magic could not control. Gora and Prye fell to fighting because of this, and he refused to pay her. So they became enemies: she disguised herself and kept the girl hidden, and his spies try fruitlessly to find her hiding place. If you want to free the girl, it's the witch you've got to deal with.

'Now, listen to this, Daniel. She can disguise herself as any woman, anyone at all, so you might end up close to her without knowing it – and I hope you do, my lad, because then you might have the chance to stick this dagger in her, which I'm going to give you now. But remember this. *Do not let her put a ring on your finger.* If you do, you will be lost entirely, and in her power forever. Promise me?'

I nodded, struggling to accept this new responsibility.

Harry handed me the dagger under the table, looking around him in case anyone thought he was acting suspiciously (and making himself look much more suspicious by doing so). Without arguing I slipped it inside my coat. I thanked him for everything he had told me, and especially for the dagger. He shook my hand, looking as though a burden had been lifted from him.

Perhaps he also felt guilty that the responsibility had passed to me, because he finished his drink quickly, made his apologies and was gone hardly a minute later.

On our own again, I was just taking a few sips of my drink and starting to relax after the night's adventures (while running my hand over the dagger inside my pocket), when Uncle stood up and gestured me to follow him. I was feeling giddy, not just from my drink, and from Harry's tale, but because the sense of jubilation all around us in the Crackey Inn was unlike anything I had ever seen before. I was reluctant to leave – it was exciting to be welcomed among grown-ups (my disguise was clearly working), and everywhere I looked I saw people telling each other stories.

Those telling the stories seemed completely caught up in the tales they were telling, and the listeners were so enjoying the funny bits, and so engrossed in the scary bits, that I could hardly bear to tear myself away.

But follow him I did, through the laughing, eating, shouting mob, to a low door in the back wall. On the other side was a room so much darker I couldn't make out anything in it.

'What's through here?' I asked.

'It's the back parlour,' he said. 'Quieter. From here, we can watch the flood that always comes with the storm. It's quite a sight.'

Uncle pushed me towards a chair, and sat next to

me. There was a low, glowing fire of blackened orange coals in front of us and he held his hands over them.

'What's out there, Sorboy?' Uncle asked loudly, apparently into the fire.

A dismissive moan came from the window where a wide-shouldered man stood leaning against the frame. 'It's really starting now,' he said. 'It's going to be a bad one, too. Is that you, Uncle?'

'It is,' said Uncle, rubbing his hands together and putting them back over the glowing coals. Looking around I could see about half a dozen people in the glow of the fire: a group of lean-faced, villainous-looking men sitting round a small table, two chubby gents in chairs side by side, and near me a sharp-faced old woman chipping at a piece of woodwork in her hands. The woman gave me an apparently careless glance that hid a moment's shrewd examination, and went on working at the wood with her knife. Behind these there were a few others scattered about in the gloom. A man stood behind a bar made from two barrels and a plank, silently refilling the cups that people held up for him.

'What's your business, then, lad?' asked Sorboy from the window.

I started to say that I didn't have one. The idea of being a surgeon had been so fixed in my mind that I kept forgetting what had happened that very afternoon. 'I . . . I collect stories,' I said. The two fat men, who had

been slightly stupefied by the warmth and the beer, snapped out of their doziness.

'What do you do with them when you collect them?' one asked.

'Yes,' said the other sarcastically, 'what exactly do you *do* with them?'

'Well,' I said, 'I mean to get them published so that people can read them. I've been hired by a publisher for that purpose.'

'Oh,' said the first man. 'What a good idea.'

'Yes,' said the other, glancing uncertainly at his friend, 'a *very* good idea, I should say. You are to be congratulated, sir.'

'I haven't done it yet,' I said. I walked to the window and peered out under Sorboy's arm. 'What are you staring at?'

'You see where the ground should be?' he asked.

The window looked out into a small street not more than ten feet across with houses crowded close together. Not an inch of road was to be seen. Instead, it was a shallow stream, running fast. It even tumbled over obstacles as if they were the stones you'd find in a real stream, making the illusion more complete.

'That's the start of it – whoa! Here goes. A wall's fallen in somewhere up the hill.'

With a whooshing sound a great foaming wave came down the street and broke against the doorways. It turned over on itself as it slipped down the gulleys between houses and as it settled, the water a foot deeper than before, I saw the swell of detritus the wave had dragged with it – lumps of wood and paper and rags, and a wash of cloudy mud.

'I wonder if we'll wake up and find the whole hill has moved downstream,' I said to myself.

'Don't joke,' said Sorboy. 'There's much worse to come. Someone for God's sake close that door and keep the racket from the next room out. Let's forget about the flood, and give Daniel a story for his collection. After all, the stories in the Underground are the best.'

The woman by the fire nodded. 'They are,' she said. Sorboy sat in a chair next to her and others moved a little closer to the fire. For a few moments there was silence except for the whishing sound of the flood outside, as everyone fell into their own reflections. The woman broke the silence without turning her head from her little woodwork, 'Rudy knows a good one.'

One of the villainous-looking men looked up. When he began speaking, I found he had a calm, educated voice and spoke in a level tone that held everyone's attention.

'I do know a good story. It's a long one, but I like it, and it's about a rich sort of a chap coming to no good. Which is the kind I always like.'

There was a murmur of approval from everyone in

the room, including those hidden in the darkness. The barman handed over pots and tankards to upheld arms, and spots of gold showed in the corners of the room where men puffed on their pipes, as Rudy began.

'It's a show-offy sort of a name for a story, but that's the name it had when it was told to me. So here's the tale of . . .

# THE MASTERPIECE

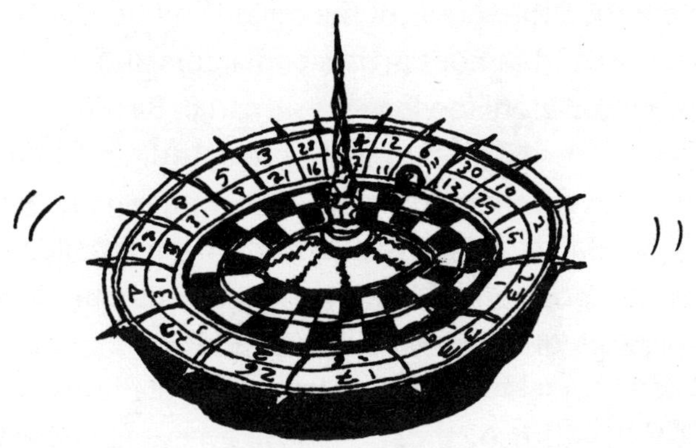

Mr Ephraim Bartle was a man who made the most wonderful clocks. He made stopwatches and alarm clocks and great big oak-panelled grandfather clocks that chimed like church bells. He prided himself on the materials he used and was sure that his were the finest made, most accurate clocks in the country. As his fame grew (as a clockmaker's will, if his clocks are as sturdy and reliable and beautiful as his were), he sought out ever more exotic types of wood and metals to improve upon his best work, and created magnificent timepieces that adorned the rooms of the royalty, all the dukes and duchesses and famous artists and actors and musicians in the land. Before too long his surname, Bartle, became the word one associated with a beautiful and valuable clock – even though Bartle is a rather ugly name.

So Mr Bartle, or just Bartle, as his friends called him, reached a position of wealth and high standing among the bigwigs of society. And such a knack and passion had he for clockmaking that he achieved all this before his twenty-fifth birthday. Almost every night he was asked along to the birthdays of earls, invited to the opening nights of theatrical spectaculars and that sort of thing. But the more he saw of it, the more he became bored of the high life, and he yearned to get back to his work, and do even greater things.

One day, feeling rather jaded after yet another extravagant party the night before (where he had been forced to drink much champagne, and put up with lots of chattering girls who were only interested in his fortune), he found himself in front of his most brilliant clock. It was a twenty-foot-tall, diamond-encrusted timepiece of such outrageous opulence that it was almost rude. In fact, now he looked at it, he decided that it probably *was* rather rude – in its showiness, its cost and its beauty. The thought made him shiver with delight. It had been bought by a prince from a foreign country and he was giving it one last look before the deliverymen wrapped it up and carted it away.

'Well,' he said, 'now I have made the finest clock that there can ever be,' and after watching it being placed into an enormous wooden crate he set off for a walk into the city, feeling rather sad for himself because now there was nothing left for him to achieve in life. He called in on an old friend and enjoyed a cup of tea and a long chat about childhood acquaintances, and when he left found himself surprised to step out into darkness.

'How funny,' he said. 'But it's only five o'clock.' He started to walk home, but after a few turnings found himself in a district of tall, overhanging buildings, and realized he was lost, because he never visited this part of town after dark. Not wanting to admit his mistake, he kept on walking and soon found himself more lost than he had ever been in the city, standing in a cobbled street of very old, dark houses, which leaned to and fro quite dangerously, as though one of them might fall over at any moment. He took out his watch again and, by the light of the moon, saw that it must have stopped at five o'clock many hours ago.

'Drat it!' he exclaimed. 'Why do they all have to stop! Why can no clock be perfect?'

So despondent was he at the thought that even his greatest clock would one day stop ticking, no matter how conscientiously it was wound every day, and so miserably did he stare up at the full moon as though he might be able to tell the time from its perfectly circular face, that at first he did not hear the voice.

'There is such a thing,' it said, 'as the perfect clock.'

'What? Who's that?' Mr Bartle said, turning round. He saw a very little old man standing in the doorway of a very little old house, which leaned so crazily Mr Bartle was afraid to go anywhere near it.

'Say that again, old man – what do you mean?'

'I said there is such a thing,' repeated the tiny man, quietly, 'as the perfect clock.' And with that he turned and walked slowly back into his house, leaving the door open.

Bartle felt unable to resist following him in. He had to duck to get in the door, and then he found himself in a tiny drawing room, so tiny that he was almost bent double. The mysterious little man had settled into a chair and was staring rather distantly through his tiny glasses, the eyepieces of which were no larger than a penny.

'Do you know how old I am?' the man asked.

'Of course I don't,' said Bartle, annoyed to be distracted from the subject of clocks.

'One hundred and thirteen years old,' said the man. 'And I've many, many years left in me yet. My father died last winter, and he was one hundred and eighty-two. And my grandfather died the winter before that, only a handful of years shy of his two hundred and fiftieth birthday.'

'That's very interesting,' said Mr Bartle, trying to settle into a corner of the room without breaking anything. 'But you mentioned something about clocks.'

'You want to talk about clocks,' said the old man, smiling. 'You know, I can tell what you're saying by reading your lips. I'm quite deaf, in fact. So long as you look straight at me when you speak, I can understand you. But clocks, yes, of course. My boy, you see the mantelpiece behind you?'

Bartle turned and saw a very plain stone mantel above a minuscule fireplace, in which seemed to be burning just two lumps of coal.

'Yes?' he said, turning back round.

'Well, do you see the timepiece in its centre?'

Blinking, Bartle looked closer at what he had dismissed as a grubby and funny-looking shell or rock, perhaps plucked from a beach many years ago.

*'That's* a clock?' he asked, incredulous.

'Aye, it is, and the finest clock in the country, even counting the fancy things that people make from gold and pearls for every dandy and millionaire who wants one. No disrespect intended.'

'None taken,' said Bartle quietly, looking more closely at the object. One could not be offended by the old man because he was clearly insane. This clock was quite the ugliest thing he had seen for years. It was made from a bulbous grey shell, out of which poked two thin splints of twig, one with a piece of string tied to it, the other with a dirty green pearl at its end.

'You can tell the time from this?' he asked, turning again so the old man could read his lips.

'Perfectly,' said the man. 'It's five to nine. When my great-grandmother was a child, she told time from that clock. And *her* great-grandmother, who lived to three hundred and two, had always told the time from the same clock; it had just kept going for as long as she could remember. There is no telling how ancient it is, yet it still tells perfect time.'

'Five to *nine*?' said Bartle, realizing what the man had just said. 'I must get home at once!'

'If you leave now,' said the little man, 'you won't never know the secret of the perfect clock.'

'Well, tell me, then,' said Bartle. 'What is it?'

'I'll tell you,' said the man patiently, 'so long as you'll make me one single promise.'

'Of course!' said Bartle, almost shouting.

'Promise me,' said the man, 'that you'll come back here.'

Bartle was confused. 'All right,' he said, taking the little man's hand in his. 'I promise.' It seemed a ridiculous promise to make – he almost laughed at how little the man demanded. Now he looked expectantly at the old man's face. 'So?'

The tiny old man turned his eyes down, and spoke softly. 'The thing which keeps a clock perfect, so it never goes wrong,' he said, 'can only be found in the human body. It is very expensive and difficult to find, but I know a man who will find it for you. His name is Mr Grum.'

Bartle stared at him. 'That's it?'

'Go to Grum,' said the man, still solemn, and looking down at the floor. Then he closed his eyes. 'You must go now,' he said. 'I have to sleep. I am, after all, very, very old.'

When he tried to get out of his chair, Bartle banged his head on the ceiling and knocked against the furniture, making himself dizzy, and once he had staggered into the street and got his bearings he could no longer see the old man's door, which must have shut behind him.

How can I return if I don't even know his name? mused Bartle, as he rushed along the streets, looking for a way home.

Bartle was going to build a single clock that would be timeless, still telling people the time in a thousand – or a million – years' time. It might even outlive humans themselves, into some far future when giant beetles walked the earth and the ageing sun burned like a huge red ball in the sky. These ideas entertained him as he began to fight through the rain, and found himself going from cobbled streets to muddy ones.

There was no use going further, he eventually realized. He was hopelessly lost, and only asking for directions would get him back to safety. The rain, which he was dimly aware always fell on this part of the town, was particularly heavy. He rested beneath the eaves of a shop and found himself standing next to another sheltering man.

'Where am I?' cried Bartle through the clattering of the rain.

The other man lifted his face briefly to look at him, as though Bartle must be joking. 'You're in Tumblewater Hill, chief,' said the man ruefully. 'And best of luck to you.'

'Tell me,' said Bartle, 'do you know where I might find a man who lives around here, who goes by the name of Grum?'

The stranger's face, dark as it was, grew darker. 'You have business with Mr Grum?' he asked. 'Then you have my deepest sympathy.'

'Never mind that!' Mr Bartle had to shout to overcome the racket of water hitting the pavement, which was as loud as the clapping of a full theatre. 'Can you direct me to him?'

The stranger nodded sadly. 'You know St Hildred's Church?'

Of course Mr Bartle knew it. It was the blackest and most forbidding building for miles around. 'Well,' said the stranger, 'you'll find Grum there behind it, in the graveyard. He's the gravedigger. If you go now, you'll find him – he works by night. A very strange man.'

'Thank you!' Bartle called, and set off at once into the downpour, much faster now and almost in a good mood. Before long he knew where he was, and found himself in the huge shadow of St Hildred's. The rain, if anything, was now worse, and water gushed at the roadside like an angry river. Bartle didn't notice that he was wet to the knees as he strode along the damp path by the side of the church. When he reached the graveyard at the back, he found it totally flooded. All he could see was the tips of a hundred tombstones sticking out of the water like decayed teeth, and the hunched figure of a man, patiently ladling mud with a bent shovel.

'Mr Grum!' called Bartle, but under the din of the rain the man could not hear him. 'MISTER GRUM!' he shouted. Slowly, the gravedigger turned round until he could see who had called his name. He beckoned Mr Bartle forward without budging from his spot and carried on digging his grave. Hesitantly, Bartle stepped from the path into the dark water, and shuddered as he found it came up to his knees. He waded until he was near enough to Mr Grum, and saw that he was a slump-shouldered old man, whose face looked as if it had never known how to smile.

'Good day to you,' said Bartle. Grum looked up at the sky, letting raindrops splash against his face for a second, then looked back at Mr Bartle.

'All right, it's not a *particularly* good day,' admitted

Bartle. 'But I have some business to talk to you about.'

'Someone dead, is it?' asked Grum. His voice was surprisingly smooth and quiet. 'Want a grave dug, do you? How big was they?'

'No, no. Nobody's dead. But I am seeking a very special item, which I think only you can give me.' He then explained, as best he could in the noise of the rain, his whole story, and how the little man had pointed him towards Grum.

Mr Grum listened, then raised his eyebrows.

'Fine,' he said.

'You can help me?'

'Course I can. But it'll cost you.'

'Anything, Mr Grum. I can pay you anything – I am a very rich man.'

'All right, then. I want a thousand sovereigns.'

'A *thousand*?' asked Bartle, incredulous. 'No, I'll pay it, I'll pay it,' he said as Mr Grum began to turn away.

'Follow me,' said Grum. 'And mind the grave.'

'What g—' said Mr Bartle as he stepped clean into the hole and vanished beneath the water.

He soon came spluttering back out, and Grum said, 'Stop fooling around, and follow me. I'm a busy man. Three graves to do tonight.'

Nervously, Mr Bartle tried to think of something to say as they waded towards the back of the graveyard, which was even darker than the rest of it, overhung by tall trees, which loomed like giants in the darkness.

'Three graves?' he asked, eager for conversation to dispel the creepiness. 'Is there some sort of epidemic in town?'

'Not that I know of,' said Grum.

'Tell me, Mr Grum. Does your work ever . . . frighten you at all?'

'Yes,' said Grum. 'I suppose it does. Here we are.'

In front of them stone steps rose out of the water to the door of a grand mausoleum, with huge grinning gargoyles sticking out from every corner. Grum ascended the steps and then reached so deep into his trouser pocket that he looked as though he was scratching his knee. At last he pulled from it a great string of keys, all jangling against each other and dripping with moisture, and held them up to squint at them.

'This is the one,' he said to himself, taking hold of a thin spindle of metal, and turning it in the lock. The door swung inwards with a dreadful grinding noise. 'Come on,' said Grum impatiently, and led Bartle in.

It was more spacious than it had looked from outside, and a slender candle burned on one wall. Around them were stacked coffins on shelves rising high above their heads. 'I come in here for me little flask of tea each night,' Grum explained, kneeling down next to the lowest and newest coffin, and working at the lid with his shovel.

''Ere we go,' he said at last as the lid came free, and he threw it aside. Laid out within the coffin was the most beautiful young girl Bartle had ever seen. She could not have been more than sixteen years old, but in her cheekbones and fair skin one could discern the gentle lines of what would have been an extraordinarily beautiful woman. The sight of such a solemn prettiness took Mr Bartle's breath away and left a terrible sadness in him.

'Right,' said Grum, and, lifting the shovel high above his head, he brought it down with all his force on to her forehead, splitting the top of her head off.

Mr Bartle cried out in shock. 'What are you doing, man?' he shouted.

'What you asked,' said Grum, stamping his foot on the spade to make sure it had gone all the way through, and then leaning on the handle for a second to get his breath back. Speechless with horror, Bartle watched as the gravedigger discarded his spade, reached down into the girl's severed skull, rooted around in the mushy matter of her brain and then plucked a little object from it, which came free with a gentle pop. He offered it up and Bartle took it in his handkerchief, examining it closely.

The size of a small pebble, it was rubbery, as though made from hard-set jelly, and soft to the touch.

'I never knew this existed,' he said wonderingly. 'What is it?'

'It's what you're paying for,' said Grum, shrugging. 'You fix that in where the winding mechanism of your clock normally goes, and it will keep going until doomsday, or so they say. Now not a word of this, you understand? We could end up in prison.'

'Of course!' Bartle insisted. Grum led them out, and locked the door. As they stepped back into the freezing water, Bartle said, 'I'll have my manservant come over first thing in the morning with your money. What will you do with it, Mr Grum – give up gravedigging?'

'Oh no,' said the old man lightly. 'I quite likes the job. Well, it's something to do since Mrs Grum passed on.'

'But even with a thousand gold pieces?'

'Well,' Grum reflected, 'I suppose I could get this shovel unbent.'

The rain continued to thunder all around them.

The following day, Bartle sprang out of bed earlier than usual, even though he had been so very late to bed.

First of all he directed his valet (which is a posh word for butler, even though having a butler is a posh thing already) to drive direct to his bank, cash a cheque for a thousand sovereigns and deliver the sum to Mr Grum's address, which was 144 Plimsole Street.

Next he sat down to a hearty breakfast, the like of which he had not enjoyed for years. He had kippers, smoked salmon, poached eggs and kidneys washed down with Egyptian coffee and pomegranate juice, and, to finish, a terrine of pig's snout on toasted soda bread.

Then he took a shower in his ridiculously extravagant

bathroom, where the water splashed in a fountain from a silver lion's head into a golden oyster shell, and afterwards he rode his favourite horse, Trumpty, around his entire estate twice, leaping over hedges and gardeners as he came upon them.

Finally, utterly refreshed and in love with life again, he went to his workshop to begin his final and most perfect clock. He assembled all the materials he needed and set to work alone, sawing wood, hammering nails, delicately applying paint and varnish, and examining every surface with his tape measure and spirit level.

This went on for weeks, which stretched into months. Bartle would blow the sawdust from a beautifully sanded corner of wood and see cold meals stacked up on trays and a growing pile of letters from the rich and famous, begging him to work for them. But nothing could drag him from his task.

It was sixteen weeks later that he emerged from his workshop, having rubbed the last touch of polish from the edges of the perfected machine. He tore down the black paper he'd plastered over the windows and stood in the sunlight for a moment, a dizzy and shambolic figure coated in paint and dirt, his clothes torn and a grubby beard making him almost unrecognizable. His valet called through the door to say that a flock of newspapermen had gathered outside to interview him about his latest masterpiece, and to enquire as to its new owner.

'Send them away,' he shouted back. 'Tell them there

is no new clock, and nor will there ever be. I have retired.' As the sound of the valet's footsteps withdrew, Bartle's eyes did not leave the face of his spotless and magnificent creation. There was only one final addition which remained. Opening his safe, Bartle drew out the small package he had purchased that night at St Hildred's graveyard, and which had remained carefully folded in his handkerchief ever since. Unwrapping it now, he tenderly took the little bulb in his palm and with his spare hand unlocked the back of the clock's head. Inside, there was a shallow bronze bowl no larger than the head of a tablespoon, specially designed by Bartle for this purpose, into which the ruby pellet fitted snugly. When he was sure it was fixed, he took two electrodes – thin copper spindles that fed into the clock's machinery – and touched the mysterious object with them, one at each end.

At once he felt a pulse of energy, heard the low ticking of clockwork and, closing the clock's door, stood back in wonder.

'It can't be true,' he whispered, walking round to see the clock from the front. But there it was – the slimmer hand switching once, precisely and magically, with every passing second. He fell into a waking dream as he watched the time pass, hardly daring to believe that he had, at last, made his eternal masterpiece.

The following day he was awoken by the clock's chimes at 8 a.m. Neither too loud nor too soft, they brought him quietly out of his slumbers without startling him. He lay in perfect peace for a few moments in the realization that yesterday he had at last achieved his one true goal, and then got up to look at his clock.

It was, of course, incredibly beautiful. Two slim gold petals, one larger than the other, formed the minute and hour hands. The hours themselves were denoted by numbers made from inlaid diamonds, and the whole clock face was enclosed within a magnificent ebony-panelled frame. As he stood watching the seconds tick by, he thought he heard a girl's voice in the next room.

'Hello?' it said. 'Is anybody there?'

Amazed and annoyed that anyone could have gained access to his private rooms, he strode across to the connecting door and threw it open. But the cavernous drawing room was empty. He went to pull on the rope that would ring a bell in another room (about a quarter of a mile away) to call his valet, but stopped. What would he say when the man arrived? There had been no sound of a door opening or closing and this room was definitely empty. He walked around it once, just to be sure, and put it down to his imagination playing tricks on him.

'That's what it is,' he said. 'I am exhausted. Apart from last night I have not slept properly or eaten well for months. I must rest.'

So instead of calling anyone he ran himself a bath and lay back in the hot water, with his eyes closed, trying to rest his mind and cure the headache that was beginning to set in.

He lost track of time, and drifted in and out of a light sleep, feeling the heat of the water soothe the pain of thousands of hours' hard work from his muscles. Then, quite distinctly, he heard a girl's voice say, 'I don't know this place.'

Once more the sound came from the next room, which was his bedroom. But it was not its nearness that shocked him and made him jump clean out of the bath and stand dripping and shivering and staring at the door. It was the deep and inconsolable sadness he had heard in those five simple words, the voice of someone utterly lost.

He stared at the door for a long time, but when no sound came, he walked towards it very slowly, trying to make no noise (although he couldn't have explained why) until he had his hand on the doorknob. When he plucked up the courage to turn it, and heard the click of the catch, he suddenly knew that he would find the room empty. He pulled the door open roughly and let it swing slowly back. No one was there.

This time he rang for his valet, and put on a robe while he waited for the man to appear, tying it tightly because after the heat of the bath, he was now freezing. After five minutes or so (it took this long to walk all the way from the servants' quarters) the valet appeared. He was a bald, serious and very neat man who always spoke with the same calm voice, no matter what you said to him.

'Smuck,' said Bartle (for that was the valet's name),

'has anyone come into the house today?'

'No, sir,' said Smuck, 'besides the baker's lad, and a couple of poor people begging for money.'

'How dreadful – you turned them away, I hope?'

'The beggars I did. The baker's lad was delivering some crumpets, sir.'

'Spare me such details as crumpets, Smuck. There was no one else?'

'Forgive me, sir. No, no one, sir.'

'And no one could have got into the grounds without your knowing?'

'No, sir,' said the man with complete confidence. 'I always keep watch with binoculars, as per your instructions. No intruders today, sir.'

Now Bartle smiled in what he hoped was a friendly way, but in fact made him seem very strange as he had never smiled at a servant before, and asked: 'Smuck, tell me. Has anyone seen or heard anything strange in the house or – or in the grounds even, over the last few weeks?

Smuck did not hesitate. 'No, sir. If they had, I would have told you about it at once. On account of the secrecy of your work, we have all been especially vigilant. May I ask, sir, if anything is wrong?'

Bartle laughed nervously. 'Why, of course not, dear Smuck! Why ever would you suggest such a thing?' and he took the valet by the elbow and ushered him to the door. 'Just wanted to check. Keep up the good work, my man!' and, patting him on the back, Bartle pushed him out, and shut the door.

Alone, he quickly felt the heavy silence in the room again, interrupted only by his fast breathing. The creeping fear that he would once more hear the voice made up his mind. He dressed as fast as he could, and went outside to walk in the gardens.

He crossed the vast lawn, walked through the rose garden and passed bed after bed of beautiful flowers until he came upon a little sanctuary he had never noticed before, square and surrounded by perfectly trimmed hedgerows. In the centre a fountain trickled quietly and he sat on a stone bench looking at it and feeling calmed by the peace of the garden and the soft breeze which was blowing.

A peacock appeared in the entrance and he watched it pause and display its extraordinary fan of feathers, bending its neck as though it was bowing to him. As he watched its feathers retract, he became aware of a voice which had been audible for some time, but which in his daze he hadn't noticed. It was a girl's voice carried softly by the wind from somewhere beyond the hedgerows, and it fixed him to his seat, unable to move.

Her words were so gentle and sad that they sounded almost like spoken song. She said how she had woken up in this strange place, and that she did not know how she had got here, only that lots of time had passed. She wondered whether this was heaven, or perhaps purgatory, and if she would be trapped here for all eternity, and whether anyone could even hear the words she was saying. She had hoped to see her family again in the afterlife, she said, as all of them were dead, and it had been the only wish of her short life to do so. But they were not here, no one was here . . . She began to sob bitterly, and then angrily, as if going mad with desperation.

Bartle remained in his seat, staring at the fountain but not seeing it, as a silence fell. A new chill began to settle into his bones as he got the sense that he was being looked at, and it intensified suddenly, with the strong feeling that someone was standing behind him.

'You!' said a voice in his ear. He shouted and jumped up, turning round. But the garden was as peaceful and empty as ever.

'*You* did this to me!' came the voice again, as close as if its owner's mouth was next to his ear. He broke into a run for the house, covering his ears, and finding that this made no difference to the voice.

'*You've* brought me here, *you've* trapped me . . .' it went on as he reached the open French windows and ran inside. The voice was dark and cold with anger. Now she was talking fast and her bitterness grew with every word.

'I will drive you mad,' she was saying. 'I'll drive you to your death. I'll haunt your every waking moment, and haunt your dreams . . .'

He was in his room now, pulling frantically on the rope to call his valet. When Smuck arrived, he was piling clothes from his wardrobe on to his bed and, without looking up, he said, 'Smuck, I am going on holiday. I leave at once. Send all the essentials on after me.'

'Very good, sir,' said Smuck, passing from the room without a sound.

Bartle pulled on an overcoat, grabbed his passport and pocket book, crammed them into his coat pocket and ran out of the house. He took Trumpty from the stables, left word of his destination and rode for mile after mile across the countryside.

He didn't want to stop until the voice was gone from his head. At first it was the pounding of hoofs on earth that drummed it out. Then, once he reached the nearest port, the clatter of the horse crossing the cobbles was even louder. He rode clear up to the side of a ship due to leave at any minute, and the crashing of the waves against the side of the vessel was louder even than the noise of the cobblestones. He paid a boy to stable the horse, and when he had secured passage on the boat he leaned over the side for the whole journey. He listened to the stormy sea, and occasionally felt very sick indeed, for he was a poor traveller at best, but for once he didn't care.

He did not relax for the whole journey by boat, even when the seas calmed and he realized he could not hear the voice any more. On the other side of the Channel, he bought a fresh horse and set out again. For four days and nights he rode until he found himself at another coast and here, at last, he rested.

He bought new clothes, rented a hotel room, cleaned himself up and poured a glass of champagne to drink while he dressed in his smart new dinner jacket. He began to hope for the first time that his madness, or his possession by spirits, whichever it was, might have left him.

When he was ready, he went down to a very expensive and delicious dinner in the restaurant that overlooked the ocean and when he was so full and happy that he could barely remember the troubles of the past few days, he walked through to the hotel's casino. He watched the games being played for a while and enjoyed the excitement of seeing rich men and beautiful women winning and losing vast sums of money, persuaded now that a few days in the hotel would be enough to make him feel well. At the table of roulette (a ridiculous game that some adults who are disappointed with life like to play, because they are bound to lose) he stopped to gamble some money for fun. In roulette, a circular board with forty numbers spins round and round and a little ball spins round it in the opposite direction, eventually landing against one of the numbers. He picked twenty-four, because it was his age, but the ball spun and dropped, and landed against the number sixteen.

'Twenty-four! I knew that'd never win!' said a female voice in his ear.

Bartle twisted round. There was no woman within twenty feet of him. 'No! It can't be! I can't bear it!' he cried. The other players stared, and thought he was overreacting a little to losing one bet, but Bartle paid them no attention. He clutched his head once more with both hands and stumbled through the casino, and out into the street.

He knew what he must do, but could not bear to think about it. In fact he was desperately trying not to think at all, lest he hear the voice again, which he feared would drive him so far out of his mind that he might throw himself from a bridge, or instantly drop dead. Without recovering any of his personal effects, and dressed quite inappropriately for the journey, he found a horse and set off for home at once.

The speed he made on his way back made the first journey seem like a relaxing jaunt. He fairly tore a hole through the countryside without stopping or eating or thinking. Three horses died from fatigue underneath him, but each time he simply ran to the nearest stable, bought another and rode on, faster than before.

Soon he was at the coast again, where, without his passport, he stowed away in the hull of a fishing boat, which reeked of stale and rotting fish. He did not care. He leaped from the side of the boat once it reached the shore on the other side of the Channel and rushed to the local ostler to reclaim Trumpty for the final leg of the journey.

He arrived home unrecognizable: thin, bearded and haggard, his torn dinner jacket hanging from him in muddy strips. Silently he let himself in with his key and stole down the long corridors towards his rooms. The voice now rang out, echoing in the chambers of his head as loud as it would have down the miles of corridor. She swore vengeance, she laughed coarsely, she screamed for minutes on end, her voice never becoming hoarse. As he reached his room, he saw the clock standing exactly as before.

'This will all be over soon,' said Bartle, walking doggedly forward. He tore one of the tall curtains down from its rail and spread it out on the floor behind the clock. Then he ran at it and barged it with all his strength sixteen or seventeen times, until finally it fell over with a heavy smash of breaking glass and splintering ebony.

'What are you doing?' asked the girl's voice.

'Shh!' said Bartle, holding a finger to his lips. He listened, but could hear no steps coming towards the room. The servants' quarters were so far away they probably wouldn't have heard if he had been conducting a sixty-four-piece orchestra, or testing a dozen of the navy's largest cannons. Taking two corners of the curtain in his hands, with all his strength he dragged the clock over acre after acre of polished floor to the front door where Trumpty waited.

The long journey he had made and the effort of dragging the huge clock told on him, and he felt weak as he tied the edge of the curtain tightly to the horse's saddle. Then, even though it was deep into the night and raining hard, he climbed wearily up into the saddle and set off back into town, and down the hill towards the bridge in the rainy district where he had first encountered Mr Grum. The strange-looking package slid along behind him, silently through mud and noisily over stone.

It was the sort of downpour usual to Tumblewater Hill at that time of night but unlike any Bartle had ever known – dense, slanting rain almost violent enough to knock you over. He struggled against it with his eyes averted and shivers running down him, his exhaustion almost defeating him. As they reached the bridge, the horse staggered with the weight of the clock and, slipping down off him, Bartle used the last of his strength to get the clock propped upright against the wall, ready to be tipped over into the thundering torrent. He stared at its face as the clock of St Hildred's on the hill behind him began to strike five o'clock in the morning. His own clock, nearly destroyed as it was, struck at exactly the same time.

'What are you doing?' asked the voice in his head, bewildered.

'It's the only way,' he said apologetically, feeling that in a few seconds his life might be his own again.

As she realized what was about to happen, she began to shout encouragement. 'Do it!' screamed the voice. 'Nothing can be worse than this! Push me in!'

Slowly, as the twin clocks struck the last chime of the hour, and at the last minute feeling a great sadness, Bartle leaned the clock back until it lay balanced across the bridge wall, and then turned it over to fall down into the raging water. He looked up and opened his mouth to sigh with relief only to find it opening wider with horror as he was pulled violently forward, tumbling over the wall himself. He managed to hang on to the edge for an instant and realized in panic that one of the straggling cuffs of his coat had caught on the corner of the clock's base before its weight pulled him down towards the mad, thrashing water. He pounded into it, and the waves crossed over each other again as though he had never existed, and he knew nothing more.

'Is that the time?' said a quiet voice that Bartle recognized.

He tried to open his eyes, happy to be alive, only to find he couldn't quite feel them. Slowly he found he could see the brown, dirty colours of a small room containing a few cheap chairs and in one of them, a very little, very old man. It was the same strange individual whom he had seen in that crooked little street so long ago.

'What am I doing here?' he said.

The little old man stared placidly back, and said, 'I am pleased with you, little clock. I thought I'd never find a replacement after that funny impatient man broke my last one. Rude sort of fellow he was.'

Trying not to be alarmed, Bartle repeated, 'What's going on? Can you not hear me? Hello? HELLO?'

The little old man sat, wearing his contented little smile. He raised a tiny cup to his lips, sipped it, raised his eyebrows in appreciation, and lowered the cup again. Slowly, Bartle realized that not only was he unable to feel his eyes, but neither could he feel his arms, or his legs, or anything at all. Then he felt the gentle, steady swish of something like an arm, or a finger, but which was not quite either. It kept moving, though, slowly, round in a circular movement that in an arm would be horribly awkward. But this wasn't uncomfortable – it felt more natural with each passing second, and it refused to stop.

The old man sipped his tea again and smiled benevolently. 'But Mr Grum came through at last. Good old Mr Grum. And now I have you, little clock. And we can look forward to many happy years together. After all, my mother only died last Christmas, and she was two hundred and forty-three. And *her* mother only died the year before that, and she was . . .'

As the old man's speech petered out and he fell into a doze, Bartle remembered his deafness, and his efforts to get the old man's attention died in the air. He thought hard, and wondered what he might do to escape. A man of his ability would not be trapped like this for long, he was sure of that. He looked around the room for something to help him, but couldn't see anything at present. That was all right. He would be out of here soon. He would wait.

When the villainous-looking man had finished his tale, there were murmurs of appreciation from the room. I saw that a few people had left but that more had joined us, and the fire had been replenished so that young flames flickered hesitantly around the fresh coals. The man who had been serving drinks was sitting near the storyteller, his chin on his hand, as if reluctant to accept that the story had ended.

Once again, I had a new favourite tale. I longed to live through the night, and the week, so that I could write them down for Jaspers & Periwether to publish. I sat on the sill and stared out of the window.

Without waiting for people to say what they thought of Rudy's story, the hard-voiced woman said, 'You like that one? Wait till you hear mine.'

So she began another story – a very good one about a miser, which I want to write down here, but I'm running out of space, so it'll have to wait for another book. And when she had finished someone else told another about a chimney sweep who made a terrible discovery. This story was followed by another, and then another.

As they spoke, I opened the silver box that I'd been holding, and discreetly looked at what was inside it. What I found consumed my thoughts for a few minutes, and afterwards I sat listening to more stories and

watching the flooded street, which had swelled to a fast-flowing river. I committed the tales to memory as I heard them, relishing their bloodcurdling endings. Outside the window the water rose as high as my neck, making it feel as though I was underwater, and the strength of the current was fearful – it was hard to believe the glass would hold it out.

As a new story began, I turned my attention back to the room, but at the last second glanced back and thought I saw a dark shape beneath the water. I looked again – it was still there: the size of a man, hovering with great strength against the current. Suddenly it coiled like an eel, and disappeared. I told myself it could have been a shadow, except there was no moon to cast it. Then I thought it could have been a sack or cloak – except that it had flowed away uphill, against the stream. I couldn't deny that it was man-sized, and that what I had seen kicking at its side looked a lot like clawed feet.

I put this to the back of my mind, pulled the silver box close to me and enfolded it with my arms, only to find that everyone in the room was looking at me, as though waiting for me to say something. I realized that someone had asked me a question, and I hadn't heard it.

The woman by the fire repeated herself: 'Daniel, you know it's only fair?'

'What is?' I said.

'Seeing as we're giving you all these stories, young man, it's only right that you should tell us one of your own.'

I hesitated. 'Until a moment ago, I would have said that I didn't have one.' The silver box was open on my lap, its contents spread around.

'But it turns out I do. This, then, is my story:

'My first memory,' I began, and now it's time to tell you, too, what had brought me to Tumblewater . . .

. . . is of being in the orphanage. I never knew my parents, and don't have even the faintest glimmering memory of them. My brothers and sisters were the other orphans who had grown up in this tall building in the countryside, miles from the nearest village. It was run by an old couple called Mr and Mrs Gammery who looked after us well but without affection, as though they didn't understand why children would need such a thing. When one of the children reached the age to leave, which is sixteen, they would find them a place to live and a place to work and put five pounds in their pocket, which is more than many parents can do, so we were lucky in that regard.

I didn't know what I was missing in not having parents, and told myself I was quite a lucky boy in that respect too. The orphanage grounds were large and had a big pond and the ruins of a cottage in one corner where

we could play and make up stories. All in all this was a much larger playground than most children have so, more than ever, I felt lucky, and didn't miss my parents, or feel too sorry for myself.

That is until a few months ago, shortly before I was to leave, when I started to hear rumours from other children that I had once had a sister. A real flesh-and-blood sister! The idea that this might be true and that it had been kept from me made me wild. I became uncontrollable, running away from home for days on end and climbing high up into trees where no one could find me. Finally I confronted the Gammerys and they admitted it was the truth. I *had* had an older sister. She had died before I was two years old.

As you can understand, the news made me inconsolably sad, and for days afterwards I was quiet and withdrawn, walking around the grounds in silence, uninterested in the other children. I couldn't stop thinking about how I had always wanted a brother or sister, and wondering what she had been like. Finally, I asked Mrs Gammery if I could see my sister's grave. Instead of answering straight away, she hesitated, and eventually said, 'Of course, Daniel. Of course you must.' She promised they would take me at the weekend, in a few days' time.

When the day came, they rode with me out to the cemetery. Mr Gammery stopped at the graveyard gate smoking his pipe, and looked away, as if to save my feelings. Mrs Gammery walked me into the mossiest, most overgrown corner and pointed between a carved marble angel and a wide, deep sarcophagus, both very decayed, to a stone twenty feet away. I walked forward carefully, not wanting to disturb anything. What I saw was not quite what I expected.

The stone was untouched – so spotless the engraving even looked fresh. For some reason, as I looked at it the sadness I had expected to feel did not come. MARIA DOREY, read the inscription. She had been fifteen years old.

Walking back towards Mrs Gammery, I looked at the other gravestones in this part of the graveyard. The most recent one I saw was over a hundred years old, and crumbling at the edges.

The next week I asked to go back again. This time Mr Gammery took me on his own and again he stopped to smoke at the gate as I went in. I had lain awake for several nights, wondering why I hadn't felt sad at seeing my sister's grave, and now I got there I realized I wasn't even interested in her grave at all, but found myself exploring the newer part of the graveyard instead, where the graves were much more recent – some of them so new that they still had mounds of earth piled on them. Without knowing what I was looking for, eventually my attention strayed to the far corner, across a patch of untouched grass, where a holly bush grew. I went over

to it and saw a stone had been leaned against the wall, hidden by the holly. It was much older than all of the other stones in this part of the graveyard – a hundred and twenty years older than those nearby – but the inscription was still quite clear. It read ELIZABETH HOPE STRANGER. The earth beneath the bush was dry and starved of sun, so it was impossible to tell if it had ever been disturbed. As I walked back to Mr Gammery, I wondered why it had been hidden away in a forgotten corner.

After that, I went back often and sat by the grave of Elizabeth Hope Stranger. I came to the conclusion that the gravestone for my sister had been made recently and placed in an old part of the graveyard to look as though it had always been there, and that Elizabeth Hope Stranger's grave had been moved to make room for it, probably because she had been dead long enough for there to be no relatives who would complain. Beyond that I couldn't fathom, and the mystery obsessed me as much as the thought that I was soon to leave the orphanage, and make my own way in the world. I watched the Gammerys, looking for a clue in their behaviour, and found none.

Eventually it was time for me to leave the old couple and the orphanage. They knew my heart was set on being a surgeon so, although they couldn't afford university, they had found a school in the city that would train me in the basics of medicine and surgery, and give me a chance of making my own way in the profession.

I can't remember now what it was that put the idea of becoming a surgeon into my head, except that I had an idea that it was what my father had been, and that it sounded like a job for a gentleman, and one which only a brave man could do. Anyway, it doesn't matter now. Most of the five pounds went on enrolling me in the course and buying the instruments I would need (a scalpel, a stethoscope, a glass syringe and a bone-saw). What was left after they had found a respectable boarding house for me and paid for my first few weeks was only a few shillings. My sixteenth birthday was fast approaching. Soon I would be out and on my way into the city. I couldn't wait.

In the final week before I left, I was leaning against the high railings one day when a rough-looking man walked past. I saw him looking the building up and down, and took him for a burglar or a crook of some kind, and told him to go away. Instead, he ambled over to me and asked in a friendly way: 'Do Mr and Mrs Gammery still run this place?'

'What's it to you?' I asked rudely.

'Quite a lot.' He smiled. 'I grew up here.'

I said I was sorry for being so suspicious, and chatted

to him for a while through the bars until he told me his age. It was the same as my sister's would be. I hesitated before I asked – had he known Maria Dorey?

At once his face fell and he moved close to me. 'How do you know that name?' he asked.

I stared at him. 'She was my sister,' I said.

He studied me carefully and when he spoke it was very quietly: 'We never knew what happened, only that she vanished one day. We heard that some rich man saw her and took her away in his carriage. Afterwards men came here to see Mr Gammery. They looked big and rough and frightening, and clustered all around the railings staring in. I remember that day so well; I was terrified. The leader of the men went into the house and we heard the shouting of insults and terrible threats. They left minutes later. Mr Gammery was quiet for weeks afterwards. No mention of Maria was ever made again.'

'Who was the man?' I asked desperately. 'Do you think there is a possibility that my sister is still alive?'

'I don't know. I'm sorry,' he said, and stood back to look at the house again. 'You know, this place was always heaven to me after my parents died.' He saw the look on my face and added, 'My parents were awful people, you see.' And he ambled away again, more sorrowful than he had come, but casting admiring glances up at the building until he passed out of sight.

Well, the morning of my birthday finally arrived, and it just so happened that the course I was enrolled on was to start in only two days' time. Gathering my satchel of medical instruments (my clothes had been sent ahead the previous day), I came down the stairs to leave. You can imagine how my thoughts had been consumed during that final week, how I had dreamed of finding the man who had stolen Maria, and despaired that I ever would, knowing nothing about him. I was still so distracted by these thoughts as I entered the playground that it was a few seconds before I saw what was different about it.

All the other children were huddled on the near side, as far away as possible from half a dozen men on the other side of the railings, staring intently at us. They looked like they could dismantle the railings with their bare hands and dismantle us in a similar fashion afterwards, and that they might quite enjoy it.

The man in charge kicked open the gate, walked to the front door and knocked hard upon it. Before anyone could have answered, he knocked again, so loud that in the house it must have sounded like gunfire.

Mr Gammery answered the door and the man charged past him and slammed it shut. At once we could hear the man's shouting and Mr Gammery's feeble replies. The man's voice rose and looking at the others I saw the fear that I felt on their faces too, the realization

that Mr Gammery was just a weak old man who couldn't protect us. I felt sorry for the children who were staying, and more glad than ever that I was going away.

Within a few minutes the door crashed open again and the man strode back out. He called to the other men and in a matter of seconds their horses were mounted, ridden away at a gallop and they were gone.

The Gammerys did not come out of the house. The children retreated to their favourite playing spots and hideaways, wondering what to make of it all.

My carriage soon came and I handed my satchel up to the driver who would take me as far as the nearest town where I would change for another all the way to the city. I wrote a note to the Gammerys expressing my thanks for all they had done for me, and promising to write to them and visit when I could. I had wanted to hand it to them, but instead I slipped it under the door, got into the carriage and told the driver to go. My heart was full of sadness and excitement and fear.

My thoughts ran at a similar speed to the road passing by the window. As I left the local landmarks behind, I wondered about what I had seen that morning, how it was just like the stranger's story I'd heard the week before. The men, I was sure, must have something to do with my sister's captor – I could only guess at why they had appeared now. The scenario I came up with was that perhaps the stranger had made what he thought were innocent remarks about me to someone. The man who had taken my sister was obviously powerful and important, and the stranger's remarks had found their way to him through some spy or informant. His anger, or suspicion, or interest aroused, he had dispatched men to threaten Mr Gammery back into silence about Maria's disappearance – a silence he had never broken.

The countryside passed by rhythmically, beautiful in the midday heat, the rocking of the carriage lulling me into a doze. I realized I had been sitting forward in tense thought all this while and leaned back in the seat, giving up on speculation.

At that moment, the wall of the graveyard flashed in front of the window, and beyond it the countless graves. An awful thought sprang to mind as I saw the holly bush pass, and I saw something near the grave that confirmed my suspicion. I called urgently to the driver to stop. Reluctantly, he pulled the horses to a halt and watched me walk towards the church gates with a look of exasperated disbelief.

I didn't go a single step towards Maria's gravestone. Why bother? I ran, instead, towards the far corner, until I saw the holly bush ahead of me and the stretch of open grass. I hadn't been mistaken: there it was. A spade, thrown aside with the sort of haste that the men had shown in kicking their horses into a gallop. As I reached

the gravestone of Elizabeth Hope Stranger, I saw what I most feared.

The ground in front of it had been dug away to a depth of two feet or more. What had been inside it was not a person's remains, but something much smaller, the size of a chess-set box or a parcel of books. And it was gone. I knelt there, shadowed from the hot sun by the prickly leaves, and saw how stupid I'd been.

Sworn to silence, the Gammerys had started the rumours about my sister on purpose so I would find out about her, and then guided me to this spot by showing me a grave for Maria so obviously fake that I would be sure to look elsewhere, and eventually find the stone that had been removed to make way for it, half-hidden in the holly bush. And there I was supposed to dig and find . . . What? They had indeed never broken the silence they had been sworn to. I had followed all of their clues, had solved the riddle and then not bothered to dig up the treasure! Whatever it was I was meant to discover, it was gone; the identity of her captor was safe. I walked slowly back to the driver, and ignored his remarks about how late we were. Nothing really mattered to me now, and although he whipped the horses into a frenzy and drove at breakneck speed for me to catch my next coach (which I did, by seconds) I was neither happy, nor sad, but empty.

Now I was alone on the coach among strangers,

heading out into the world with no more knowledge of my sister's whereabouts than you who listen to me now. I watched the countryside become greyed by clouds and spattered with rain as we approached the city, and looked up at the first clouds of the thunderstorm that's above us now, thinking I would never have a chance of finding my sister.

When I reached this point, I told the listeners what had happened to me since arriving in Tumblewater, how I had seen the girl who I felt the mysterious connection to, met the witch and stolen the silver box with her help.

'I couldn't be sure the girl I had seen, and who had been kidnapped by Prye, was my sister until I opened this box on my knees. They are letters, loving letters from my sister to me. Each one was sent to arrive on my birthday. I had never seen any of them until a moment before I began this tale.'

And inwardly, as I said this, I realized why Prye's men had known about me so soon. They'd read the letters they'd stolen from the grave and knew I existed – and knew my age too – so they'd been on the lookout. I saw how lucky I'd been to be turned away from my 'respectable' lodgings (where Prye's men would have found me in a minute) and forced into the shady back-streets.

Reaching the conclusion of my story, I looked up. A peace had descended while I spoke, which I had put down to the audience paying rapt attention to everything I said. But I saw now that two things had happened: the furious rain had calmed while I was talking; the storm had passed. And I had spoken so quietly that I had sent everyone to sleep.

Even Uncle had joined them, giving in to his tiredness after so many countless hours on the streets and in the passages, most of them in constant danger looking after me. He lay sound asleep at the table, his pipe still in the corner of his mouth. It was the first truly peaceful moment I had known since I had got here, but although I longed to join them the discovery of the letters had left me wide awake, thinking of the risks I now faced and the chances of getting my sister back. The childhood I had enjoyed until a week ago seemed a long, long way away.

I looked out of the window and saw the water in the street was a standing pool, sinking even as I watched it, broken by drips from the overhanging gutters. What's more, the storm's passing had left the sky almost light – or as near as it could get in Tumblewater – a bright blue that shone down through the spitting rain and at that moment felt as dazzling as bright sunshine.

I walked as quietly as I could through the room and passed back into the main parlour of the Crackey Inn, where many more people were slumped over (or lying under) tables, and the only sound was rough and regular snoring. I wanted to walk the passages a while and think about what I would do next and, allowing the latch to fall behind me, I began an exploration of the tunnels and pipes and holes Uncle and I had traversed on the way here.

Families and groups were beginning to stir from their overnight hibernation to make their way tentatively back through the passages, and I began to get a sense of the strange unknown population that lived here. The tunnels were indeed, as Uncle had said, far from deserted.

After a few minutes, the passage led through the hallway of a deserted house and I saw a group coming from the other direction, a large family bearing a lot of furniture in their arms, telling people to get out of their way. As the group barged through, knocking against the walls and arguing between themselves, I moved to one side amongst the people who had spent the night asleep in the hallway, some of them waking and grumbling at the family with irritation. Above their talk I heard a noise: a scratching of metal in the lock of a door. Turning, I heard the voices of two men trying to get in by the front door of the house.

That's funny, I thought. I didn't think people who used these passages were supposed to come in through

the street doors. And then I heard the bustle of hushed panic behind me. The family with furniture split up; half of them ran forward and the other half ducked back into the hole they had come from. The snoozing vagrants scuttled on their hands and knees, suddenly awake, worming between the legs of others. All at once the hallway was totally empty. It had taken less than two seconds. The men outside would be here in an instant.

The twisting of the key grew fiercer as the man battled impatiently with the lock and shouted angrily at it. At the last second, unsure which way to run, I made a fatal hesitation. A crowd of fearful faces peered out of the left-hand hole where a dozen bodies were crammed into a wall-space not even designed to fit a single body. A man was lifting a square plank of wood into the square gap in the wall. He waved me away angrily – 'The other one! Go to the other one!'

I turned to see the other hole shutting on invisible hinges. I pushed it back desperately. A voice behind it said, 'Try the other side – no room!' and the person behind shoved it closed.

The key finally twisted in the lock behind me.

'There's the damned thing,' said the angry voice beyond.

My skin prickled as the handle turned. I had no time. My legs trembled as I threw myself up the stairs three at a time.

The front door banged open and the men came in still talking to each other. I had stopped near the top, just out of sight, and pushed my hand into my mouth to stifle my heavy breathing. The men walked straight towards the stairs so I went up two steps at a time, as fast as I could while keeping my tread silent. I wanted to run but they would hear me, so I stayed just round the corner, a few steps ahead of them.

We went past the first floor and up to the second. As I reached the last flight of stairs, I heard one of them say, 'Next floor up?'

'To the top,' said another. Reaching the top and using the witch's power I swiped the door open and passed through.

I found myself in a very small, poor flat, completely deserted except for a great pile of objects in one corner that looked like stolen goods waiting to be reclaimed.

There was no door out of this room, only a window. I ran to it, thinking blindly that if the spell worked on drain covers it had better work on windows as well and, finding that it did, slid over the window sill, my feet nearly missing the lead gutter beneath me. Holding tight on to the sill I ducked down just as the window swished back into place and the door swung open.

Clambering out of sight, I leaned back on the steep roof and breathed hard, feeling the rain on my face. When I was a little calmer, I tested the gutter with my

foot. It seemed sturdy enough, but I was high up now and had to tread carefully. Slowly I crouched so I could peer into the street below to see the best way down. It was empty. There was no sign of life, only wrecked and deserted barrows, decaying rubbish and broken glass. The sort of street where no one lived to clear it up. I leaned back again, and looked to my left. The roof of the next building connected to this one. If I could find my way into another deserted dwelling through a—

Suddenly an alarm bell in my head stopped my train of thought. I had started climbing to the top of the roof, so I could inch along more safely with one leg on either side of the steep tiles, but now I looked down again into the empty street – what I could see of it. It looked like any one of a hundred streets I'd walked through, or been told about in the Grisly Tales. Still, a voice urged me to look yet again, so I did. The more I looked, the less I saw.

I reached the top of the roof and straddled it like a horse's back. Still unsure, I made my way along to the roof of the next building. It was a storey higher so instead of climbing I inched around the wall very gingerly, holding on to little nails and hooks and holes in the brick with my fingers, and walking along a narrow ledge. When I came round to the front, I got to a window and held on to the ledge. Then I caught my breath. Yes – I was right!

Both ends of the street below were completely enclosed by houses, the only entrance a low passageway through a thick stone wall. Opposite me was a rusted and forgotten lamp post whose glass had been smashed out with stones years ago, and which had rusted red-brown. The last time I had seen the cobbles on this road they had been shiny and clean, with not a speck of the rubbish that covered them now.

This was the street where I had seen my sister. And yet it wasn't.

The street I had seen was some kind of a vision from another time – the moment of my sister's capture more than a dozen years ago when it had been smart and well kept. Not like now, when all that filled it were the rotting remains of a forgotten market.

Standing on the narrow ledge, I realized that I was almost above the spot where I had seen her, that she had appeared to me in the next window but one. I moved my feet cautiously, inch by inch, terrified of falling now that I was so close.

As I came level with the first window, I could grip the outside of the sill and move a little faster. I looked in: the whole of the building's insides were gutted. From the basement up to the roof, it had been scorched black by fire and then doused by years of rain into a sodden mess. Spikes of broken wood stood out in the space where beams had been, and water had gathered in a

grey pool where the lower floors once were. My hopes fell, but still I knew I must look in through my sister's window, and for what seemed like an hour I inched until my hand touched the next window sill, and with a few more cautious steps I could see in.

It was not the slightest bit scarred by fire, but painted cold white. And totally bare – until, creeping forward, I saw the edge of a table. Now my heart rose to my mouth and my fingers tightened on the window sill as I saw the back of a person sitting at the table, facing away from me.

With a sickening repugnance I saw the sack still placed over her head. The anger gave me strength to ignore the danger and I reached upward and swiped my hand across the window so it disappeared into its casing, but the movement made me lose my balance and I fell backwards, clutching at the sill. My fingers closed over it as my feet fell and I hung there for a second, terrified, kicking my legs to find a foothold, before my toes found the ledge again and I pulled myself up. Breathing hard, I stumbled over it into the room.

It was breathtakingly cold and utterly still. The window closed behind me without a sound. I didn't say anything, but crept forward, wondering. No one could survive in this cold. Was she under a spell? Was she alive at all, or a ghost?

Standing behind her, I reached out and held the tip of the cloth bag. As it shifted at my touch, I recoiled in the fear that she would jump or scream. But she didn't move. Steeling myself, I drew it smoothly away from her head until I could see the dark curls of her hair. Released from the sack, they fell halfway down her back, exactly as I had pictured them. I walked slowly round the table until I was facing her. There was a chair opposite and I pulled it close to her. Her eyes were open, looking downward, and she was blinking, adjusting to the light. She looked very frightened. I didn't dare touch her for fear of scaring her (and myself, if she jumped in shock).

Finally she lifted her eyes and looked at me. Every feeling I hadn't felt at the graveside poured into me now – the years on my own, wanting to speak to her and ask her questions – but I controlled myself and met her gaze calmly. After our eyes had held for a few seconds, a look came upon her as though she was seeing me for the first time. She realized I wasn't her captor. I saw thoughts passing behind her eyes as she worked out who I was, and then she grew stronger. I was sure she felt the same as I did – the feeling of recognition, even though I knew for certain we had not seen each other for more than fourteen years.

She smiled distantly.

'You've rescued me,' she said softly. Then she

dropped her eyes again, and tears began to fall down her cheeks. As though provoked by the sight, they began to fall from mine too, unstoppably, and it was with a great strength of will that I held myself back from grabbing her in a hug for which she was still too frail.

'I hoped you would come,' she said. 'All those years when I wrote the letters, and willed you to get old enough to come and find me. I hoped and hoped, for day after day. I can't believe – it's actually—'

Crying overwhelmed her for a moment and I pulled her head to rest on my shoulder and put my arm round her.

'It's all right,' I said, and thought this was far and away the most grown-up thing I'd ever said, because it was so very much *not* all right, but I couldn't tell her that yet.

'Oh, Daniel,' she said, leaning back to look me in the eyes again. 'I never thought I would have this chance . . .' And while her hand fumbled in a pocket for something I took the opportunity to wipe away my tears, hoping she hadn't noticed them.

'I never thought,' she said again softly, 'that I would be able to give you this.'

She held out her hand. In her palm was a ring.

I opened my mouth to speak, but the words got jumbled in my throat.

'There are only two of them,' she said, looking down

at it. 'This one was for you; it belonged to our father. I wear the other, you see?' She held up her hand and I saw it on her middle finger.

Again I opened my mouth and again the words caught on each other. She took my hand and hers felt familiar, not like a stranger's at all. I closed my fingers around hers and spoke urgently.

'We can do that later,' I said. 'We must leave now, do you understand? The witch will know that we are here. She will be on her way.'

'Daniel,' said Maria again, 'I must see this on your finger before we leave.' And her eyes met mine with the look of love I had gone without for so long that it had had a terrible effect on me.

I pulled my hand back.

A film covered her eyes as she watched the hand retreat, and she became as distant again as when she had first awoken.

'Maria?' I said, putting my arm round her again. 'Be strong – we have to leave!'

'I can't leave, not until you put it on,' she said, holding a hand to her head as though suffering from a violent headache, and her voice became scratchy.

'I – I can't . . .' I said apologetically.

She threw her head into her hands and let out a strangled groan, her hair hanging down like a curtain.

'What's happening?' I asked, getting up and taking a few steps back.

She tried to speak, but just a croak came out at first. Putting my hand back to the window, I felt the hoarfrost that had grown there since I had come in. It was an inch thick.

'Just put on the ring . . .' she said, not looking up, sounding exhausted, hopeless. Her voice had changed entirely now; it had retreated, as though coming from far away. Or – it reminded me of something, and I tried to think what – not from far away, but from *within* something . . .

I felt the bitter taste of horror and defeat in my mouth as I realised – her voice sounded as though it was coming from the bottom of a well.

'Gora,' I said, anger and hate surging through me. 'I know it's you. Where is my sister?'

She looked up at me sharply. Her hair was thrown back and I saw Maria's face melting, wrinkling into Gora's. The eyes were shut and the mouth was open – her face was disappearing into her mouth, the skin shrinking and folding. Her whole body shrank in a sequence of bone-crunching convulsions so that the clothes appeared to grow around it and cover it up. Only the face remained visible, but it kept wrinkling so that the flesh seemed to sink. It became deathly white, the face of an old woman, and then kept shrinking smaller and smaller. The wrinkles fell over her eyes so I couldn't see them and she peered out through pea-sized gaps in the skin. Her nose retreated to a tiny button in the folds with the pursed hole of her mouth no wider than a penny. She became smaller and smaller until she was a mean little shape made out of frowns and creases, no taller than my knee.

'So now you see me,' she said. 'And you've brought me that little box I sent you to fetch, haven't you, like a good little boy?'

Repulsed, I nodded slowly and reached inside my jacket, where the letters were tucked in my pocket. Her mouth hovered open and although they were invisible I could sense her eyes were watery with anticipation as they watched my hand. When I brought it out again it was holding Harry's blade.

Her whole face and body shook violently and a change came over her. She grew suddenly tall and more muscular, and her skin darkened. The hood and cloak fitted her again, and her looks became beautiful, bronze-coloured – those of a tribe from some far continent.

'You'll never find your sister,' she said with satisfaction. 'I've hidden her through a doorway you could never find. I can send myself anywhere, through any door. You'll never catch me,' she said with a smile, retreating to the door that looked out over the building's empty insides, and pausing on the threshold. 'After I go

through, you'll never see me again. Goodbye, boy.'

'I've still got your spell,' I said, walking forward with the blade. 'It stays on a door for five seconds after you've used it – I've counted. And you're tired from using your magic to try to trick me – that's why you couldn't stay looking like my sister for long enough. Transport yourself where you like, I'll be there after you!'

She looked at me for a second as though she was going to speak, but spat viciously instead. Then she turned through the doorway and vanished into midair.

I ran forward. I could see out into the gutted core of the building – a drop of fifty feet down into the bricks and ash. Only the glint of fear and anger in her eyes as she spat at me told me I was right about the spell, and this was my only chance to catch her. So with my eyes closed I jumped through, taking a breath and trusting that the doorway would take me where she had gone.

I landed hard, winded, but found myself in a large kitchen, cooks all around with their knives out, confused and outraged by Gora's sudden appearance and disappearance. They were shouting at each other and pointing at the door to a tall ice-box. I squeezed between them and swiped at the door before a hand could grab me.

It switched. I dived through.

I skidded on a slippery patch of blood and skin between two rows of fishmongers' stalls into the marketplace. As I caught my balance, I ducked a handful of fish guts thrown over a fishmonger's shoulder and felt them slither over my neck. Staring around, I saw the skirts of a woman disappearing through a tavern door on the other side of the street and sprinted for it. My hand reached the door just as I saw it slipping back into place, and I slid it back hard.

I staggered through it into the cells of the police station. A policeman was right in front of me, staring around him, bewildered, and the second he saw me he reached and grabbed my neck. The grip felt hard enough to squeeze the life out of me, and as I twisted round to get out of it I met the eyes of Inspector Rambull barely ten feet away. He stared at me coolly, raised his eyebrows and walked forward, flexing his fists with satisfaction.

Another policeman ran past him to help restrain me and I wriggled and squirmed as only a thin lad could, feeling the hands holding me slipping and then grabbing again more fiercely than before. As I fought, I looked around and thought bitterly what a clever trick this was for Gora to play. There were five cells in front of me, men cheering from the doors of four of them, but in the nearest a terrified drunk was shouting about a ghost in his cell. I gave a final wriggle with all my strength, slipped through the policeman's arms just as Rambull reached me with his fist raised, and dived forward.

I swiped the cell door, leapt through and found myself in a store of general supplies, with every kind of implement and appliance piled on to shelves and hanging from the ceiling. In its centre stood a burly well-dressed man holding up a sign saying GARSTANG & PEGLEY. As I appeared, a dour-looking bespectacled man who had been examining the sign stopped in the middle of saying, 'I think PEGLEY & GARSTANG sounds better . . .'

He looked at me and then at the burly man with deep cynicism. 'Another one! Are you *sure* you locked the back door, Garstang?' he asked.

'Which way?' I asked. 'Where did she go?'

'That way!' shouted the burly man, pointing excitedly out of the front, before turning again to his friend. 'GARSTANG & PEGLEY surely has a better ring . . .'

Ten feet ahead of me, I saw the witch jump up on to the step of a fast-moving carriage and yank the door open. I sprinted behind and caught it, wrenching it open just in time and tumbling through. Falling confused into the wet mud, I looked around to find I had been transported but was still on the same street.

Where has she gone, damn it? I thought, sticking the dagger back into my inside pocket so that it tore a deep hole. I had disappeared through the door of one carriage and jumped out of the door of another a few yards down the street, going in the opposite direction.

I spun round, struggling to get my bearings. For a second left was right and right was left.

But the witch was exhausted, I knew, or she would have used her power to cast herself further and further away, not back into the same street.

I heard a sudden, aggressive screech behind me and saw a man angrily pulling along a creature that refused to be dragged. It was Stanley the Sapient Pig, squealing and pointing with one of his trotters back over my shoulder.

Turning, I saw a woman leaning tiredly against the wall twenty yards away, and ran towards her. Gora had changed her disguise to a pale red-haired woman, but her anger and panic as she saw me couldn't be hidden. She took a breath and dived through the nearest door. I started to run, even though I knew I couldn't make it in time, and heard another squeal of the pig, and a man shouting, 'Here, miss! Watch out, you daft . . .' as footsteps ran behind me.

Barely ten feet behind me, Gora was running across the road to an alleyway between two shops. She had tried to double back on me.

Now I knew I could catch her. She had hardly any magic left. With a burst of energy I tore down the alleyway behind her. It went steeply downhill and one of us was going to slip in the mud any second. But we came out at the other end on our feet and I pulled out

the knife again as I gained on her, but she dived left round a corner into a narrow, unlit alley.

It was incredibly steep and impossible to keep your footing. The witch slid ahead of me in the mud and I fell face forward behind her, tumbling over and over. I had been here before a few days ago, at night time, sliding helplessly in the drumming rain, and I knew where we would come out. As the hill levelled and we slowed to a stop, I saw five men opposite. It was the tall, melancholy man from the post office and his four tiny helpers. He looked on with no expression while the others yelped and cheered and pointed. One pushed another over into the mud in his enthusiasm.

Nothing would distract me. As Gora got to her feet and squirmed down a tiny, almost invisible passageway, I was only inches behind.

Through a thin crack of light we stumbled on to a tiny jetty, a makeshift thing cobbled together from river flotsam, and not a single boat moored to it. The river itself was a hundred yards away beyond high brick warehouses. Brown water lapped quietly, making the jetty lean from side to side as Gora retreated down it ahead of me. I followed her. The frail structure sank under the weight of my boots so that one of them went under the water for a second. She looked around desperately. There was not a door or a window anywhere to be seen.

‘How do I find her?’ I said. ‘I’ll let you go. Just tell me!’

She shook her head, and spat at me again. She put her hand to an inner pocket and produced a small metal key, and looked at me defiantly. She bent her arm and leaned back to throw it as far as she could – I ran forward.

At once the water exploded. Falling backwards I saw a shape launch into the air and land on the jetty, making it shudder dangerously. It was a huge, scaly creature, a tiger in fish form, and in one movement it landed and snapped its mouth around the witch’s neck. It shook and trembled with the effort of clenching its jaws, and closed its eyes, digging its claws into her sides to hold her still. Drops of water showered all around. It had webbing from its arms to its body and wide flaps behind the ears; a ridge of scarred bone rose from above the holes where its nose should be over the top of the head. With a great final tensing of face muscles it tightened its jaws and a wet snap came from Gora’s neck.

The creature’s pinprick eyes opened and the fire went out of them. It took long breaths, as though in satisfaction. For a second it looked almost as though it was kissing the side of her neck. Blood poured from its mouth like a tap as it took two steps to the edge with a hunchbacked gait, the witch’s neck still in its teeth, her whole body hanging from its mouth. Then it bent down

to the water, slid in and swam away calmly, making a meandering S-shape in the water, the witch's dress flowing in the same pattern like a rag.

The jetty swayed gently to and fro, with no sound but the trickling lap of the water against brick. The only evidence that someone had been there was a tiny object on the wood where Gora had stood. I looked closer and saw that it was the key she had been about to throw, half resting on the edge of one of the rickety planks.

I crawled carefully over and reached out to pick it up. I put it inside my coat pocket and, when I could stand, I did so, and walked back to the street. The silly, grubby little men had gone. Rather than walk past the post office and arouse their curiosity, I turned in the opposite direction and kept walking.

The streets were full and bustling with the day's business as I walked through them. I knew it was dangerous for me to be there, but I didn't care any more. I didn't have a drop of fear left, so I trudged on, turning my collar up so that it covered my face up to my ears, and not meeting anyone's eye.

Either the danger towards me had passed overnight, or Nuala's disguise worked perfectly. No one approached me, or even noticed me, that I could tell.

I watched all the hours of the day pass as I walked, the business going on at the streetside, the sweeps and lamplighters coming at the end of the day and the beggars rising as the light faded to shake off the day's rain and find a hole where they could rest as warmly as possible away from the policeman's stick. Many – most of them, perhaps –would find their way to the Underground.

The night came on and the streets emptied, but still I saw evidence everywhere of people sleeping alone, wet and cold. Yet gaping windows showed empty houses on every stretch of the hill, for streets at a time. I passed up the main road to the crossroads, and beyond into the rich squares and beautiful houses in the north of the city, then back down through the heavy factory district with its thick grey fumes resting in the foggy air, waiting for the machines to start up again in the morning and get them churning afresh.

I found myself walking through crooked streets past riverside inns where singing sailed out of the windows, and through terrifying slums that never slept where murderous characters lurked at each corner, and past the Courts of Justice, and over the river, and back again.

In those hours the course of my life, which I had already begun to see taking shape, became set as hard as stone. I reached the district of Tumblewater again. In a few short days this place had given me three burning purposes for living and I'd stay here forever if that was

what it would take to find my sister and destroy Caspian Prye. And then I would keep walking these streets until there were no more stories to write down. But I knew that that day would never come.

Light began to show on the river.

I walked through the south side of the district towards the corner I hadn't yet seen. This close to the river it wasn't quite raining, but water hung in the air in a dense yellow fog. With no one else to be seen or heard, and able to see just twenty yards ahead of me, I felt as though I was walking through a myth. Out of the fog came a wall, then some railings. Behind them, with a gentle wind swirling the cloud, I saw rows of gravestones. Each one was engraved simply with a name, and they leaned to and fro like drunkards – not from age, but as though they had been kicked over, or hastily put up. In the corners there were stacks of stones neatly piled, although whether these were stones waiting to be used, or old ones pulled up for lack of space, you couldn't tell. The grass grew wild and thick with weeds, and garbage thrown over the fence lay on the nearby graves.

Who hates these people? I thought. Why do they disrespect these dead?

Then I realized I had come to Ditcher's Fields, where Prye's victims were hanged. I walked on with foreboding, feeling the disease of the place, as though the very air and earth were cursed and dying. A dry creaking sound came from a few feet away and a gust of wind burrowed a hole in the mist. I stopped, staring upward.

Above me hung the body of a boy, gently pushed by the breeze. He was no more than sixteen, a boy who looked so like me that for a second I was paralysed with the fear that I was trapped in some dream after death. Then I knew why no one had noticed me on the street, why no alarm had been made, why I had passed safely through the length and breadth of Tumblewater in every direction.

It was the body of Benjamin Bright.

Prye thought I was dead.

I was tiring as I came to the bottom of the hill, and nearly asleep on my feet. I came to the offices of Jaspers & Periwether before I knew where I was, and leaned exhaustedly on the door for a second. Then I stood back and swiped my hand across it. I was too tired to care about how I would explain how I had got in – I would simply have to come up with something when Jaspers arrived and found me inside.

Nothing happened.

Frowning, I did it again, and waited for the door to move. Then again, and again, looking over my shoulder in case anyone was watching me. But nothing happened – I was just making a fool of myself in front of anyone

who happened to be passing.

That was when I realized that the witch was truly dead, and my power had gone with her. I crouched in the doorway, hugging my knees, and slept until someone arrived to let me in. Some time later I was woken by a nervous little laugh, and found myself looking up at the bespectacled Cravus.

'You are early for your first day,' he said. 'Mr Jaspers will be impressed.'

'And I've dressed up for it too,' I said, gesturing down at my mud-spattered front as he unlocked the door. He gave his nervous little laugh again (it went on for several seconds this time) as I sat heavily in the chair that was to be mine, which was next to the one belonging to the unpleasant blond-haired boy. If that laugh was Cravus's reaction to everything, I rather bad-temperedly thought, then I could almost imagine why Mr Jaspers treated him the way he did. As I thought this, Cravus bustled back into the room, hooking his coat with difficulty on the coat rack (which was rather too tall for him) and offering me a morning cup of tea.

'Cravus,' I said, 'I have never admired a man more in my whole life than you for making that suggestion.'

'So that's a yes?' he asked nervously. I nodded, and as he went out leaned back and put my feet up on my desk. Then I saw something on the other side of the room that caught my attention. It was behind the large waterlogged chest beside Mr Jaspers's desk (from which I now noticed some plants seemed to grow), on top of the bookshelf made of books and crammed in underneath lots of papers: a dark bronze lamp, octagonal and with oriental-style designs running up its sides. I got up, stood on a chair and fished it out, causing a little landslide of paper down the back of the chest.

I took it back to my desk and looked at it until Cravus came in carrying a tray of tea things.

'What sort of lamp is this?' I asked.

'It's one of those candlestick-makers' lamps.'

'That's what I thought. Thank you, Cravus,' I said, taking my cup from him and sipping it.

He shrugged. 'It's nothing at all. Nice to be asked a question. No one ever listens to me around h—'

The door burst open and Mr Jaspers strode in, smiling.

'Cravus, is it your birthday?'

'No, sir.'

'Then what are you doing here? I've no present for you. You can retire to your hammock in the store cupboard until I poke you with my umbrella in three quarters of an hour's time.'

Cravus began to speak, but Jaspers turned to me. 'Mr Dorey, I'm pleased to see you prompt on your first day!'

'As a matter of fact, I've been up all night on an assignment, Mr Jaspers, and have another to go to now, so you won't see much of me.'

'Good, good,' he said, settling at his desk and opening the latest edition of *Old Git* magazine with relish, so that the pages made a snapping noise. 'You carry on. I like half an hour's quiet in the morning before I awake Cravus and his infernal questioning.'

I took the lamp from my desk, drank the last of my tea and walked out of the front door and up the hill. I was on my last legs and could hardly think of anything except the bed I would be in soon. But there was something I had to do first.

First I found the market, and then the street where the costermongers lived. Sitting on a doorstep near the corner I saw a little girl I recognized, who didn't seem to notice the other children playing around the newly lit fire.

'Hello,' I said. 'Are you Jenny?'

She nodded shyly up at me. I offered her my hand. 'My name is Daniel,' I said. I smiled encouragingly. She offered her hand and I shook it, and squatted down.

'Now,' I said, 'you've been sitting here for a long time waiting for your father, is that right?'

She didn't answer, because she had already seen the lamp in my hands and she was watching me solemnly.

'Jenny,' I said, 'he asked me to come and visit you, and give you this, and tell you he's sorry he can't come himself. And I'm very sorry too.' Her mother had appeared at the door and was looking down at us both. I said confidentially, 'It's not his fault. A very bad man has taken your dad away, and won't let him come back. And you and I both hate that man and will do anything to make him pay, won't we?'

She nodded.

'Now, I'm giving you this lamp because your dad wants you to think of him as you light it each night. He wants you to stop watching for him to come round the corner, and play with the other children instead. Will you do that?'

She listened so hard and peered up at me so seriously that I had to struggle to overcome the tearing pain in my heart. I held her eye and she nodded. I took her hand again, as though sealing a formal agreement.

'I'll be back to see you,' I said. 'And somehow I'm going to get revenge on the man who sent your dad away, and I'll tell you how I've got on. Is that a deal?'

She nodded, and I got up and walked away, not wanting the tears in my eyes to show. At the corner I looked back and saw her already placing the lamp in the window, as her mother stood behind, holding out a match for her to light the flame.

# THANKS

I find 'acknowledgements' a bit lofty. I don't want to *acknowledge* anyone, but there are lots of people I'd like to thank. This is not in any order of importance, but roughly chronological:

Firstly to Jon Butler, who suggested and then encouraged these stories. I owe you an enormous debt in all sorts of ways. Next, and most of all, to Nicola Barr and Emma Young for both being really passionate and a great agent and editor respectively. Then there are lots of people who were kind enough to read early versions and give feedback. I'm sincerely grateful to you all, and I really hope I haven't left anyone out: Rebecca Saunders, Georgina Difford, Jane Cramb, Lucy Pessell, Anna Carmichael, Mark Searle, Catharine Vincent, Ben Vincent, Will Atkins, Matt Hayes, Catherine Richards, the Why family and Eli Dryden.

Thanks very much to Charlie Whiteside and Eden Lloyd for being a test audience. Your kind letters were really appreciated! And thanks to Georgina Ikin for 'Slurgoggen' – more suggestions, please . . .

And lastly to my mate Tom Wharton for his encouragement.

BRUNO VINCENT

I came to Tumblewater an innocent orphan and had to survive by my wits. Follow me, stick to the shadows and don't make a sound. We both might escape with our lives.

In the creepy town of Tumblewater Daniel Dorey is on the run from sinister millionaire Caspian Prye, who kidnapped his sister. To escape he must venture below the rain-drenched streets, where he unwittingly enrols in a very strange school. Here kids learn the tricks they need to survive – from safe-cracking to double dagger-throwing, from disguises to practising surgery on chunks of corpse. This is one school where naughtiness never goes unrewarded! But will Daniel learn his lessons in time to confront Prye and rescue his sister?